I've travelled the world twice over,
Met the famous: saints and sinners,
Poets and artists, kings and queens,
Old stars and hopeful beginners,
I've been where no-one's been before,
Learned secrets from writers and cooks
All with one library ticket
To the wonderful world of books.

THE PEACOCK PAGODA

Two of John Anson's wishes were granted on the same day. He was offered an important post in the State of Gaupal and Sandra Beauchamp promised to marry him. On that day he also met Rose Lian, the beautiful girl, who, he was told, was of mixed French and Gaupali blood. Their destinies and that of Charles Garrison, a figure from Sandra's past, were to be strangely linked in this romance set against a far eastern background.

Books by Alex Stuart
in the Ulverscroft Large Print Series:

ALEX STUART

THE PEACOCK PAGODA

Complete and Unabridged

ULVERSCROFT
Leicester

First published in Great Britain in 1959
Mills & Boon Ltd.,
London

First Large Print Edition
published April 1988

British Library CIP Data

Stuart, Alex
    The peacock pagoda.—large print ed.—
Ulverscroft large print series: romance
Rn: Violet Vivian Mann   I. Title
823′.914 [F]   PR6063.A38

ISBN 0-7089-1793-3

Published by
F. A. Thorpe (Publishing) Ltd.
Anstey, Leicestershire
Set by Rowland Phototypesetting Ltd.
Bury St. Edmunds, Suffolk
Printed and bound in Great Britain by
T. J. Press (Padstow) Ltd., Padstow, Cornwall

For my sister and brother-in-law, Betty and Thomas Bustard, in the hope that it may evoke pleasant memories for them both.

1

"MAJOR ANSON—His Excellency will see you now. Come with me, if you please."

John Anson rose slowly to his feet, towering head and shoulders above the messenger who had summoned him. The Ambassador's secretary was a small man, his round, earnest, brown face half hidden by the heavy horn-rimmed spectacles he wore. Dressed in an impeccably cut morning coat and beautifully pressed grey trousers, he spoke perfect English and his manner was correctly dignified.

Yet, despite all this, he gave the impression of a little boy, carefully acting an adult role. A hint of a smile hovered impishly at the corners of his pursed mouth and lurked, only half-suppressed, in the dark, slanting eyes behind their absurdly large glasses. Watching him, John Anson expected him to make some childish, wholly incongruous joke and then laugh aloud when he had made it.

But he did not. Moving silently, he crossed the luxuriously furnished room, with its shining parquet and priceless, hand-woven rugs. Reaching the door, he paused for a moment in front of it as if suddenly undecided, his neat, golden-brown hands clasped in front of him in an odd little gesture that was almost a plea, if not for patience, then, at least, for indulgence.

"Major Anson—" he began, and broke off, glancing up uncertainly into the Englishman's face. The hint of laughter had vanished from his eyes, and although he still resembled a small boy, he now looked an acutely anxious one.

"Mr. Anson, if you don't mind," John amended gently. "I have retired from the Army."

"Yes. Oh, yes, of course, I know." The little secretary nodded vigorously. He added, obviously proud of his understanding of the circumstances, "You have been axed from the British Army, like many other distinguished officers, and you have come here to seek employment of a congenial nature in my country."

He had stated as much in his application

2

for an interview, John reflected, but he winced to hear it put so bluntly into words by this odd little brown man. Still, it was the bitter truth. The War Minister's axe had fallen on him, as it had fallen on hundreds of others of his age and rank. The British Army was being cut down and reformed: it was to be in future an army of highly trained specialist technicians, and there was no place for him in its ranks. After sixteen years' service—three of these wartime years, fighting in Burma, for he had joined up on leaving school—he was a civilian again, thrown on his own resources with a not ungenerous gratuity, but with no training for anything save war.

An advertisement in *The Times* had brought him to the Embassy of the ancient kingdom of Gaupal. Its wording had attracted him; the advertised post had sounded, from his point of view, almost too good to be true, since he possessed all the qualifications it demanded. But no doubt many other ex-officers besides himself would have applied for it. He had come optimistically, but had forced himself not to entertain too serious a hope that his own application would be successful. Thinking this, he turned again to the secretary. It might be as well to know the sort of competition he was up against.

"I suppose," he said, his tone deliberately casual, "His Excellency has received a great many replies to his advertisement for this post?"

"Many hundreds," the secretary confirmed. "But—" He smiled, a confiding, little boy's smile and his hands unclasped themselves. He extended them towards John appealingly. "You are the first to be summoned for an interview, Maj—I beg your pardon, please—Mr. Anson."

"Am I?" John was visibly disconcerted. "Good heavens, why should I be?"

"You are the son of Sir Michael Anson, the very distinguished surgeon. His name is not unknown to us in Gaupal." The secretary's smile widened.

"Is that so?" John's bewilderment increased. His father's name was respected in his own sphere, but it seemed incredible that it should carry sufficient weight with the Gaupali Ambassador to ensure his own preferential treatment.

The little secretary inclined his smooth, dark head.

"Indeed yes, Mr. Anson. If you . . . how do you say it in English? If you play your cards correctly, the appointment you seek will be yours—no one else will be asked to come for interview. It was this which I wanted to tell you before conducting you to His Excellency's presence. Speak to him of your father and of St. Ninian's Hospital, where he is working, and there will be no need for you to look further than Gaupal for employment."

"Thank you," John said, masking his astonishment as best he could. "Thank you very much for telling me."

"Please," the secretary begged. He flung open the door of the ante-room with a flourish. "If you will be so good as to follow me, Mr. Anson." He led the way down a wide corridor and tapped discreetly on a door at its far end. In response to a muffled command from within, he opened the door, announced "Major Anson, Your Excellency" in ringing tones and then stood aside, bowing politely. John stepped past him into a large, oak-panelled room, comfortably furnished as a study, with a massive mahogany desk in the centre and half a dozen leather covered armchairs grouped about the fireplace. Books lined three walls and the fourth was occupied by a vast leather sofa which stood in front of a high window, overlooking the Park.

On this, reclining at full length with a tea-tray set with silver beside him, was a handsome, grey-haired man in Gaupali dress who smilingly waved him to a chair.

"Forgive me, Major Anson, if I do not rise to greet you, but I am, as you may observe, temporarily incapacitated." A gesture indicated the heavily bandaged foot, propped carefully on pillows. "Gout," explained the Ambassador briefly, "for which, it seems, there is no treatment save rest."

"I'm extremely sorry to hear that, Your Excellency."

"Ah, well!" The Ambassador sighed with resignation. "These ills beset us all at times, do they not? I am at least fortunate in having the best of medical advice for the asking. My daughter, Major Anson, is a doctor, recently qualified and at present studying here in London. At St. Ninian's Hospital where, I believe, she has the honour to listen quite frequently to the lectures given by your father, the famous Sir Michael Anson. She considers herself privileged to have such an opportunity."

Light dawned then. The reason for the little secretary's friendly advice was now abundantly clear, and John's spirits rose appreciably. Perhaps, thanks to an unforeseen and happy coincidence, he might, after all, land this wonderful job in Gaupal. His father was in a position to bestow favours on the Ambassador's daughter, which was an incredible slice of luck . . .

He listened as the Ambassador talked of his daughter, warming to the note of pride in the older man's voice as he spoke her name. Rose Lian. Rose . . . it was an attractive name. Dr. Rose Lian. Probably she was an attractive girl. He was surprised that his father hadn't mentioned the fact that he had a Gaupali girl amongst his students, but then he was very busy and preoccupied these days, desperately overworked with a large consultant practice, in addition to all he did at the hospital. And in any case, John reflected guiltily, he had been at some pains to avoid the Harley Street house and his father's company of late. He had been too busy job-hunting himself to have much spare time, and his efforts had hitherto been too unproductive for him to wish to endure more of his father's well-meant advice and probing questions than he could help. It was humiliating, at thirty-four, to come to the end of what had seemed a promising career and, after months of searching, to be unable to find anyone willing to employ him . . .

"My daughter," the Ambassador said, "will soon return to Gaupal in order to practise medicine there. She is to work at the new hospital in Tauling, the capital. Please"—he waved an inviting hand in the direction of the laden tea-tray—"will you not take tea with me, Major Anson? Perhaps you will pour out for both of us."

John complied. As he sipped the fragrant China tea from an eggshell-thin cup, he found himself trying to picture Dr. Rose Lian. She would bear a superficial resemblance to her father, he supposed. Her features would be of Oriental cast, her skin golden brown, like his, her hair smooth and jet black. The Gaupalis were hill people and they were small, the women tiny.

The Kingdom of Gaupal lay, John knew, in the mountains between Burma and Indo-China. It had been allied to Burma before the coming of the British, its King paying token allegiance to the Burmese Crown, whilst maintaining political independence and firmly closing his frontiers to foreign traders. With the fall of King Thebaw of Burma, the brief alliance had ended. But the two peoples were closely akin. Gaupalis wore much the same dress as the Burmese, worshipped at the same Buddhist shrines, and their language was the language of the Shans. Like the Gurkhas of Nepal, Gaupali warriors had offered themselves as soldiers under the British flag and had served with valour in both world wars. John himself had never served with them, but he knew that their reputation had been second to none in the XIVth Army.

"I imagine," the Ambassador suggested, setting down his cup and reaching for a cedar-lined box of black Burma cheroots

9

which he placed hospitably at John's elbow, "that you know very little about my country, Major Anson?"

"Thank you, sir." Accepting a cheroot, John sniffed at it appreciatively before lighting it. "I don't know a great deal about Gaupal, I must admit, although of course, since replying to your advertisement, I've found out what I could." He listed, very briefly, all that he had been able to learn and the Ambassador smiled when he came to the end of his recital.

"That is not a great deal, is it? But it is enough, it would seem, to induce you to offer us your services?"

"Yes, indeed, Your Excellency. The idea of going to Gaupal appeals to me very strongly. I served in Burma during the war —I liked the people and what I saw of the country. I believe that I have the experience you require and that I should be able to carry out the duties you would expect of me as tutor to His Majesty's eldest son."

"H'm." The Ambassador glanced down at an opened folder which lay across his knees, and John recognised his own handwriting on the letter clipped to the front of the file. He had set out fully his experience and qualifications and, as the advertisement in *The Times* had requested, had given his reasons for applying for the post. There was nothing, really, to add to what he had already said, so he waited in silence for the Ambassador to continue. After one or two questions concerning his education, the Ambassador said, "I see that you state here that you speak Burmese and Urdu to interpreter standard. Have you any knowledge of the Shan dialect?"

In honesty, John was forced to shake his head.

"I'm afraid not, Your Excellency. But I don't find it hard to pick up languages."

"You were in the Indian Army during the war?"

"Temporarily, yes, sir. But I transferred to Force 136, which was a commando unit, and—"

"And you were awarded the Military Cross, I believe, for gallantry in action?"

John's smile was wry. "I was the only survivor of the action, Your Excellency, that was the reason I was decorated."

"That is not quite what is stated in your citation," the Ambassador demurred. "I took the liberty, Major Anson, of obtaining a copy of it from War Office records. But we will let that pass, since you obviously wish it . . . at the end of the war you were re-drafted into the British Army, were you not? You served with the Airborne Forces and were in action in Malaya and at Suez?"

"Yes, sir."

"And obtained a bar to your MC. It seems strange to me, Major Anson, that the British Army can find no further use for an officer of your calibre. An officer of proven courage, twice decorated and with, I see, a pilot's qualification. Surely that is unusual in an Army officer?"

"Not really, Your Excellency. A few of us took the opportunity, when we were serving in Malaya, to do a flying training course with the RAF." And we qualified in Auster scout planes, John reminded himself bitterly. We were very useful in operations against the bandits in the heart of the Malayan jungle. But how much more sensible and far-sighted it would have been if we'd been offered courses in radar or rocket launching or if we'd qualified as physicists or nuclear weapons experts! The wings he had worn on his tunic had been worth very little, when the Powers That Be had come to weigh up his usefulness to the new scientific army . . . "I wasn't a technician, Your Excellency," he ended a trifle stiffly. Conscious of his own heightened colour, he was at pains to avoid his host's gaze. "The tendency is all for specialization now, you see."

"I see," the Ambassador confirmed. His tone was sympathetic. "But I am sure that we shall be able to make use of many of your non-specialist qualifications in Gaupal. Not least, Major Anson, of your courage. Our country is undergoing something of an upheaval—we are ringed about with enemies, we are not finding it easy to preserve our jealously guarded independence. There are elements amongst our people whose loyalty to the King is a matter for doubt, and the man into whose hands the education of our young heir apparent will be placed must be one who will protect him at the risk, if necessary, of his life. Are you such a man, Major Anson? Would you be prepared to guard your young charge's life with your own if this should be required of you?"

John answered, without hesitation,

"Yes, Your Excellency, if it should be required of me."

The Ambassador's round, ageless face relaxed in a satisfied smile. "I had imagined, from your record, that you would give me exactly the answer that you have given. I believe you to be the man we are looking for, Major Anson, but before I can formally offer you the appointment, there are one or two other questions which I must ask you. These are of a personal nature, but I trust that you will understand why I have to ask them and that you will reply to them quite frankly."

"Certainly, sir." John waited, inhaling smoke from his cheroot. He could guess, from the Ambassador's slight but obvious embarrassment, the trend of the questions he was about to be asked. The first two or three, which concerned his family, he answered briefly. Then the Ambassador asked, "Have you, for example, any close personal ties, Major? I am aware that you are unmarried, of course, you have stated this in your appplication, but are you, perhaps, engaged to be married? Do you contemplate matrimony in the immediate future?"

14

"I—" Sandra's lovely, serene face floated for an instant before John's eyes. His hesitation was perceptible, but finally he shook his head. "I'm not actually engaged, sir, but I have hopes of becoming engaged in the near future—hopes which, to be honest, had to be deferred until I had found myself a job."

He forced himself to speak quite lightly, yet, in spite of this, something of the intensity of his feelings reached the man reclining on the couch. The Ambassador's dark brows rose in swift question. "You mean that you might wish to marry before leaving for Gaupal? You might wish to bring your wife with you?"

Did he? John wondered. Had he really any serious hope of that? He hadn't, of course—his relationship with Sandra Beauchamp had been, perforce, a casual one, with no promises either on his side or hers. She had realized that he was in love with her, he imagined, although he had never put his feelings into the form of a proposal. Circumstances had made it impossible for him to do so and she had known that. He had met her for the first time a little over six months ago and,

15

within a week of making her acquaintance, had received official notification from the War Office that his services were not to be retained.

It hadn't been the most propitious moment at which to begin a courtship, yet all the same, he had begun it. For Sandra's sake, he had spent the last six months of his Army service replying to advertisements, seeking interviews, looking for the sort of job that would enable him to ask her to become his wife. Up till now he hadn't found one, but that hadn't stopped him taking her out, seeing her as often as she would let him, making love to her. They had gone about regularly together, to parties, theatres, dances: Sandra had many friends and she led a busy social life, but John knew that he had occupied more of her time than anyone else. He knew that she was fond of him and that he attracted her, knew, too, that he had no serious rival, but . . . it was a big but . . . Sandra was a very successful career woman. A dress designer by profession, she had worked extremely hard to win the recognition she wanted. She now had her own small, exclusive salon in the West End and it was coining money.

Would she abandon this, would she sacrifice all that she had worked for in order to marry him? Perhaps. But would she be willing to go with him to a remote, Far Eastern native State, which few Europeans had ever heard of and fewer still had ever visited? It seemed doubtful in the extreme and yet . . . he had to hope she would, in time. He had to believe, if he left her now, that she would wait for him: he had to convince himself that if he extracted a promise from her to join him there, she would love him enough to keep it. And he *did* believe that. If Sandra gave him a promise, she wouldn't break her word . . .

He drew a long, sighing breath.

"Well, Major Anson?" prompted the Ambassador softly. John braced himself. "I think, Your Excellency, that in all fairness I should tell you that I should *like* to marry before I leave England and that I should like to bring my wife with me to Gaupal. But I don't think for a moment that it will be possible. The most I can hope is that my—that is, the young lady in question may agree to join me there in, say, six months' or a year's time. Would there be any objection to such an arrangement?"

The blandly smiling brown face opposite betrayed neither approval nor disapproval. "No objection at all, Major Anson," the Ambassador stated simply. "I think it would be a most sensible arrangement. A year would give you ample time to settle down in Gaupal and to get to know the country and its people, as well as the royal family and, of course, your pupil. The appointment is open to a married man and a house and servants will in any case be provided for you, whether or not you are married."

"But you would prefer it if I were not?" John suggested.

"Initially, yes, Major Anson." The Ambassador stubbed out his cheroot. "I have been empowered to choose a mentor for the Prince," he went on, "and the choice is left entirely to my discretion. You were my first choice. I confess, however, that the fact that you were unmarried influenced me to a certain extent in selecting you for interview before any of the other candidates. Mine is a backward country by Western standards, you will understand, and life in Tauling might be very lonely for a young Englishwoman accustomed to living in London. I am sure you will have the good sense to realize this —you have served in Burma and Malaya and will know what I mean. You would not take as a wife a woman who could not adapt herself to our conditions and share them happily with you. After a year's experience of them—even after six months —you would be in a position to judge what they are and to make them comprehensible to the young lady whom you propose to marry, would you not, Major Anson?"

"Yes, sir, I think I should."

"'Good." The Ambassador sat up, smiling. "I am glad that you agree. In a year's time—who knows? The British community in Tauling may be quite numerous. At present, apart from your Ambassador, we have only three Englishmen living there—officials of an oil company. And—this is confidential, of course—it is likely that His Majesty the King may grant them concessions in Gaupal which they have long wanted. If he does, then we may expect many radical changes to take place. This is one of the main reasons for His Majesty's decision to seek a British tutor for his son, Major Anson. He feels that—even if he himself cannot do so—his son should learn to keep pace with Western thought and knowledge, since Gaupal can no longer afford to remain isolated. And with much of Burma in a state of unrest and uncertainty, it is conceivable, is it not, that our oil may yet become an important commodity in Western markets and a source of profit and employment for our people?"

John inclined his head thoughtfully, concealing his surprise. During his quest for information about Gaupal, he had heard whispers concerning the discovery of oil and the possibility of its development by a British company, but this was the first time that he had heard it stated as a definite fact. He knew that it was tremendously important, and knew, too, that the official representative of Gaupal would not have mentioned it had the matter not progressed a long way beyond the realms of conjecture.

The exchange of diplomatic representatives between Great Britain and Gaupal was a recent innovation and had taken place only within the last three or four years. And, as one of his informants had pointed out, John recalled, it was significant that these representatives were of ambassadorial, rather than of ministerial status. Until this moment, he hadn't fully appreciated the significance of this subtle difference in rank, but now he was beginning to do so.

And—he drew in his breath sharply, remembering the Gaupali Ambassador's earlier question as to his willingness to risk his own life in defence of that of his young charge. The significance of this was becoming apparent too. Where oil was involved, other interests were also involved, and his military training had taught him that the preservation of oil supplies could, at times, even lead to war. Her oil supplies were vital to Britain—had not Suez been the proof of how vital? There would be other interests, hostile, perhaps, to his own country as well as to the small kingdom of Gaupal, which might oppose the King's plans by intrigue, if not by force. The Ambassador had spoken guardedly of elements amongst his people whose loyalty to the King was a matter for doubt . . . it all fitted together, like the pieces of a jigsaw puzzle . . .

"Well, Major Anson?" The Ambassador was sitting up, regarding him expectantly, a hand poised above the bellpush at his side. "Are you willing to accept the appointment as tutor to His Highness Prince Maung Saw? If you are, then I shall summon my secretary and he will bring you the contract to sign. You would be expected to leave for Gaupal within the next two to three weeks, which I take it you are willing to do. Your air passage will, of course, be provided, and if there are any points in the contract which do not meet with your approval, I feel certain that we shall be able to adjust them to our mutual satisfaction. The appointment would be for one year, with an option to extend it for a further year, and the salary, as stated in *The Times*' advertisement, the equivalent of two thousand pounds sterling a year, to be paid in whatever proportion of sterling to taus you may elect in due course. With, as I have already mentioned, a house and servants . . . and the rank of Colonel in the Gaupali Army."

John felt his pulses quicken. This was a job after his own heart, a job for which he was fitted and which he knew he could do. As a soldier, it appealed to him strongly. He would be serving his country in far-off Gaupal as, all his adult life, he had been trained to do. And in England, it seemed, he was unemployable. Sandra would understand that, she would realize why he was taking this opportunity when it offered. And if she loved him, she would come with him when he asked her to, she would share this adventure with him, as she would share his life.

He had a swift, mental vision of Sandra's face as he rose to his feet, a hand extended.

"Thank you, Your Excellency," he said formally. "I shall be pleased to accept the appointment."

The Ambassador took his hand. Then he depressed the bellpush and the little secretary came in, beaming, with a type-written document which he offered for John's inspection. It took a few minutes to read, but there was nothing in it to which he could possibly object. The terms of his new employment were fair and generous. He took the secretary's pen and signed his name firmly at the foot of the document.

He left the Embassy with a spring in his step and a new lightness possessing his spirit. He had a date for dinner with Sandra that evening, but it was still only a little after five. He decided to walk through the Park and fill in the time of waiting at his club, over a whisky and soda. He would need to give some thought to the form his proposal should take, and he might do a lot worse, he told himself, than rehearse what he intended to say to Sandra before they met, for it wasn't going to be easy to break the news of his impending departure to her. Or, if it came to that, to ask her to wait a year for him . . .

Striding briskly along the crowded pavement, John was brought to a halt by a set of traffic lights, on an island halfway across the road. He waited there without impatience for the lights to change, the long, seemingly unending stream of cars and buses crawling past him at snail's pace on either side. A small two-tone sports car, its hood down, drew up a yard from him and he glanced at it idly, attracted first by its gay, flamboyant colours and then by the glimpse he caught of the girl at the wheel.

It was only a fleeting glimpse, for the car moved on almost at once, but he thought, as he watched it go, that never in his life had he seen a more beautiful girl. Normally unimpressionable, he found himself staring after her. She was quite young, about twenty-three or four, as nearly as he could judge, slim and poised and charming, with a lovely oval face whose skin was close to perfection and a pair of frank, smiling brown eyes, their laughter echoed by a scarlet mouth, innocent of make-up. Her hair, dark and iridescent as a raven's wing, flew out behind her in the tiny breeze of the car's passing, caught but insecurely held by the jaunty little flowered hat which was perched on top of her head. John did not notice the dress she was wearing, for she had gone before he could do so, but he received the impression that it was dark— a woollen dress, probably, or a suit, with vivid touches of colour at neck and wrists.

Conscious of no disloyalty to Sandra but

only of his own swiftly awakened curiosity, he followed the progress of the small car through the traffic, admiring the skill of its driver.

To his surprise, he saw it come to a standstill opposite the steps of the building he had just left, the Gaupali Embassy. The girl slipped gracefully from her seat, mounted the steps to ring the doorbell and, a moment later, vanished inside the house.

And then the lights changed and John was caught up in a surge of hurrying pedestrians, intent on crossing as quickly as they could. He wondered, as he followed perforce in their wake, what business the beautiful, dark-haired English girl in the sports car could have with the Embassy of Gaupal, but, entering the Park at last, he put her out of his mind. Her business was no concern of his and he would probably never set eyes on her again. Perhaps she was a friend of the Ambassador's daughter, calling to take tea with her, or a society girl, employing her time usefully as a confidential and highly paid stenographer. It didn't matter who she was: they had met without recognition or acknowledgment and passed each other by. Only her destination had been a coincidence, her beauty a brief delight, but—he had other things to think about and decide before he called to pick up Sandra. Suddenly impatient, John hailed a taxi. He would drive to his club and ring up Sandra from there. Perhaps, if he asked her, she would manage to get off early this evening . . .

"Pall Mall," he directed the driver, "this end. I'll tell you where to stop."

He got in and the taxi swung back into the line of cars heading slowly for Hyde Park Corner, the driver whistling tunelessly under his breath.

2

SANDRA BEAUCHAMP was busy with a customer when her assistant came in diffidently to call her to the telephone.

"I can't possibly come now, Elizabeth," she objected. "Say I'll ring back, or take a message, will you?" Her voice trembled on the edge of irritation, for it had been a long day and she was tired. In spring the thickly carpeted little showroom always seemed too small and stuffy, almost as if it were a prison for her restless, dissatisfied spirit. On days like this, Sandra longed to escape from it, to go out, locking the door behind her, never to open it again, and yet . . . she bit back a sigh. When the chance to escape offered, she never took it, she carried on, driven by an ambition whose demands took heavy toll of her but which, it seemed, she was powerless to resist.

She was now twenty-nine, and there had been so many lost chances, so many might-have-beens. She sat back on her heels, surveying her handiwork with half-closed eyes.

"I think," she said, "a little more fullness in the skirt, Mrs. Lane." But her mind wasn't on what she was doing as, automatically, she reached for the pins and despatched Elizabeth to summon a fitter from the workroom upstairs.

So many lost chances . . . this time, the sigh refused to be suppressed. There had been Peter, who had been her first love, but she had dismissed him as an adolescent dream and hadn't regretted it. Peter and Ted and George, all of whom had belonged to her youth. They had been fun, but that was all. Vince Leyman, the American surgeon, had been more serious. She had almost married Vince, but—he had been killed in an air crash and, while his memory still hurt a little, it was beginning to fade. After Vince, there had been Charles. Charles, who could have given her so much, who would have bought her all the things for which she had forced herself to work . . . Charles, who had gone away because she had refused to accept either his love or the gifts he had wanted to shower on her . . . she bit her lip.

Now there was John. Sandra's face, hidden from the customer as she bent to adjust a hem, suffused with warm colour. John was a darling—gentle, chivalrous, sweet, utterly without guile. He wasn't her type at all, really, but he attracted her more than she cared to admit. He was so tall and good-looking, with his tanned skin and his clean-cut profile, his blue eyes, that should have belonged to a seaman rather than a soldier, and the fair hair that was beginning to grey a little at the temples. Oh, she was fond of John: she enjoyed his company and his devotion, his good manners and the way he protected her, his air of breeding and the fact that, in a world whose standards were topsy-turvey, he was so undeniably a gentleman. But . . . would she marry him, if he asked her? Or would she let this chance slip through her fingers when it came, as she had let all the others slip, when they came?

She didn't know. That the chance *would* come, she could not doubt: it was only a question of time until John found a job, and then, of course, he would ask her to marry him. A man like John, who was upright and decent, always did ask the girl he loved to marry him: he would want her in no other way. She wondered if he had succeeded in getting the job he had gone after today and then, pinning busily, wondered what sort of job it was. He hadn't told her, but he had seemed quite hopeful for once. Perhaps the telephone call had been from him, to tell her about it. She must remember to ask Elizabeth when she came back . . .

"I like it," Mrs. Lane told her, turning this way and that in front of the triple mirrors. "Yes, I like it very much, Sandra. You're a clever girl."

"Thank you," Sandra replied, without elation. Mrs. Lane was an old customer and a faithful one, but she was easy to dress and easier still to please. It was really no achievement to sell her a dress.

The fitter came in and, rising to her feet, Sandra issued crisp instructions. The fitter nodded. Her work had been done for her and all she had to do was to help Mrs. Lane out of the dress. As she did so, Elizabeth whispered, "Miss Beauchamp, that was Major Anson. He told me to ask if he could call for you at six-thirty instead of seven. If it's not convenient, will you ring

31

him at his club. I wrote down the number."

So it *had* been John . . . Sandra glanced at her watch. It was a quarter to six now and she had the day's accounts to check, as well as the order for Melanie et Cie to attend to, before she could possibly leave. And Mrs. Lane would have to be seen off the premises with due courtesy—the purchase of a sixty-guinea cocktail dress entitled her to this. She might even expect a glass of sherry in the office before she left.

"I can't," she told Elizabeth, "I can't hope to get away a minute before seven. Get through to Major Anson's club, would you, and explain that I'm tied up?"

"Yes, all right," Elizabeth promised dutifully. She was a pretty girl with a lovely figure and she wasn't at all bad at her job. But she had no imagination, Sandra thought, as she watched her assistant cross the showroom and pick up the telephone in the outer office, to dial the number with a languid, beautifully manicured hand. Her face was remote and expressionless, her thoughts—if she had any—obviously miles away. She would

32

simply deliver her message in a toneless voice and then hang up. On impulse, Sandra followed her, taking the receiver from her unresisting hand.

"I'll do it myself," she said brusquely. "Go and look after Mrs. Lane. Tell her there's sherry in the office and that I won't be a moment." To the respectful male voice which came to her across the telephone wires, she said, forcing herself not to sound impatient, "I'd like to speak to Major Anson, please. Tell him it's Miss Beauchamp."

"Very good, madam. I will ascertain if Major Anson is still here." There was a long wait. Sandra drummed restless fingers against the ivory-coloured base of the telephone, regretting the impulse which had prompted her to speak to John herself, instead of letting Elizabeth do it. This was such a hideous waste of precious time . . . when, at last, she heard John's voice on the line, she was unable to conceal her annoyance.

"John, really . . . where do you hide yourself in that club of yours? I've been waiting simply ages and I'm up to the eyes . . ." She cut ruthlessly into his apology. "Oh, it doesn't *matter*, and I simply haven't time to listen to involved explanations now. I just rang up to tell you that I can't be ready before seven. In fact, with all this delay, I'll be lucky if I'm ready then."

"That's all right, my dear," John answered equably. However rude or impatient she was, he never seemed ruffled, never lost his temper with her, Sandra reflected ruefully. There were moments when she almost wished he would. "I'll be along at seven. I can wait if you haven't finished, there's no hurry. I've booked a table for a quarter to eight, at the Savoy. I thought we could have a drink first—I've got quite a lot to tell you."

There was a note of eagerness in his voice, Sandra realized, and he sounded pleased and excited, as if someone had unexpectedly left him a fortune or as if . . . she caught her breath.

"John—you didn't get that job, did you? The one this afternoon?"

She heard his deep, pleasant laugh. "I did indeed, my sweet."

"Is it a good one? Oh, darling, I'm so

pleased." And she was, genuinely pleased, for his sake. It had worried him and struck at the roots of his male pride when his earlier attempts to find work had proved so unsuccessful, Sandra knew. She asked again, "*Is* it a good job, John?"

"Two thousand a year, Sandra. And a house. But—"

Again she cut him short, her tone sharp, "A *house*?"

"That's right. But it's a long story, which will have to keep till I see you, if you don't mind."

"Of course I don't mind. But—two thousand a year! John, that's wonderful."

"And a step up in rank," John said. "I'm a full colonel. So long, darling. See you at seven."

Infuriatingly, he didn't wait for her to question him further but rang off. Sandra stood with the receiver in her hand, staring down at it blankly. Had he persuaded the Army to take him back? How extraordinary! But a house and two thousand a year *and* promotion—that could scarcely mean anything else.

It also meant—Sandra replaced her receiver on its rest with a little click—it also meant, of course, that John would ask her to marry him this evening. That was why he'd booked a table at the Savoy, why he'd been in such a hurry to call for her and why he'd sounded so happy and excited on the telephone. She was about to be offered another chance of escape . . .

Sandra looked round the small salon with uncertain eyes, studying it as if she were seeing it for the first time. Subdued voices reached her from the fitting room —Mrs. Lane's, Elizabeth's and the fitter's. They were talking clothes and were absorbed in their discussion, oblivious of her, indifferent to her, interested in nothing else. A fading shaft of light from the window fell on a sheaf of patterns she had beed sorting when Mrs. Lane came in. They lay where she had thrown them down, soft greens and yellows, a swatch of lilac coloured silk and, beside it, the sketch she had started to do before the interruption. She glanced at it, made a gesture of annoyance and crumpled it up. For some reason she couldn't have explained, even to herself, tears came to prick painfully at her eyes. She was tired, she told herself, bending to gather up the silks. Tired and a little disillusioned, perhaps. The spring always had this effect on her, made her wonder if she hadn't lost the substance for the shadow, made her doubt whether the considerable success she had won had been worth the effort it had taken, the worry, the fear.

And the loneliness. A woman's life was lonely, it was incomplete if she lived it by herself . . . *for* herself. Women were odd creatures. To be fulfilled, they needed love and marriage, children—a home. A career wasn't enough by itself . . . not really. It never could be, for a woman with a heart.

Sandra stood up, squaring her shoulders. Her reflection stared back at her from half a dozen angles on the mirror-hung walls. She saw a tall, elegant woman in a fashionable spring suit, with a perfectly groomed head and an expertly made-up face which, in spite of the make-up, looked tired and rather sad. A suspicion of a bitter droop to the carefully outlined scarlet lips was already there, giving them a hardness that made her want to cry out loud in protest: and the traces of tears in her grey eyes gave them a washed-out look, like the sea after rain.

She dabbed at them hastily and went blindly into her office, closing the door behind her. There was a framed snapshot of John on the desk. She picked it up. He was very nice, she thought. It shouldn't be hard to love him . . .

When Mrs. Lane was escorted into the office by Elizabeth, Sandra was her usual assured and charming self. She drank sherry, chatted with her customer and saw her to the street door, a quarter of an hour later, as if nothing untoward had happened.

Afterwards, she dismissed Elizabeth and heard the workroom staff clatter downstairs. They called good night to her and she answered them abstractedly. The account books were piled up on the desk in front of her and she dealt with them mechanically, scarcely aware of what she did, only part of her mind on them. The rest of it, like Elizabeth's a little while ago, was a long way away . . .

John's ring on the doorbell came punctually at seven. Sandra rose, put away the books and covered the typewriter, setting out a tray of sherry and glasses in their place. Before going to open the door to him, she carried in the great bowl of daffodils from the showroom and placed them on one side of the desk. Then she went to the door. Her fingers shook a little as she fumbled with the catch. "Come in, darling," she invited, and smiled up at him. John followed her across the showroom in silence, his feet making no sound on the thick, pearl-grey carpet. Reaching her office door, she halted and turned to face him. "Oh, John," she said, her voice not quite steady, "I'm so terribly pleased about your new job—more pleased than I can begin to tell you, darling!"

"So am I, Sandra," John answered gravely. He took both her hands in his, drew her to him and held her close. "It gives me the right to do this at last . . ." She felt his mouth on hers, felt the strong, eager beat of his heart as he held her imprisoned against him. His kiss was long and passionate and demanding and, with a little sigh, Sandra relaxed in his arms, her lips soft as they yielded to his. She was aware of him as never before, the blood leaping to new life in her veins, her heart racing. They were both a trifle shaken by the intensity of their emotions when he finally released her, to stand looking down at her, his blue eyes bright. "Darling, I didn't mean to do it like this . . . here, in the shop. I'd planned to come out with it all pat at the Savoy. I love you, Sandra, I think you know that, don't you? And you know that the only thing that stopped me asking you to marry me before was the fact that I hadn't a job or any prospect of one."

Sandra let her head fall on to his shoulder. She enjoyed the sensation of his fingers gently caressing her hair.

"Yes," she admitted, "I—I thought that was why. Are you asking me to marry you now, John?"

"Yes, darling, I am. If you'll have me . . . I want you terribly, Sandra, I doubt if you realize how much. I'd like to marry you tomorrrow, only—that won't be possible, I'm afraid. You see, my new job's abroad, in the Native State of Gaupal, and I'll have to go there for a year first, before we can be married. But there's a house, as I told you, and servants, the terms are extremely generous and—"

Sandra raised her head, staring at him, the colour slowly draining from her cheeks. "You mean you want me to wait for a year, while you go abroad? To—to Gaupal, wherever that may be?"

John's hand gripped her shoulders hard.

"Yes, darling, that's about the size of it. We'd be engaged and either you could join me in Gaupal in a year's time and we could get married there, or I'd come home in order to fetch you and we'd have the wedding here in London and fly back together. You see—"

"I think," said Sandra shakily, "that you'd better come in to the office and we'll have a drink, while you explain to me, in words of one syllable, what all this is about. Where *is* Gaupal, for heaven's sake? And what are you going to do there? You said you'd been made a colonel—are you going to command the Gaupal Army or something? You"—her laugh was strained and it held little amusement—"you really have rather taken the wind from my sails, you know."

"Have I? Darling, I'm sorry." John again drew her to him. "I'll explain, of course, and I'll show you exactly where Gaupal is on the map. I'll tell you everything I know about it and about my job in a moment, I promise you. But the

41

important thing, the thing that matters is whether or not you love me. Do you, Sandra—do you love me enough to marry me in a year's time? Do you love me enough to wait a year, without me, while I get to grips with my job and make a home for you? Please, darling, tell me the truth . . . do you love me enough for that?"

Panic seized Sandra. So this, she thought, was to be her escape. She was to go to some outlandish, uncivilized Native State on the other side of the world—with John. She was to give up her work, her salon, her life and all that she had built up with so much effort and at so great a cost, in order to become John's wife, in order to bear John's children, in order to keep John's love . . . she choked on a sob.

She couldn't face it, she couldn't, and yet . . . what was the alternative? To stay here, to go on working, to go on fighting, alone? To be unfulfilled, unless she married someone else—and *who* else? She wasn't getting any younger and she was so tired of most of the men she met in the course of her work or at the parties to which she dragged herself, with increasing lack of enthusiasm, when John wasn't with her.

Oh, God, what was the answer? John was waiting for her to say something, a hint of pain dawning in his eyes. But what could she say to him, what answer could she give when, in her heart, she wasn't really certain how much he meant to her or if she really loved him. If only his job had been in England . . . if only he'd given her a little more time.

But—*hadn't* he given her time? Wasn't he offering her a year in which to make up her mind? An engagement wasn't final, like marriage: an engagement could be broken off if one didn't want to continue with it . . . of course, that was the answer!

She raised her face to John's, brushing his cheek with her lips very gently, without passion. "I love you enough to wait for you, John darling," she whispered, "and we'll get engaged if you want to . . . announce it before you go, if you like. Dear John—" She felt his arms tighten about her and again became conscious of a sensation of breathless ecstasy as he kissed her. But, an instant later, she freed herself from his embrace.

"Come!" She held out her hand to him, smiling. "I want you to tell me about Gaupal—and show me where it is on the map. I want to hear all about everything, darling. And I need a drink!"

The daffodils, in their handsome copper-coloured bowl, nodded their stately heads in unison as she brushed past them. Sandra touched them lingeringly. Daffodils were a symbol of spring, she thought, and turned to look back at John. He raised his glass. "To you, my darling," he said softly. "You've made me quite unbelievably happy, you know."

It was a little after ten when John let himself into his father's Harley Street house. His mood of quiet happiness persisted, even after he had left Sandra. They had celebrated with a magnificent dinner, they had danced and toasted each other in champagne. It had been a wonderful evening, an evening, John thought, that he would remember for as long as he lived. Now he was anxious to have a talk with his father, to acquaint him with the change in his circumstances and the fact that he was engaged to be married.

It was going to be quite a *lot* for the old man to take in all at once, but he'd be pleased, of course. He would undoubtedly be very pleased. He had met Sandra a couple of times and had seemed to approve of her, and he could not possibly fail to approve of the Gaupal appointment.

There was no one about on the ground floor and all the consulting rooms were in darkness. John mounted the stairs two at a time and, seeing a light under the door of his father's study, tapped on it softly.

"Father—are you busy? D'you mind if I come in?"

The door opened and his father stood framed in it, his lined, tired face creased into a smile of welcome. "John, my dear chap, come in, come in! I was afraid you weren't going to show up until the small hours, and I've someone here from the hospital whom I want you to meet. Doctor, this is my son, about whom we've been talking. John—Dr. Rose Lian. She's the daughter of His Excellency the Gaupal Ambassador, and I promised I'd introduce you to her."

John went into the room. His hand was extended, but he withdrew it, his jaw dropping in ludicrous astonishment as he recognized his father's guest.

Dr. Rose Lian was the girl he had noticed driving the sports car earlier that day. Seen thus, at close quarters and in evening dress, she was even lovelier than he had imagined. And, only a few inches shorter than himself, she looked as English as any girl he had ever met.

"Good evening, Colonel Anson," she greeted him politely. "I have been hearing so much about you, both from your father and my own. I believe that we shall be travelling to Gaupal together quite soon."

3

IT was midnight when Rose Lian returned to St. Ninian's Hospital, escorted there, in a taxi, by John Anson. As a post-graduate student, awaiting the results of the examination for a Diploma in Tropical Medicine, she had no duties to perform and held no specific appointment at the hospital. But she had the freedom of the wards and often availed herself of this at night.

She liked the hospital at night. While frequently no less busy than by day, the night hours were hushed and strangely peaceful, the great, echoing entrance hall all but deserted. The Out-Patients Department—a hive of bustling activity during the daytime—was lit now by a subdued light, and, as she glanced in through the double glass doors, it seemed to Rose to be peopled by shadows.

She skirted the porter's lodge, hearing the shrilling of a telephone as she passed. It was the only sound. Apart from the staff, who moved softly and spoke in lowered voices, only the seriously ill were wakeful in the hospital at night: only in the theatres and in Casualty were there lights blazing and people moving about as normally as they did by day, for these departments never closed and time meant nothing to anyone working there.

Rose made her way down a long, silent corridor to the Theatre Block. A list, pinned to the notice board just inside the first pair of swing doors, told her that four of the theatres were busy. In Number Two, an emergency operation for decompression was being performed by one of the senior consultants, on a case she had herself examined earlier that day.

Rose donned a gown and mask and went in to watch it, but her mind, usually so eagerly attentive on these occasions, began to stray, after a while, from the surgeon's deft, purposefully moving hands to her own hopes and dreams and plans for the future.

Surgery had always interested her more than medicine. She was through the preliminaries for the Edinburgh Fellowship— she had held a junior house surgeon's appointment for a year at her training hospital and had been attending a special course in general surgery at St. Ninian's, following the diploma course—but now time was running out. She knew that it was no use dreaming of staying on, in the hope of being able to sit the Fellowship examination a year hence. She had said as much to Sir Michael Anson this evening, when he had sought to persuade her to stay on, offering, as inducement, an appointment on his own firm at St. Ninians. It had hurt a great deal to say it and it had hurt still more to have to refuse so unexpected and gratifying an offer, but . . . she had had no choice.

In a fortnight's time, she must return to Gaupal, to take her place in the splendid new hospital which the King had caused to be built in Tauling.

Rose expelled her breath in a long-drawn sigh. She had a duty to her country: trained physicians and surgeons were desperately needed to staff the new hospital and, besides, it meant so much to her father that she should go back. His heart was in Gaupal, in spite of the fact that he had lived more than half his life away from it, in selfless exile.

At the thought of her father, Rose's mouth curved into a smile behind the concealing mask. There were few people in the world, she thought proudly, who could compare with her father, for he was an exceptional man. Soldier, poet, statesman and now diplomat, he possessed a brilliant intellect and more than his share of far-sighted courage. In a society which was not remarkable for these qualities, he was wise and generous and kindly, a just master and a loyal servant. And he had been so good to her, had given her so much, loved her so deeply . . . she sighed again. Now it was time for her to prove that she was worthy of the trust he had placed in her and the love he had lavished upon her—the years, the care and the money he had expended on her education and training. He had no son. She was all he had and she must not fail him. For her mother's sake, if for no other, she must endeavour to repay the debt they both owed him . . .

"We shall see, gentlemen, that the diagnosis of subdural haemorrhage has been correctly made in this case . . ." The surgeon's voice, raised so that the dozen or so watchers in the tiered seats of the semi-circular gallery might hear it, reached Rose faintly, bringing her mind abruptly back to the present.

She had been the first to make the diagnosis of subdural haemorrhage. Neither the casualty officer nor the senior house surgeon had shared her opinion when the patient had come in that morning. She was relieved to learn that her instincts hadn't been at fault. In the early stages, it was frequently very far from easy to make the differential diagnosis in head injuries of this nature, but something about the sick man's appearance, when she had first looked at him, had warned her that he was more seriously hurt than either his history or the casualty officer's report on the accident had suggested. And the X-rays had borne her out, revealing a closed, depressed fracture of the skull, involving the vital motor area of the brain, with loose fragments of bone which . . .

". . . we observe that the dura mater is torn, a spicule of bone having entered it below the site of the injury. You should study the radiographs in this case, gentlemen. The fracture is much more extensive than these lead one to expect, which is almost always the case in this type of fracture. I am now going to remove the loose fragments of bone, excising the dura mater at this point, in order to evacuate the clot. The Horsley's seeker, Sister, if you please . . ." The surgeon's voice faded into silence as he resumed his patient, meticulous task.

The little group of green-robed figures about the operating table was still, as the theatre sister slapped the instrument he had asked for into the surgeon's gloved palm. In the gallery, those students who, despite the lateness of the hour, had come to watch and learn, leaned forward in their seats, rapt and absorbed. Only one, seemingly indifferent to the tenseness of the scene being enacted below him, wrote up notes, seldom raising his eyes from the scrawled pages of his notebook. The stertorous, laboured sound of the patient's breathing and the small, metallic clatter as a discarded instrument was thrown down, was all that disturbed the silence as the fight for a man's life went quietly on. Time passed slowly and most of the watchers in the gallery were tired, but none made any move to go.

Rose, too, remained where she was, but again, after a time, she found her thoughts beginning to wander. It was a long time since she had thought of her mother, but she thought of her now and wondered, remembering, whether her father's memories were as fresh and painful as her own.

Her mother had been French . . . Marie Claude Antoinette de Chaumont. The daughter of a distinguished French Colonial administrator, she had been only seventeen when she had made her first marriage to an officer of the Foreign Legion, whom she had met at a ball in Hanoi. They had made a runaway marriage, within twenty-four hours of making each other's acquaintance, although why they had done so had never been quite clear to Rose. Her grandfather, she knew, had held an important Government post in Indo-China and was a man of wealth and influence—perhaps he had hoped for a better match for his daughter than the one she had so precipitately made for herself. At all events, the young couple had eloped and M de Chaumont had washed his hands of them.

After a brief honeymoon, spent in Saigon, they had set out for the bridegroom's military station, an isolated outpost of the Legion in Laos, close to the Gaupal border. Tragedy had struck very soon after their arrival there, when a band of marauding dacoits attacked the post— in the absence from it on patrol of the majority of its defenders—and, overcoming the depleted opposition, entered the village and put the few survivors to the sword. Her mother had somehow escaped into the mountainous jungle with two women servants, after being compelled to witness the murder of her husband. And there, after days of terrified wandering, her mind all but unhinged, she had been found by a Gaupali hunting party led by Rose's father, half starved and desperately ill, unable to give a coherent account of what had befallen her.

Her father had made camp at the spot where he had found the three exhausted women, so as to avoid subjecting them to the ordeal of a further journey across the mountains, and, with the kindly tenderness that was typical of him, he had nursed all three back to health. Finally, when her mother had recovered sufficiently to be moved by litter, he had taken her back with him to his own palatial residence in Tauling.

Their marriage had followed a few weeks later. Rose had never fully understood the circumstances which had led up to her parents' marriage, but she knew that her mother had obstinately refused to return to Indo-China or to get in touch with any of her relatives, either there or in France. She had, it seemed, been content to remain in Gaupal, making no move even to inform M. de Chaumont of her safety and, in fact, keeping his existence a secret from her rescuers. Her one desire, apparently, had been to renounce her own people and forget the past. Rose imagined —and her father had never denied this— that her beautiful young mother had suffered a blow from which her mind had never quite recovered. Certainly there were gaps in her memory: it had been months before she could be prevailed upon to tell the full story of what had occurred during the dacoit attack, and years were to pass before she consented, at last, to seek out the father from whose house she had fled, at the age of seventeen, with her unwelcome suitor.

Rose herself had never heard the story from her mother's lips. What she knew, her father had told her after her mother's death, which had occurred when she was still a schoolgirl, completing her education at a British school.

They had lived together, a happy, united little family, first in Gaupal, later in India, during the war, when her father had been attached to Lord Louis Mountbatten's staff, and finally, up to the time of her mother's death, in England, France and Switzerland, where her father had headed various trade and military missions, returning periodically to Gaupal.

Rose had given her mother a child's unquestioning devotion and had felt her loss very keenly. She remembered her as a frail, gentle, soft-voiced woman of exquisite beauty, who had petted and caressed her but who had never seemed, even to her young eyes, fully adult. Her mother had borne no responsibility for household affairs, she had performed no housewifely duties and made no decisions. Her father was always the ultimate authority and he had treated Rose and her mother as if they were much of an age—two pretty children who were very dear to him.

Even to the servants in the vast Tauling palace, her mother had been known as Madame. She had spoken French and English fluently, Gaupali hesitantly and with a strong accent, and her constant companion, when Rose was at school, had been a Chinese woman servant called Marthe Hong—now pensioned off—who had escaped with her from the dacoit raid. Marthe Hong had gone everywhere with them, acting as ayah, cook and housekeeper and relieving her mother of all domestic worries.

The fact that she was the wife of a man of a coloured race had never caused the small, delicate Madame the slightest concern. Rose had accepted her mixed parentage with equal unconcern. In his own country, her father was the titled head of an old and noble family. A cousin of the reigning King, he had held a succession of increasingly eminent posts, which had included command of the Army of Gaupal and had culminated in his present appointment as Ambassador to the United Kingdom. He was the doyen of the newly created Gaupal diplomatic service and, in his years abroad, had always been in a position which entitled him to respect, as the accredited representative of his country.

Occasionally at school, Rose had heard herself referred to in uncomplimentary terms as the daughter of a Gaupali, but in general she had met with little prejudice in England and none at all in France, where she had commenced her education. She knew that she resembled her mother much more closely than she did her father and was aware that most people, meeting her for the first time, mistook her for a European and were puzzled by her name. Once, years ago, a friend to whom she had confided her mother's story had suggested that she was, perhaps, only the adopted daughter of the man she knew as father, and Rose had been horrified. That this was a possibility she was forced to admit, but it was not one she desired. She had never told the story to anyone else and, even now, grown up though she was, would have bitten her tongue out rather than question the Ambassador on the subject. She had accepted him as her father and loved him all her life: it would have hurt her unbearably to doubt their relationship now.

It was only sometimes . . . she bit her lower lip, feeling it quiver . . . sometimes, when she met a man like John Anson, that the look of surprise, glimpsed for an instant in his unguarded eyes, was hurtful, for she could read the thoughts which had prompted it. And she could feel the barrier—never admitted but always there —that her birth set between them.

"You seem so English . . . so French . . . so European," the look said, as it had said many times in the past. She ought to have become inured to all it implied by this time, Rose reflected ruefully, but she hadn't. It always hurt a little more each time she met it.

But she liked John Anson, was glad that he was the man whom her father had chosen to act as tutor to the young Prince Maung Saw, and it pleased her to think that—as he himself had insisted—she might have helped his cause in some small measure. Certainly she had talked a great deal about Sir Michael Anson to her father. She had conceived a deep admiration for the distinguished surgeon and his name had been frequently on her lips, but she was aware—knowing her father—that this, while it might have caused him to remember the name of Anson, would not have influenced his choice, had he considered the younger Anson unsuitable for the post. That this was likely to be a very difficult and responsible one she realized, with much depending on the character and personality of the man who undertook it.

The King and his family lived a completely secluded life in their enormous, sprawling palace in Tauling behind formidable, heavily guarded walls. None of them had ever left Gaupal. Surrounded by sycophantic courtiers, ringed about by archaic ceremonial and regarded as gods by the common people, they knew nothing about the Western world, save what they had read or were told—and they were not always told the truth. The King prided himself on his progressiveness, it was true, and he had done much that was good in his fifteen-year reign. But he was out of touch with the vast majority of his subjects, a remote, unapproachable deity, hearing of them only through the lips of his ministers, seeing them only through the curtained windows of a fast-moving car, whose escort let none approach too close.

The Prince's upbringing had been along traditional lines and, Rose thought, John Anson would find him an unreceptive pupil, unless he were able to devise some method of approach which would kindle his enthusiasm and break down the wall of reticence with which, hitherto, he had been surrounded.

"All right, I think he'll do now," the surgeon announced. His voice was low and controlled, devoid of emotion, but, as he turned from the operating table, Rose saw that his eyes were tired and that the expression in them belied the promise his words had held out. He had done his skilled best, but he knew that even his best might not be good enough—knew and accepted the fact that, in this case, he might have failed. He issued brusque instructions to the houseman who had assisted him and then, stripping off his mask with a weary gesture, disappeared into the changing room.

The theatre became full of bustling movement following his departure. A porter wheeled in a trolley, the patient was transferred to this and, almost before the trolley with its burden had vanished from sight, the work of clearing up had begun. The surgical team made for the basins to scrub up afresh, talking in lowered voices. A runner collected their discarded gowns, and a second, holding a pair of long-handled forceps at arm's length, prepared to take sterile gowns from the drums when they should be ready to don them. A tray of instruments was brought in from the sterilizer and the theatre sister, already freshly gowned, set to work to check these, her gloved fingers quick and deft as she arranged them in precise order for the next operation. A second trolley was wheeled slowly in from the anaesthetic room.

The whole busy, concentrated scene was being enacted once again and would be, probably, several times more before the night ended. To the staff there was no drama in this constant battle against death and injury and disease. Familiarity with it had reduced it to a routine, so far as they were concerned. It was a job they did, from which, at stated hours, they were relieved: a job they would do the next night and the next and the one after that. Soon, Rose thought, it would be *her* job, in the hospital at Tauling . . . she slipped out into the corridor, feeling suddenly, inexplicably, drained of energy.

It was late—past one o'clock—and time she got to bed. She had, for convenience, taken a room close to the hospital, but her bedroom at the Embassy was always kept ready for her and she decided, as she got into her car and pressed the starter, to go there now. It wasn't much further, and at this hour the traffic was comparatively light. She should be in Kensington in twenty minutes. Her father would be pleased if she were there, in the morning, to take breakfast with him. They had all too few opportunities, these days, to talk together as they had been wont to do in the past, he and she, for their work tended to keep them apart.

To her surprise, when she entered the Embassy, using her own key, there was a light still burning in her father's study. He heard her and called out to her and, wondering what could be amiss, Rose hurried to his side, joining her hands in the customary dutiful greeting before bending over to kiss his smooth, dark-skinned cheek.

"Does your foot pain you, Father, that you are awake still?" She looked down at him with concern. "Is there anything I can get for you? Some aspirin, perhaps, or would you like me to make you tea?" She spoke, from force of habit, in English.

He smiled and shook his head, gesturing to the tray at his elbow. "This tea is quite hot, my child—Tun Min made it for me before he retired for the night. I made him leave an extra cup, in case you came . . . I was hoping you would come, as a matter of fact, Rose. Pour yourself some tea and refill my cup for me, if you please. My foot is quiescent for the moment, I am pleased to say, and so, if you are not too tired, there is a certain matter that I should like to discuss with you."

Obediently, Rose picked up the small, delicately patterned teapot. An odd note in her father's voice, a note of strain, perhaps, made her ask curiously, "It is something that worries you, isn't it?"

"Yes," he confessed, accepting the cup she passed him. "It worries me a little, but that is because I am a selfish old man, my dear, and being so, I do not like to face the fact that I must soon lose you."

"You mean . . . ?" Rose hesitated, watching him anxiously. It was unlike her father to be evasive, yet he avoided her gaze and did not answer her unspoken question until she prompted, "You mean when I return to Tauling, Father?"

"That, of course, child—although I expect to be recalled within a few months of your departure, at any rate for a short time." The Ambassador smiled. Setting down his cup untasted, he reached for Rose's hand. "There is the matter of your future to be arranged, is there not?"

"But my future *is* arranged!" Rose protested. "Am I not to take up an appointment at the hospital? I thought that was what you had decided, what you wanted me to do, Father—"

"It is, child, it is." His slim brown fingers tightened about hers. "That is what I want with all my heart, that you should return in triumph to Tauling with a string of letters after your name and the skill you have acquired there for all to see, when you choose to demonstrate it . . . oh, yes, that is certainly what I want. But"—his eyes met hers and there was a wealth of significance in the glance he gave her—"you are a woman; Rose. You are now twenty-five."

"I . . . yes." She stared at him miserably, not pretending to misunderstand, and wave after wave of warm, alarmed colour crept slowly up into her cheeks.

"In Gaupal," her father pointed out gently, "it is usual for a girl to marry long before she reaches the age of twenty-five, Rose."

"I know, Father. But in my case—"

"Your case is, admittedly, exceptional. You have studied to become a doctor of medicine. I am proud of what you have achieved and, had she lived, I am sure that your dear mother would have been as proud as I. Rose, your presence in my house delights me—you are the light of my life, you are all I love and hold dear, and it will break my heart to let you go from me. Yet I must let you go. I must fulfil this last of my duties towards you by arranging a suitable marriage for you, according to custom."

"Is my training to be wasted, then?" Rose questioned, with a hint of rebellious bitterness in her voice.

The Ambassador patted her hand. His tone was gentle as he said, "No, child, it will not be wasted. I have received an offer for your hand which . . ." he broke off, searching for words, as if fearful of hurting her by employing those which offered any possibility of misunderstanding or doubt. Finally, since Rose appeared too stunned to give him a reply, he went on, smiling down at her with compassionate tenderness, "You are of your mother's race, Rose —in tastes, in appearance, in education and upbringing. Therefore, in spite of the years you have spent in my country, you are not of Gaupal and will not be, unless you wish to be. I shall not force this marriage upon you unless it is what you desire. Although, from the depths of my heart, I want it for you, since it will give you the place amongst my people that I long for you to have. An honoured place, my daughter, as the wife of an upright and distinguished man whom I should welcome into my family."

Rose drew away from him. She felt tears aching in her throat and burning unbearably behind her eyelids. Quickly she averted her face, lest her father see the tears and read into them evidence of her dismay. She could not have explained the overwhelming sense of grief and shock which had swept over her at his words. They had been unexpected, yet—there was no reason why they should have been. Had she not always known, had not her father told her that when the time came for her to marry, he—according to the custom of Gaupal—would choose a husband for her? And surely, if she had thought about it at all, she should have realized that, inevitably, his choice would fall on a man of his own race . . . as, now, it had?

For a moment, standing there beside her father with her head averted, Rose had a vision of John Anson's tanned, attractive face. She saw him, in that moment, not as a person but as a type. A good-looking, well-bred Englishman, the type of man she had come to know during her years at school and as a medical student in England —the type of man she had worked with and with whom, quite naturally, she had been on terms of friendship and equality. Even on one or two occasions, she recalled, the type of man for whom she had felt a strong emotional attraction. She had been too dedicated to her work and too dutiful a daughter to do anything save suppress such emotions in the past, too sensitive of the racial barrier to encourage any of the young men who sought her company to expect more of her than friendship. But she had enjoyed their friendship. She had danced with them, gone to their parties, driven in their cars, studied and worked beside them: she had shared their laughter, their triumphs, their fears and their anxieties and their long, exacting hours of toil. But always the barrier had been there . . . for her, if not for them. She had held herself aloof behind it, as if it were a secret armour

69

she wore. Not afraid but cautious, not mistrustful but wary—and conscious always of the fact that she had a life apart from that of her fellows to which, in the fullness of time, she must return.

Only once had she ventured to ignore the barrier. Once, five years ago, when she had been too young and inexperienced to understand what she was doing . . . Rose sighed. The result had been a hurtful lesson which she had never been able to erase from her memory.

Perhaps, she thought, her throat contracting, it would be as well if she were to remember it now, to recall how close she had come to disillusion and heartbreak all those years ago, when Jeremy had let her believe that he was in love with her. Jeremy, who had married the daughter of his erstwhile chief a few months afterwards and who—ambitious as always—was already making a name for himself in Harley Street, in partnership with his father-in-law. Jeremy whom she had loved, for whose sake she had been ready to forget her filial duty and sacrifice the principles which had governed her whole life . . . Jeremy who had told her, with his lips on hers, "Rose, I can't marry you, darling, you must understand that—the Old Man's expecting me to take Laura off his hands. But until I do, what's wrong with our having fun together, hitting the high spots a bit? Who's to know . . . ?"

The scraping of a match roused Rose from her brief, unhappy reverie. Her father set down the matchbox and inhaled smoke from his cheroot, leaning back against the sofa cushions, his eyes narrowed and pensive as he gazed up at the thin blue cloud of his own creation. His expression betrayed nothing of his thoughts or feelings, but Rose knew that he was waiting for her to speak, waiting for her to give him an answer to the question he had posed.

She dropped to her knees beside him, suddenly overwhelmingly conscious of her affection for him and of the ties of kinship which bound them together. He was her father. But in spite of this, he had never insisted on obedience to any of his wishes since she had left school, he had always left her free to decide matters of importance for herself, only giving her advice when she asked him for it, always listening with grave attention to any views she wanted to express. Even her choice of a career, she reflected, had been hers and hers alone, and he had never begrudged the years she had devoted to it, never reminded her that it was her duty to marry so that his line might go on . . .

"Father," she said, hands clasped and held out towards him, "it shall be as you advise me and as you think best."

The Ambassador let his cheroot fall into the ashtray. Leaning forward, he took Rose's outstretched hands between his own. "I am glad, child," he told her softly, "I am very glad. I have waited in order to see whether your choice would fall upon a man of your mother's race. Since it has not, then it is better that it should be a man of mine. He whom I have chosen for you is a good man and one whom you will be able to admire and respect."

Rose lowered her gaze. She asked in a small voice, retaining his hands in hers, "May I know who he is, Father?"

"You will meet him soon," her father returned. "He will attend our reception here next week. But already"—he smiled at her, putting two fingers beneath her chin and raising it, so that he might look down into her eyes—"already he has seen you when you were unaware of it, and he is enthralled, my daughter . . . he has told me so himself."

Rose's heart missed a beat but she remained silent. The Ambassador went on, "He is the new Director of the Army Medical Service, Colonel Kim San Myint, and he will be in official command of the new hospital in Tauling as soon as he returns. So you will be able to work together, if that is his wish and yours, at least until you are married. After that, of course, it will be for your husband to decide, but I think he will be reasonable— he has served for ten years with the British Army in Burma and Malaya and in Korea with our Gaupal Brigade. He has just spent six months here in England, attached to the Royal Army Medical Corps. His outlook is as Westernized as your own. And as a man he is well-favoured, in his late thirties, I believe, of good family, an experienced surgeon and a courageous soldier, decorated by the British in action during the Burma campaign and by the Americans in Korea.

I understand, from what he has told me, that he numbers our friend Colonel Anson amongst his acquaintances and that he is anxious to meet him again . . . well?" He regarded Rose expectantly. "Is my choice for you the right one? What do you think, Rose, my child? Tell me the truth."

Rose took one of the hands she held and bore it to her brow. She answered, her voice quite steady, "If Colonel Myint is your choice, Father, then he will also be mine."

She rose from her knees, made him a graceful obeisance and withdrew, closing the door very quietly behind her.

Left alone, the Ambassador finished his cheroot, his brows knit in an anxious pucker. But when it was done, he did not immediately prepare to retire for the night. Instead, rising with difficulty, he limped across to the big mahogany desk and seated himself there, drawing pen and paper towards him. After some thought, he began to write, covering four sheets of paper with his beautiful, ornate script before he was satisfied.

Finally, with a tired sigh, he selected

two of the pages he had written, thrust these into an envelope and sealed it carefully, tearing up the discarded sheets and setting a match to them, the burning paper making a tiny bonfire in the ashtray at his elbow. Then he picked up his pen again and addressed the envelope to Father Jean Delarge, care of the Tauling Mission. Across the corner, in heavy capitals, he wrote: PRIVATE AND CONFIDENTIAL.

For several minutes he studied the envelope, his mouth compressed and his frown deepening. Then he got up and went to a small safe set in the wall on the far side of the room, opened it and placed the letter inside, amongst his confidential papers. When he returned to his desk only a heap of greying ash remained of the pages he had sought to destroy. He touched the ash with an exploratory forefinger and it disintegrated into formless dust, save for one small scrap which the flames had missed. On this, four words in his own handwriting leapt to meet his eyes. ". . . *le père de Rose* . . ."

With a stifled exclamation, the

Ambassador lit a second match and held it, his fingers not quite steady, to the scrap of curling paper. It burned at once.

4

IT was John Anson's last week-end in England and he had planned to spend it with Sandra at an aunt's house in Sussex. He thought, as he strode briskly along the cobbled mews which led to Sandra's flat, that, when the time came, he would not be sorry to go. It would be a wrench leaving Sandra, of course—that would hurt like the very devil—but he was impatient to get to grips with his new job, to explore its possibilities, to begin the life that she would eventually share with him.

It might, after all, not be necessary to wait for a year before he sent for her to join him. Once he had their house organized and the staff trained and had picked up sufficient of the language to make himself understood, there would really be nothing to stand in the way of his marriage, providing Sandra agreed. He was hopeful that she would. An engagement was always rather a trial at the best of times, and for himself and Sandra, who weren't children, it was proving more of a trial than he had believed possible. With the thought of their long parting to haunt and torture them, with Sandra over-working and himself very fully occupied with packing and preparing for his depar-ture, their meetings had, perforce, been strained. These took place mostly in the evenings, when she was tired after a long and harassing day and he, loving her so much and longing desperately to comfort her, could find no words to express what he felt and had to fall back on platitudes.

He wondered, at times, whether he had disappointed her, whether she wanted more of him than he gave her, more tenderness, more reassurance . . . more time. Oh, there were moments, a great many of them, when he held her in his arms and was exultantly conscious of her eager response to his lovemaking: moments when they were alone together in the flat, in the salon after it had closed, in the car he had hired for their last fortnight . . . moments when she was wholly his and he could have no doubts. But there were others when, fight against them as he might, the doubts returned and he was afraid. He was asking so much of her, demanding so great a sacrifice: leaving her so soon and then being able to offer her so little . . . Standing outside the gaily painted door of her flat at last, his finger on the bellpush, John found himself wondering whether he hadn't been a fool. Perhaps he ought to have tried harder to find a job in England, for Sandra's sake. Or, having decided to go to Gaupal, perhaps he ought to have asked for a month's grace, instead of only a fortnight, and married her before he left. Perhaps . . .

The door opened and he stepped forward eagerly, hat in hand, a smile lighting his eyes. Sandra said, her voice flat, "Oh, it's you," and his heart sank as she lifted her cheek and permitted him to brush it with his lips.

"Of course it's me," he retorted, trying to make a joke of it, "surely you weren't expecting the Gaupal Ambassador, were you?"

She didn't answer, but turned and led the way into her small living-room in silence. The table was strewn with account books and he saw that she had been working on them, for the ink on one page was wet and a half-finished cup of coffee stood on a corner of the table, cold now, the cream congealing on its surface.

"I suppose you missed lunch?" he accused.

She shrugged. "I hadn't time. As it was I had to bring all these wretched books home with me. We had a ghastly morning, going flat out all the time."

"Well, it's a good thing if you're busy, isn't it, darling?" John made to draw her into his arms, but she eluded him. "Not now, John, for God's sake. I'm a mess. I simply must get into a bath, even if it holds us up. Sit down and make yourself at home. I'll be as quick as I can. Where did you park the car?"

"At the end of the mews." He forced a smile. "Off you go then and have your bath. I'll make you an omelette or some-thing and some fresh coffee while you're having it—it'll be quicker than trying to get a meal outside. And if you like I'll square up these books for you—I used to be quite an efficient book-keeper when I was in the Army, you know."

"I hate books," Sandra said. She swept

them from the table, her movements impatient, her hands trembling perceptibly. John saw that she was wearing his ring on the third finger of her left hand. It was a fine solitaire diamond which had belonged to his mother and which he had had reset for her in platinum, but he eyed it unhappily. Sandra hadn't been enthusiastic about the ring, although it was a much better one than any he could have afforded to buy for her. Obviously she had expected more of him, but—at least she was wearing it, which he supposed was what mattered.

When she had gone and he heard the bathroom door slam behind her, he picked up the heavy ledgers and set to work on them. It took him some time to finish them, and he was thoughtful when he made his way into the tiny kitchen to begin preparations for her meal. If Sandra's accounts were kept accurately, she wasn't only coining money, she was raking it in. Her overheads were heavy, it was true, but even so . . . he bit back a sigh. What could he give her to compare with what she was earning herself? Despondently, he started to break eggs into a basin, looking about him for a whisk. From the bathroom he heard Sandra's voice, humming a remembered tune . . . a tune to which they had danced, the night before last. Did she love him, he wondered, did she really love him enough? He wished, from the depths of his despair, that he knew. And then the milk he had put on to heat for the coffee boiled over and, cursing under his breath, he went to rescue it.

Sandra looked lovely when, a quarter of an hour later, she joined him. The bath had evidently refreshed her, for her cheeks were glowing and the pinched lines had vanished from about her mouth and eyes. She went into his arms and he held her to him.

"Darling, I love you." He said it ardently, lips in the soft fagrance of her hair and she breathed a sigh, raising her face to his. "I know you do . . . and I'm a beast to you, aren't I? A sulky, ill-tempered beast."

"You're nothing of the kind, darling," John denied.

"I keep you waiting, I'm always tired and then I bite your head off. I don't know how you put up with me. And—oh, that coffee smells heavenly . . . in spite of all I do to you, you go and make me coffee and a gorgeous-looking omelette and you never reproach me. You're a darling and I simply don't deserve you, John. Shall I eat the omelette now? I must say I'm famished, although I'd no idea I was, until I smelt the coffee."

He settled her at the table and watched indulgently as she demolished his omelette, pouring coffee for her and refilling her cup when she had done, offering her his cigarette case.

"I shall miss you quite desperately when you go, John," Sandra said suddenly, breaking a little silence which had fallen between them. She took a cigarette and John had to steel himself not to touch her, as he held his lighter to its tip.

"Will you?" he answered, careful to steady his voice.

Sandra patted his cheek. "You know I will. No one ever made me feel as—as precious to them as you make me feel."

"You *are* precious to me," John said. He captured her free hand and bore it to his lips. "Sandra, you are going to come out to me, aren't you? You are going to marry me?"

She looked down at the ring on her finger and smiled.

"I'm engaged to you, aren't I?"

"Yes, I know. But—"

"Either I'll come out or you shall come home to fetch me—if Gaupal proves to be at all possible. I shall have to trust you to decide that for both of us, shan't I? I must say . . ." She hesitated, and John was conscious of her eyes on him, an odd, half-teasing, half-serious expression in them.

"I must say," she went on, "the only Gaupali I've seen so far is extremely attractive. I'm not at all sure that I like the idea of your travelling out with her to Tauling, as I believe you're supposed to be doing, according to her."

John stared at her, puzzled. "What in the world do you mean? Sandra—*who* do you mean?"

"Dr. Rose Lian," Sandra returned. She smiled. "She came into the salon this morning to buy a dress for some reception her father's giving at the Embassy on Monday evening. I gather that *your* father recommended me to her. John—" She rose, looking up at him, a question in her eyes.

John rose with her. "What, darling?"

"I think I'd like to attend that reception after all. You did say we'd been invited, didn't you?"

"Why, yes," he admitted, "of course. But you said, since it was our last evening, that you'd rather not go to it, and I thought—"

"I've changed my mind," Sandra told him sweetly. "We'll go darling, if you don't mind. I want to."

John was silent as he led her out to his waiting car.

Sandra closed the salon half an hour earlier than usual on Monday evening, dismissing Elizabeth's plea to be allowed to remain in temporary charge with a scornful, "Oh, good heavens, no! You'd lose more custom than you'd bring in."

She turned a deliberately blind eye to her assistant's hurt expression and threatened tears, sent her off with the workroom staff and then retired to her office, to deal with the day's quota of orders. For once she had plenty of time and, since this was a rare luxury, Sandra poured herself a glass of the expensive dry sherry she kept for her best customers and permitted herself ten minutes' relaxation, with her feet up and a cigarette to accompany the sherry.

John was to call for her at the flat and give her dinner before taking her on to the reception at the Gaupali Embassy but he wasn't due until seven-thirty, so that there was no need for her to rush. In any case, she didn't feel like rushing. The weekend had been so peaceful that she was reluctant to shatter the mood it had induced.

Sandra slipped off her shoes and sat back, closing her eyes. She had enjoyed every moment of her week-end, spent with John at the home of an elderly aunt of his, who lived in a lovely, unspoilt Sussex village which had held an unexpected charm for her. They had driven down in leisurely fashion, in bright sunshine, the fields and woods they passed all clad in the brilliant new green of spring, and the gardens—even in town—gay with daffodils and narcissi, their bright faces upturned to the sun.

The aunt's house, though small, had been efficiently staffed by old-fashioned maids and run with pre-war elegance. Early morning tea and breakfast in bed had been brought to her, Sandra recalled, in a bedroom furnished in dark oak and curtained in chintz, with a beaming, white-haired housemaid in starched cap and apron to turn on a bath and bid her courteously not to think of rising until she felt so inclined.

There had been log fires, the scent of beeswax and freshly ground coffee, to mingle with the fragrance of country flowers and the delightful, unfamiliar smell of new-mown grass wafted in from the lawn outside—even a gardener, rejoicing in the name of William, to say "Arternoon, ma'am" and touch his cap to her when she went out to admire the result of his labours.

The small house had dreamed serenely in the sunshine, shut off from the outside world and from time and stress and motion, like the other houses which neighboured it. There had been an atmosphere of brooding quiet about the whole place, Sandra reflected, a sense of timelessness, a complete absence of haste. No noisy coaches parked by the single inn, to decant a crowd of thirsty passengers to fill its oak-panelled parlour. No stuttering sports cars with loud, inadequately silenced exhausts roared down the village street to scatter the geese on the green or drive the small stream of returning church-goers to seek refuge on the path beside the grave-yard wall. And there had been neither radio nor television to disturb the firelit quiet of after-dinner conversation or bring the news of strikes and crises to destroy its calm.

Sandra sighed. It had been a long time since she had experienced such content-ment as she had known during the last two days. She wished that it might always be so, for herself and John . . . but John was going away, thousands of miles away. He was going to Gaupal and would expect her to follow him there.

She was engaged to him . . . she crushed out her cigarette with sudden viol-ence. She had come closer to falling in love with John during that week-end than she had ever been before. He was a charming companion, considerate of her smallest wish, courteous, kindly, anxious only for her happiness, yet possessive and ardent enough to excite in her a warm response. A countryman by birth and upbringing, he had taken her fishing and for long walks across the smiling countryside, had stood beside her in the bar of the little inn, talking easily to the people about him, fitting perfectly into the village setting because, for him, it was home. She envied him his background. Her own had been so different. A Yorkshire mining town, grey and cold and unlovely, with the grim shadow of the pit always hanging over it in a smoky pall, with the spectre of poverty and unemployment so lately removed that it still haunted the memories of its inhabitants.

Sandra had left it for ever before she was out of her teens, she had risen above it and nowadays never spoke of her childhood, but—one didn't forget. One couldn't, unfortunately, however hard one tried. She shivered. She had never told John anything about her earlier life, he hadn't been curious and had asked no questions. She had simply said that her parents were dead and left it at that, allowing him to infer what he could from the vague hints she dropped, from time to time, of a once well-to-do family in a Northern city. Even the facts disclosed in her part of the engagement notice hadn't been entirely truthful . . . *Sandra Kathleen, only daughter of the late Commander and Mrs. Neville Beauchamp of Brocklehurst, Yorks* . . . No one was likely to refute her claim. No one knew the truth.

Except Charles. She frowned at the name. Charles Garrison was the only person with whom she had been entirely honest, but he had gone out of her life more than two years ago, back to the East. And it had been partly because she had been honest with him that she had let him go. She had learnt wisdom since Charles's going—a great deal of it from him. He . . .

The telephone rang with shrill abruptness. Stifling her annoyance at the interruption, Sandra lifted the receiver. Who on earth could be ringing her here, at this hour? It was now well past her usual closing time, although perhaps John, having tried the flat and obtained no answer, had decided to ring her here, on the chance that she hadn't left.

"Yes?" she said into the mouthpiece, without announcing her number, her tone noncommittal. If it should prove to be anyone to whom she didn't want to speak, she could always make the excuse of a wrong number . . . "Who is it you want?"

"Sarah?" The voice was a deep masculine one, faintly accented and startlingly familiar. What strange trick of fate was this, that Charles Garrison should telephone her at the very moment when she had been thinking of him? No one else called her Sarah nowadays. It *had* to be Charles. Sandra's fingers tightened convulsively about the receiver. She was shocked to notice that her hand was trembling. "Charles," she said, trying to repeat the name lightly, as if the sound of it amused her, "*Charles*! It *is* Charles, isn't it?"

"You know perfectly well it is, my dear," Charles returned.

The flat drawl was unmistakable, and Sandra drew a quick, uneven breath as panic seized her. Charles was the last person she wanted to see or talk to, the very last. She had got over him, he had ceased, months ago, to hurt . . . it was ages since she had thought of him, months since she had missed him.

"What—what do you want?" she asked, an edge to her voice. "Why have you rung me up? I thought you were abroad."

"I got back last week." . . . She could picture his lazy, mocking smile, imagine him sitting at his desk, his big body relaxed, his long legs stretched out in front of him. He would have a glass of whisky at his elbow, a decanter and siphon in a tray beside him. He drank sparingly, but always, when he did drink, it was Scotch, iced, with a dash of soda. One of his idiosyncrasies was that he hated the telephone and, when he had to use it, he invariably fortified himself for the ordeal with whisky. How absurd that she should remember that! With a return of her feeling of irritation, Sandra asked brusquely, "Well, what do you want? I'm rather busy and—"

"But not too busy, surely, to talk to me?" he challenged reproachfully. "Especially when I rang in order to congratulate you on the announcement I saw in the *Telegraph* this morning? Come now, it's not like you to bite my head off when I'm only trying to be civil."

"All right," said Sandra, making a great effort to control her voice, "you've congratulated me, you've been civil and honour is satisfied. Have you anything more to say or shall we ring off?"

"I've a whole lot more to say," he put in, with infuriating patience, "but I'd rather say it in person than on the phone. How about having dinner with me? I'm staying at the Westbury."

"I'm sorry," Sandra replied, without contrition, "I'm already dining out this evening."

"With the boy friend—with this chap Anson?"

"Of course."

"Is he a decent chap? I'd like to meet him."

"He is, *very* decent. But I'm afraid you won't have the chance of meeting him, Charles—even if I were prepared to introduce you. He is going abroad. He's leaving tomorrow and—"

"He's going to Gaupal, I take it?" Charles suggested. There was an odd note in his voice which surprised Sandra as much as his knowledge of John's destination. But before she could question him about it, he went on: "I heard he was going there from a mutual friend—a man who has interests in Gaupal and keeps his finger on the pulse of things. The appointment of a British tutor to the heir apparent is quite a thing, you know."

"Is it?"

"It certainly is, my dear."

"But why? It's just a job, isn't it?"

"Well . . ." Charles hesitated. "It could have pretty far-reaching consequences for a number of people, as it happens. Including this friend of mine—the one who told me that Anson had been appointed to the post. I didn't think much about it when he told me, of course—the name Anson didn't mean a thing to me then. But when I saw the announcement of *your* engagement to the self-same fellow, why, the coincidence struck me, that's all. So I overcame my aversion to this infernal telephone and rang you up . . . Look, Sarah my dear, I'd very much like to meet him before he leaves. Couldn't it be arranged somehow?" His voice took on a persuasive note. "Why

94

don't you both dine with me this evening, eh? Or failing that, come and have a drink?"

"I don't see how we can," Sandra objected. "We're going on to a reception at the Gaupali Embassy after dinner. And in any case—

He interrupted her with cool insolence, "Oh, then that simplifies matters a lot. I'll get myself an invitation to the Embassy and chase round and find a white tie. You won't go and cut me, will you, Sarah? I can rely on you to present me to your future husband, can't I?"

"Why in the world should I, Charles?" Sandra was at a loss to understand his persistence and more than a little piqued by it. "I see no reason why I should."

"I can see absolutely no reason why you shouldn't," Charles returned equably. "I'm interested in the fellow who's supplanted me in your affections. After all, I'm an old friend of yours, aren't I . . . apart from anything else? A *very* old friend. Used to know you in the Brocklehurst days . . . or had you forgotten that?"

Sandra sensed his amusement, although she couldn't see his smile, and her heart sank. She had once loved him, but she had few illusions about him. Charles Garrison was a financier of international repute with interests in oil, a wealthy and ambitious man who had fought his way to the top of his particular tree with a ruthless disregard for those who opposed him. A generous and powerful friend, he was an adversary to be feared and he was always at his most dangerous when he appeared to be amused, as she knew to her cost. Their parting had been a bitter one, of her making more than of his: for which, she was aware, he hadn't forgiven her. He had been very much in love with her and he wasn't accustomed to having any woman refuse him anything. She didn't think that he had ever quite realized why she had rejected him, but he had left her in no doubt that her rejection had wounded him deeply. Did he, she wondered in dismay, hope to take his revenge on her now? Through John perhaps . . .

"I suppose," she suggested, with unconcealed resentment, "you intend to have a nice long talk with John about . . . about Brocklehurst? Is that why you're so anxious to meet him?"

"My dear little Sarah!" Charles laughed aloud. "Such a thought never entered my head. *I* shan't give you away—what sort of an opinion can you have of me to suppose that I should? If you must know, I want to have a nice long talk about Gaupal with your John. Surely you've no objection to that, have you?"

"But why? *Why* do you want to talk to John about Gaupal?" Sandra's tone was suspicious. She heard him laugh again. "Darling, you've changed. Becoming a successful business executive has made you uncharitable and hard."

"Never mind about that. Just tell me why."

"Strictly business, I give you my word. By a strange coincidence, I've recently taken over a company with interests in Gaupal, and in fact I've just been out there. Does that satisfy you? In any case, I don't propose to say any more on the phone, with the lord knows who listening in to us. Come and have a drink with me and I'll tell you all about it. I have no secrets from you, Sarah, my once beloved."

Sandra glanced quickly at her watch.

There would just be time to see him, if she changed here. She could take a dress from stock and leave the orders until tomorrow. Her curiosity was aroused, as well as her suspicions, because it *was* a strange coincidence that Charles should have interests in Gaupal. It was more than strange, but at least it explained his phone call.

"All right," she said, "I'll come. Give me half an hour."

"Fine, my dear. The Westbury. Suite on the second floor. Just ask for me. I'll be waiting impatiently to see you."

He replaced the receiver with a little click.

The telephone rang again as Sandra was zipping up the dress she had chosen. She answered with an abrupt, "Yes? Who is it?"

This time it was John. He said apologetically, "Darling, an infuriating thing has happened. I've only just been told that I'm expected to dine at the Embassy this evening. It's in the nature of an official command, so I can't get out of it. There are people His Excellency wants me to meet before I leave. Will you forgive me?

I'll be round to collect you, at the flat or anywhere else you say, the instant dinner's over, and then—"

Sandra cut him short. "It doesn't matter, John. In fact as it happens, it fits in rather well . . . I've had an invitation to dine too. An old friend, Charles Garrison, who's been abroad for ages, asked me to meet him. I *was* only going to have a drink, but he'll give me dinner and he can bring me to the Embassy."

"Yes, but—"

"He says he's going to the reception anyway. I gather he wants to meet you. Don't worry, John dear—I'll be perfectly all right with Charles."

"I hate doing this to you on our last night, darling." John sounded so miserable that Sandra's heart went out to him.

"There'll be tomorrow," she offered consolingly. "And I'll see you at the reception."

"My father would give you dinner—" John began. She brushed that aside. John's father had come down for part of their week-end: she had been dutifully polite to him and that was enough. The idea of dining tête-à-tête with Sir Michael

Anson held no appeal for her: he was a cultured, charming man, but they had little in common. "No," she answered firmly, "I'll dine with Charles. See you later, darling—bye!" She rang off before John could voice any further objections.

She thought, as she finished her dressing, that it might, as things had turned out, be quite a good idea to spend the major part of the evening with Charles. While she could scarcely hope, in the circumstances, to win back his friendship, at least she might succeed in putting an end to his enmity. She didn't relish the thought of having Charles as her enemy now that he was back in London, for she was still, she realized, a little afraid of him. And with reason . . .

Sitting in front of a mirror in the showroom, she studied her reflection with critical eyes. She hadn't changed very much. She was still as beautiful as Charles had always told her she was: the two years that had passed since she had last seen him had taken their toll, but it wasn't apparent tonight. Her make-up hid the tiny maze of lines about her mouth and eyes, and the dress—although she *had* designed it herself—was lovely. Charles, as a connoisseur, would appreciate its subtleties . . .

She rose, took up her wrap and went to the door. A cruising taxi halted at her signal. Sandra locked the door of the showroom behind her and the driver leaned across from his seat. "Where to, miss?"

"The Westbury, please," Sandra told him. She got into the taxi and leaned back against its stiff, upholstered cushions with half-closed eyes. Her weariness had gone and a pleasurable thrill of excitement set her heart beating faster than its wont. In spite of everything, it would be good to be with Charles again. He wasn't gentle and chivalrous like John and he had never made her feel that she was precious to him. But he was an exciting person and she understood him. They were birds of a feather, he and she. They were both ambitious and they both made dangerous foes . . .

The peaceful week-end memories faded as the taxi sped down Piccadilly. Sandra sighed as other memories came flooding into her mind.

5

THE Gaupali Embassy was ablaze with lights when John reached it, a little after seven-thirty. He was shown into the Ambassador's study by a soft-footed native servant, who announced him as Colonel Anson and then stood aside with a low salaam.

There were already a number of other guests assembled in the lofty-ceilinged room, several of whom he recognized. The Ambassador, resplendent in the blue and gold of his official uniform, still limping a little but his foot free of its encumbering bandages, moved amongst them at the far end of the room. John bowed to him formally and the Ambassador returned his salute.

"Come in, Colonel Anson, come in!" It was the little secretary, beaming at him in respectful welcome and looking more boyish than ever in his impeccable tails. "What will you have to drink, sir? A cocktail, whisky, sherry, gin?" He signed to a servant when John asked for sherry, issuing orders rapidly in his own tongue. "Now, sir, His Excellency is anxious to introduce you. May I ask that you come with me, please?"

John followed him to the Ambassador's side.

"Good evening, Your Excellency."

"Good evening to you, Colonel Anson." The Ambassador extended a slim brown hand, his smile warm and friendly. "I regret the interference with your plans for this evening, my dear Colonel, but I thought it important that you should make the acquaintance of some of your new associates before you leave England. I trust that I have not inconvenienced you unduly?"

"Certainly not, Your Excellency," John assured him politely. "I am honoured and delighted to be here."

"It is good of you to say so. Tonight we shall be a small and exclusively male party at dinner—my daughter and, of course, your charming fiancée will be joining us afterwards, I hope. We have the head of our Trade Mission here—the Maharaj Kumar Chand Rewal, who arrived in

London only yesterday for talks with your Government. And our new Military Attaché, Major Thakin Sao. Also, I believe, an old friend of yours whom you knew in Burma—Colonel Kim San Myint of the Army Medical Service."

"Kim Myint?" John echoed, pleased. "Yes, indeed, Your Excellency, I remember him well."

"Then come, I beg you, and renew your acquaintance with him, as well as making that of my other guests." A hand on his arm, the Ambassador led him to a group gathered round the flower-decked fireplace. "Gentlemen, I should like to present Colonel John Anson, of whose appointment to the service of Gaupal you will have heard. Colonel Anson—Maharaj Kumar Chand Rewal . . . Colonel Taw Sin Gyi . . . Major Thakin Sao . . . Mr. Gilbert Gregory of your British Foreign Office . . ." the names followed each other in swift succession. John bowed and shook hands, striving to memorize the faces which smiled courteously back into his own. There were a number of other Englishmen present besides himself, private individuals as well as Foreign

Office representatives. He recognized an Under-Secretary from the Board of Trade and a distinguished Member of Parliament, who had commanded a division in Burma, and then his hand was being warmly clasped by a slim, middleaged officer in the green and gold of the Gaupal Army mess kit, whose badges proclaimed him a colonel in the medical service.

"John, my dear fellow! It is good to see you again, after so many years."

"And you, Kim." John returned the handshake with equal warmth. "It's extremely good."

"You haven't forgotten me, then?"

"Forgotten you? Lord, no—as if I could!"

"I shall leave the two of you together," the Ambassador announced, "to exchange reminiscences, as I am sure you will want to. How long is it since you have seen each other?"

"Rangoon in August '45, wasn't it, Kim?" John hazarded.

"Yes, I believe it was. I missed you in Singapore the following year . . . by a few days, I was told. Your Excellency, John Anson and I were in Force 136 together—

quite a pair of desperados we made, didn't we, John, by the end of our time?" Kim Myint chuckled. "Do you remember the time we spent with the Myosa's Defence Force in Korsang, recruiting guerillas? And old Chu Wen Li . . . and that landing, on our second trip, when a Jap post unexpectedly opened up on us and killed the pilot? This is the man, Your Excellency"—smiling, he put an arm about John's shoulders—"who took over the controls of a Dakota and put us down in a very small jungle clearing east of the Salween River, after we had lost part of a wing and our pilot and were crashing in flames. I don't pretend to know how he did it, but the fact that we're both here tonight is proof of what I say."

The Ambassador's dark eyes lit with a fugitive gleam of interest. Then he smiled. "I wish I might stay with you both and listen to the memories you have to share with each other. But I see that Tun Min is waiting to announce dinner. We must keep to our schedule, lest we be discovered, still seated at the dinner table, when the first guest arrives to attend the reception. Kim San, look after Colonel Anson for me, please."

"With the greatest of pleasure, Your Excellency."

"And afterwards . . ." the Ambassador's hand rested for a moment, lightly, on Kiru Myint's green-clad shoulder, "come to me afterwards so that I may make my daughter known to you."

"Your Excellency!" Kim Myint drew himself up. He bowed stiffly and then, his gesture the Gaupali sign of dutiful submission, touched his brow with the fingers of his right hand. It was the gesture a servant made to his.master, a sepoy to his officer or—a son to his father and, recalling this, John stared at his companion. He said, as the Ambassador moved away from them, "You admire him very much, don't you?"

"Indeed I do," Kim Myint replied. "But—" He took John's arm and added, lowering his voice, "I am to become his son-in-law. This evening, after the reception, I am to be betrothed to his daughter, Rose."

"To . . . Dr. Lian—to *Rose* Lian?" For some reason which he couldn't have

107

explained, even to himself, John was shocked. He looked into the other's face, taking in its Oriental cast, the dark, slanting eyes, the smooth brown skin, the black, close-cropped hair. He had always liked Kim Myint and found him a fine soldier and an excellent companion, the best and most loyal of friends. But as a husband for Rose Lian, for Rose who was white, for Rose who was the loveliest girl he had ever seen in his life . . . John shuddered. It simply didn't bear thinking about, it was—oh, it was quite abominable, a tragedy he would have given a great deal to prevent. It wasn't his affair, and he had no right to question it, no right to interfere—no right, if it came to that, even to protest. But it took all the self-control he possessed not to do so. He opened his mouth to speak and closed it again, fearful of what, in his unreasoned anger, he might say.

Something of his thoughts must have communicated themselves to Kim Myint, for a faint flush came to darken the tan of his cheeks and he asked, his tone abrupt and trembling on the edge of bitterness, "You've met Rose, have you?"

"Yes," John managed, "I've met her. She's been working at St. Ninian's where my father is on the consultant staff. He thinks very highly of her as a surgeon, I believe—in fact, when I met her the other evening, she was with him at his Harley Street rooms, and he told me he'd been trying to persuade her to stay on here and sit for her FRCS. Needless to say, she refused. I gather that she—"

"She has a post waiting for her in our new hospital at Tauling," Kim Myint put in. His face relaxed, the colour fading. "Your father is, of course, Sir Michael Anson—I'd forgotten that. I am glad that he has so high an opinion of Rose's work."

"He wanted to give her a house job at St. Ninian's," John supplied. The Ambassador was leading the way into the dining-room and he fell into step beside Kim Myint, glad of the interruption the move had provided. The last thing he wanted to do was to offend the man at his side, the very last thing, especially now, right at the outset of his new career, when Kim Myint's friendship was likely to be an extremely valuable asset.

He stifled a sigh. It was, he supposed,

Rose Lian's affair whom she married. In these enlightened days no coercion would be put upon her, and her father, he felt sure, would leave her complete freedom of choice. Or almost complete. She must realize what she was doing, she must know what marriage to a native Gaupali, however distinguished, would mean to her. He was being a fool to let it worry him—a stupid, prejudiced fool. She was her father's daughter, and that meant that she was half Gaupali.

But as they seated themselves at the long, elegantly set table, with its gleaming silver and highly polished glass, John felt his companion's eyes on him, a question in them.

"Rose looks like a European, doesn't she?" Kim Myint said softly. "Her mother was French. A very beautiful, very tragic woman whom Rose resembles most strikingly. Perhaps you know her story?"

John shook his head. "No," he answered. "No, I don't."

"I thought that she might have told your father of it. Well, briefly"—Kim Myint helped himself to the first course and, when he had done so, he turned to look directly at John—"it was this . . ." He talked on, and John listened with growing interest, as course succeeded course and the conversation of the other guests rose and fell, a meaningless sound which he heard but did not assimilate.

After that, losing his earlier constraint, Kim Myint engaged in reminiscence. They were back on their old terms of easy, undemanding friendship by the time the meal was over and they rose to drink the first toast.

"It is good to find you again, John," Kim Myint told him. Seated once more, he raised his glass. "To you, my friend— to success in your new appointment and a welcome to my country where, I confess, I never thought to see you. But I am glad that you are coming to join us and more pleased than I can begin to tell you that you are the man His Excellency has chosen to come. He could not possibly have chosen a better man if he had searched the entire British Empire."

"Thank you," John answered, reddening. "It's very kind of you to say that. But—"

111

"I mean it, my dear fellow, from the depths of my heart."

"Then thanks again. I am extremely pleased to have been given the post. I hope that I shall justify your faith in me.

"We've talked mostly about myself," Kim Myint reminded him. "I don't know what has been happening to you since we last met. Come"—following the Ambassador's example, he got to his feet —"while we're waiting for the reception to begin, fill in the gaps for me. Are you married? Will you be bringing a wife with you to Tauling?"

Slowly John shook his head. "I'm not married, Kim. But I have recently become engaged."

"Recently?" There was a slight congestion by the door of the dining-room and they halted there, waiting for the Ambassador and his principal guests to precede them. "You mean—"

John smiled faintly. "Yes. It was announced this morning, as a matter of fact. Quite a coincidence, isn't it?"

"Indeed it is. I am very pleased. And who is the fortunate young lady?"

"Her name is Sandra Beauchamp. She's

a dress designer, quite a successful and well-known one. You'll meet her this evening, she's going to join us here for the reception. I hope you will allow me to introduce you when she comes."

"My dear fellow, I shall be most honoured." Kim Myint looked genuinely delighted. "This way, I think—after you." He motioned John to go first. "Tell me, will Miss Beauchamp follow you to Gaupal?"

"That is our intention," John confirmed. "Either that or I shall come home to fetch her . . . in about a year's time, or possibly"—he hesitated—"possibly sooner. It depends."

"On whether or not you like Gaupal?" Kim Myint suggested shrewdly.

"Partly that. But mainly I think it will depend on what I'm able to make of the job. I've never done anything like it before and frankly—well, I may find it's beyond me. I shall do my best, of course."

"I am sure you will. And I am equally sure that you will make a tremendous success of it. His Highness is a nice young man and he will like you. You are—how can I put it? You are the type he will admire. We shall be travelling to Gaupal together tomorrow, you know, so that I shall be on hand in Tauling at any time you may wish to call on me. For anything, John my friend—for anything at all. That is understood, isn't it? Whether you want my help in choosing a dhobi or in working out a curriculum for His Highness' studies, it is yours for the asking."

"That's damned good of you, Kim," John said, with sincerity. "But I don't see why you should put yourself out."

The other smilingly shook his head. "I haven't forgotten our first 'drop' together," he returned, "nor that minute island of mud by the Salween River. I am always ready and willing to put myself out for you, so I hope you will remember it. But now, if you will forgive me, I must wait on His Excellency who is to present me to my betrothed . . . we have not met officially as yet. I have seen her, but she has never set eyes on me. It is rather an anxious moment for me, as you may imagine." He paused by the door of a cloakroom. "I expect you'd like a wash and brush up, wouldn't you? You'll find the rest of the party in here. Come into the ballroom when you are ready—I shall be there. Rose will have to stand at her father's side to receive the guests, so I shall be looking out for you."

John held out his hand. "Let me wish *you* luck," he offered, "and may I also congratulate you? Dr. Lian is a very charming girl." It was, he thought, the least he could say.

Kim Myint took the proffered hand. "Thank you," he acknowledged quietly, smiled and was gone.

In the washroom, John found himself in conversation with several of the British guests, all of whom seemed interested in his new appointment. He entered the ballroom in company with two of the Foreign Office representatives and was in time to see Rose come in on her father's arm. Kim Myint, looking erect and soldierly, walked on her other side. His expression was inscrutable, but when Rose turned to him to make some casual remark, his dark eyes were lit suddenly as if from some inner radiance and John heard him catch his breath.

Rose Lian seemed to John, as he watched her, more lovely even than he had imagined. She was wearing a deceptively simple dress of jade green chiffon—Sandra's creation, John remembered, and was struck at once by its beauty and by its aptness. The pale, delicate shade of the dress set off to perfection the creamy pallor of her skin, its cut, without drawing attention to her tall slimness, managed nevertheless to enhance it. Hers was a rare, elusive beauty, he thought, and wondered anew that it should be so . . . surely there should be some hint of her mixed blood? Yet there was not, so far as he could discern. Her hair was dark but not unusually so: it had bronze lights in it and, even at a distance, was obviously of a fine, soft texture only European women possessed. Which was very strange, for he had never seen a Eurasian with such hair and, in the course of his service in the East, he had seen many Eurasians.

He heard Gilbert Gregory draw in a quick, astonished breath, heard his bewildered, "My God! Is *that* HE's daughter? It can't be," and anger rose in him as it had earlier that evening, when Kim Myint had told him of his betrothal.

"Yes," he said savagely, "it is," and was

shocked by his own fury as he said it. He turned his back on the Foreign Office man's astonishment and dived blindly into the crowd, conscious that Gregory and his companion were both staring after him. He had progressed only a few paces when he heard a commanding voice call him by name. He halted and found himself looking into the cold blue eyes of General Sir Lancelot Mayne, MP.

"You're Anson, aren't you?" the General demanded.

John stiffened. "Yes, sir, I am."

"Good. I'd like a word with you. There are a couple of chairs over there. Let's go over, shall we?"

"Certainly, sir." John followed him to the side of the room, waited until he had seated himself and then drew up the second chair. Sir Lancelot stared at him. "I know your face, don't I? We ever met before?"

"We did, sir, yes—only it was quite a long time ago. At the end of the war, sir, in—"

"Wait, I've got it! Don't often forget a face. Rangoon—on the V J Parade, wasn't it? You were Hodgson's ADC—and you were Force 136, weren't you? Right?"

"Absolutely right, sir, though I don't know how—"

A flicker of amusement touched the frosty eyes. "You were a damnably scruffy ADC, me boy. Noticed you particularly. Collection of ruffians, Force 136, y'know —more like brigands than soldiers. But 'pon my word, I don't know what we'd have done without 'em. They did what was needed and did it damned well. Not that *I'd* have chosen an ADC from that bunch of yours, Anson. Hodgson must have been out of his mind."

John laughed. His anger had faded and he was genuinely amused. Sir Lancelot was expressing the Regular Army's view, of course, and he had heard it too often to take offence. "General Hodgson is an uncle of mine, sir," he explained.

"Is he, now? Ah, well, I suppose he had his reasons. Uncle of yours, eh? H'm. Tell me, Anson, why are you taking this job in Gaupal? Weren't you happy in our peace-time Army? Find it too dull, perhaps, after the cloak and dagger stuff?"

"Oh, no, sir—I was very happy. But

apparently I didn't quite succeed in convincing those in higher authority of the fact. I was declared redundant, sir."

"With your record? Good Gad! Well, I suppose there must have been some reason for it. Probably you went on thinking in terms of the commando unit after the need for that sort of thing had passed. The fighting soldier's a bit of a misfit in a peacetime army very often. You found that, surely?"

"Yes, I suppose I did, to a certain extent, sir."

Sir Lancelot Mayne took out his cigarette case. He passed it to John, frowning. "*I* found it," he admitted. "Fighting soldier meself really, if the truth be known. I had the choice of a seat on the board of half a dozen industrial companies I didn't know the first thing about or standing for Parliament. I think I made the right choice. At least I'm beginning to learn me job in the House and perhaps I even do a bit of good there. I don't know. I didn't like retiring either, Anson. Well" —he puffed thoughtfully at his cigarette— "I'm glad you've got this Gaupal post. I think you're the right man for it. But see you make a good job of it, won't you? It could be quite tricky, y'know."

"Yes, sir, I realize that. I hope I'll be able to do it reasonably well."

Sir Lancelot grunted. He asked a few brusque, very much to the point questions concerning the appointment and the responsibilities it carried, which John answered to the best of his ability, very conscious of the shrewd, searching blue eyes on his face as he did so.

A band at the far end of the ballroom struck up and a few couples took the floor. Among them John noticed Rose Lian and the slim, green-clad figure of Kim Myint. They made a strangely ill-matched couple, he thought, and looked hurriedly away from them. He glanced down at his watch. The room was rapidly filling, it was time that Sandra made her appearance. He wondered whether he could make his escape from Sir Lancelot without seeming discourteous, in order to go in search of her, but the old man was launched on his pet hobby horse and gave him no opportunity to excuse himself. He waited, concealing his impatience. The music swelled to a lively climax and then ceased.

The dancers began slowly to leave the floor.

". . . want to watch your step with those fellows," Sir Lancelot said heavily. John scarcely heard him. He saw Sandra coming across the floor towards him and he made to rise "If you'll forgive me, sir, my fiancée—"

Sir Lancelot followed the direction of his gaze.

"Your fiancée, me boy? The girl in red? Why—" He broke off, his grizzled brows coming together in a scowl as he took in the fact that Sandra was not alone. "Good Gad, she's brought Garrison with her, Charles Garrison."

John hesitated. "Do you know him, sir?"

"Know him? I should think I do. You ever heard of Pagoda Oils? I don't imagine you have, but you're going to when you get to Gaupal. The Peacock Pagoda Oil Company . . . Garrison is their chief shareholder, with a seat on the Board. Yes, you're certainly going to hear a good deal about the Peacock Pagoda when you get to Gaupal, Anson." His tone was brusque. "I suggest," he ended dryly, "that you go

121

and meet your fiancée. Get her to introduce you to Garrison. And then, if you'll take my advice, you'll steer clear of him. His job and yours won't mix."

He turned abruptly on his heel, leaving John to stare after him helplessly.

And then Sandra was beside him, smiling up at him.

"John dear," she said, "I want you to meet Charles Garrison"

6

THE next day, Tuesday, was the day of John's departure. The Gaupal party was to fly as far as Rangoon by the regular BOAC service and thence, by charter aircraft, across Burma to Tauling. The flight was scheduled to leave London Airport at nine-thirty.

As they had previously arranged that she should, Sandra drove John to the airport. She was unusually quiet during the drive, answering only when he spoke to her and giving all her attention to threading a way through the heavy traffic. Already depressed by the nearness of their parting, John could find no words with which to break through the barrier of her silence. The few he attempted to utter met with an indifferent response and earned him, at best, a preoccupied ghost of a smile, so that, after a time, he too relapsed into silence, bewildered and wretched.

They breakfasted at the airport restaurant—frugally, since neither was hungry and the hour an unaccustomed one —to the accompaniment of despairing small talk on his part and brittle laughter, which held no amusement, on Sandra's.

All the warmth, all the easy, happy companionship they had enjoyed in the past seemed to have vanished, John thought painfully, leaving no trace of its existence. He asked at last, unable any longer to keep up the pretence that all was as it should be, "Sandra, what's wrong, darling? Are you miserable because I'm leaving you, or is it something else—something I've said or done that's upset you?"

"Oh, no." She shook her head, avoiding his puzzled, searching gaze. "It's nothing you've said or done—how could it be? You've always been perfectly sweet to me."

He reached for her hand across the table and held it. He wanted to ask her if her depression had anything to do with Charles Garrison and, because he was afraid of what her answer might be, refrained from mention of it. Instead, he questioned gently, "You're not worried about our engagement, are you? You aren't regretting that you promised to marry me?"

Sandra lowered her gaze but not before he caught the glint of tears in her eyes. "No," she returned, her voice muffled and indistinct, "no, of course not, John. I'd be every sort of a fool to regret that."

"Well, then?" he persisted, his fingers closing about the hand he held. "What is it, darling? You aren't yourself, you're— oh, God, it's almost as if we were strangers. I can't get near you, you've shut me out so that I can't even help you, don't you see?"

"I wish you'd leave it alone, John." She spoke harshly, with a quick flash of anger in the eyes she raised to his face. "I hate your going—isn't that natural, isn't it understandable, for heaven's sake? Do you expect me to jump for joy, to go round screaming with laughter because you're leaving me and I shan't see you again for the best part of a year?"

"Of course I don't," he conceded, but was aware, as he said so, that she wasn't telling him the truth. His going and the necessity for it was something she had accepted weeks ago: it was hard to believe that it could so profoundly have affected her now, at the eleventh hour. She hadn't argued about the year of separation and waiting—it was he who had wanted to shorten it. He drew a deep, strained breath.

"Sandra," he demanded, "if I asked you to follow me almost at once—say in a couple of months' time—what would you say? Would you agree?"

"You know that's not possible," she said flatly, and rose, glancing at her watch. "Isn't it time I—"

"Not yet," John pleaded. "Let's go somewhere where we can talk." He took her arm, sensing her reluctance as he led her from the restaurant. "Darling, we've got to have this out, you know. I can't leave you on these terms."

"There's nothing to have out," Sandra returned. She moved restlessly over to a window which overlooked the main entrance and went on, not looking at him. "Unless you regret our engagemeut, unless *you've* changed your mind about marrying me."

"I? Oh, good heavens, darling!" He was appalled. "You must know that's the last thing I'd do. I love you, don't you understand? I want, more than anything else in the world, to have you as my wife . . . surely you believe that, don't you?"

"I . . . yes, I believe it."

"Well, then—"

"I don't know what's the matter with me," Sandra said helplessly. "It's probably nerves." She shivered. "Don't worry, John, I'll get over it, it's just that I—oh, I don't know."

John put an arm lightly about her shoulders. "You don't love me, do you?" he suggested quietly. "Is that what you're trying to say?"

"No, I . . . wasn't." She sighed and leaned back against him. "I care for you very much, John."

"And I'm to be content with that?" he countered bitterly. Again the name Garrison trembled on his lips, but he didn't utter it. Sandra stood beside him, with his arm about her, yet they might have been a thousand miles apart, they might—as he had said a few moments ago —have been strangers.

"Sandra—" he began, "Sandra, you . . ." and felt her stiffen. She said abruptly, pointing to a large black saloon car which had just drawn up at the entrance to the terminal building, "They're here—Dr. Lian and the others. Your travelling companions."

John followed the direction of her pointing finger and recognized Rose Lian and her father. Kim Myint emerged from a second car and went to join Rose. He was followed, more slowly, by the retiring military attaché, Major Aung, with his wife, a tiny, brown-faced woman to whom, John recalled, he had been introduced the previous evening.

"Who is that, with Dr. Lian?" Sandra asked.

"That's Colonel Kim San Myint, director of the Army Medical Service. I knew him in Burma. He's"—John said it reluctantly—"he's to marry Rose Lian."

Sandra was silent for a long moment, watching Kim Myint, a puzzled frown puckering her smooth brow. Finally she said, "I see." Then, losing interest in the party below them, she looked again at her watch. "John, you'll be leaving soon, I— I don't think I'll wait, if you don't mind. I don't want to have to speak to them, become involved. Goodbyes are awful anyway and I'm in no state to endure an audience when I say goodbye to you. Let's say it here and—and get it over. Please, John, I—"

John opened his mouth to protest and closed it again. What the devil was the use of asking her to stay? They could decide nothing here, in these circumstances, with a crowd milling about them and his own departure now only ten minutes away. Sandra was obviously at the end of her tether, tense and strung up, finding the whole thing an unbearable strain. It was needlessly cruel to try to keep her with him any longer. He took her arm and offered, as he tucked it under his, "I'll see you out, then."

"No. There's no need, honestly. I'd rather you didn't. Just—just come with me to the door."

He did so, walking stiffly and unhappily at her side, racking his brain for words, any words, which would reach her and put an end to his torment. But no words would come, his throat ached and his mouth was dry, his brain seemingly frozen. There was nothing he could say, little, even, that he could do, save cling to her hand and hope for a miracle, aware that the hope was vain.

When the moment came for their parting, Sandra lifted her face to his so briefly that he could do no more than touch her cheek with his lips. He felt the salty dampness of tears on his mouth and longed, quite desperately, to take her in his arms and crush her to him. As if sensing his longing, she drew away from him, freeing her hand from his clasp, shaking her head to the mute entreaty in his eyes. "No . . . I can't take any more, I . . . goodbye, John. I hope you'll have a good journey."

Cursing himself for his own inadequacy, John mumbled a gruff goodbye and watched miserably as Sandra turned and left him, to be swiftly swallowed up in the crowd.

His flight was being called to go through Customs, but he stood immobile, straining for a last glimpse of her, feeling as if, with her going, the light had gone from his whole existence. It was a strange sensation, of helplessness and frustration, mingled with a sense of deep and abiding loss. He could have no real conviction now that Sandra loved him, he must always doubt, in spite of the fact that she wore his ring and had promised to marry him. He could no longer believe, in his heart, that their parting meant to her what it meant to him, nor, try as he might, could he believe that, when the time of waiting should be over, she would keep her promise to follow him to Gaupal.

He wished that he could believe it, but last night, seeing her with Charles Garrison, seeing the change which this had wrought in her, his faith had been shaken. Badly shaken. And Garrison had shaken him too. It hadn't needed Sir Lancelot Mayne's dryly phrased warning to make him realize, within a few minutes of meeting him, that Garrison was not a man to be trusted. He had found himself disliking the loud-voiced fellow heartily, not only because of the possessive attitude he had adopted towards Sandra but also because, under the thin veneer of conventional charm and good manners, he had glimpsed a ruthless hardness in the man which repulsed him.

Not that Garrison had said anything

openly to anger him . . . John moved slowly towards the door marked Customs. He had, in fact, gone out of his way to be pleasant, hinting, indeed, that John's good luck in his engagement to Sandra was his own misfortune. He had hinted at other things too, less pleasantly, as the evening wore on and his consumption of the Ambassdor's whisky increased slightly. Recalling some of the hints and the covert sneers, John's mouth tightened.

Garrison had affected to know a great deal about Gaupal and the Gaupali Royal Family, as the result of a recent visit to Tauling on his way back from Australia. He hadn't made the smallest attempt to hide his contempt for the King and the system of government. He had talked loudly, with no apparent thought for anyone who might overhear him, of primitive conditions, an illiterate people, archaic laws and corruption in high places, stating emphatically that it was necessary for those Europeans who concerned themselves with the country to stick together and present a united front.

"You and me, for instance, Anson . . ." His tone had been heavily jocular, John remembered, with a shiver of distaste. "It's possible that, although you may not realize it yet, the occasion might arise when we could do each other a good turn. I can think of one good turn I could do you right now, if you'll let me. You'll be wanting a car when you get to Tauling, it's a necessity . . . steep hills, hot climate, you won't want to walk far. Don't touch any of the local dealers, they're rogues and all they'll have to offer is secondhand, *very* secondhand, and they'll make you pay through the nose. Leave their stuff alone. I'll get the oil company boys to arrange delivery of an American car for you—a new one. Why, great heavens"—he had cut short John's objections—"it's no trouble, simply a matter of sending a cable to Harry Walters in Tauling. He's got one or two cars going spare and he'll do it to oblige me. Why shouldn't he, when I'm one of his bosses? And if you're worrying about repaying me, then don't, old chap. As I said just now, we Europeans have got to stick together or we'll get ourselves precisely nowhere. You can pay for the car when you feel like it, either out there or in sterling back here in London. No hurry. And who knows, the occasion might arise when you could do me a good turn and we could forget about the car, eh? On the principle that one good turn deserves another . . ."

For Sandra's sake, he hadn't dealt with Garrison's offer as he had been tempted to deal with it, John thought, although he wished now that he had. He had simply refused it and turned his back on the man, making a great effort to control the cold rage that filled him. A more blatant attempt at bribery and corruption he had seldom heard in his life—and Garrison had sneered at the Gaupalis for doing it! He wondered how the man had come to own a major interest in the Pagoda Oil Company and then, angrily, how it was that Sandra, of all people, had come to be on terms of friendship with him. If it was a coincidence, it was certainly a very unfortunate one. Oh, damn Garrison . . . damn Garrison and all his works!

"Is this your baggage, sir?" He had halted, instinctively and without consciously seeing it, beside the pile of his own cases, John realized. He nodded. "Yes, this is mine. What do you—?"

"Colonel Anson, sir, I have been looking for you." It was the Ambassador's secretary, peering at him short-sightedly through his heavy, horn-rimmed glasses, a typewritten list in his hand. "The others are all on their way now to the airliner. I have seen to their baggage and would have seen to yours also had I been able to find you. Perhaps you would care to leave matters to me, or at least—" He turned to the Customs Officer. "This gentleman is in the Embassy party, sir. May I ask that you will expedite the clearing of his baggage?"

The man smiled. "No trouble at all, Mr. Min." He signed to a waiting porter, "All these can go on board the Rangoon aircraft. Right, sir," he addressed John. "Straight ahead. Your aircraft is waiting."

John thanked the little secretary, who wrung his hand warmly, and then made his way out to the waiting airliner.

Kim Myint joined him at the door of the cabin, as a stewardess checked his name against the passenger list.

"Ah, so here you are! We had begun to wonder what had happened to you. Come, we are all sitting together on the port side.

His Excellency asked me to bid you *bon voyage* and to apologize for not having seen you himself—he had to return at once for an important conference, you understand."

John followed him over to where the rest of their party were seated. Dr. Lian gave him a smiling greeting. She looked subdued, John thought, shaking hands with her gravely and bowing to Major Aung and his wife. He had scarcely settled himself in his own seat when the cabin door was closed and a sign flickered on above the door to the flight deck, requesting passengers to fasten their seat belts preparatory to take-off. The airliner taxied down to the runway and halted at the end, its engines increasing their steady hum as the pilot began his cockpit check. The take-off, a few minutes later, was smooth and effortless. When they were airborne, the sign flickered off. John unfastened his seat belt and lay back wearily, his eyes closed. To his own surprise, he instantly fell asleep and remained so until the stewardess roused him for lunch.

Zürich was the first stop, but it was a

brief one, lasting only forty-five minutes. They took off again for Beirut, where they were scheduled to land for dinner.

John slept for part of the afternoon. Accustomed to flying in Service aircraft, he was impressed by the high degree of comfort enjoyed by civilian passengers and by the excellence of the food, impeccably served by two attentive stewardesses. After tea Kim Myint, who with sympathetic tact had left him alone until then, came to join him. They talked in desultory fashion of the war, of Burma and the many mutual friends they had shared, and finally—the topic introduced by Kim Myint—of Gaupal.

Kim was a brilliant talker, and on the subject of his homeland he spoke with eloquence and enthusiasm, for clearly, it was very close to his heart. In sharp contrast to the scornful assertions made by Charles Garrison, his criticism was kindly and constructive, his judgment without prejudice and his praise sparing and sincere. That there was corruption in certain of the ministries he admitted, but —and his voice hardened—this was due in part to foreign commercial interests, vying

137

with each other for preferential treatment and also in part to outside political factions, whose aim was more sinister. He mentioned no names, but his omissions were, in themselves, significant. He assured John earnestly that steps were being taken in an attempt to stamp out the evil, and that heavy punishment was meted out to any offender who was caught accepting a bribe, large or small.

"We are a backward country, as His Excellency has no doubt told you," he went on thoughtfully. "Our people lack education and the benefits it confers. But we are learning. The new hospital is a step in the right direction and schools will follow the hospital, in increasing numbers. We hope to derive financial benefit from the development of our natural resources and to put the foreign capital we gain to constructive use. In time, perhaps, we shall learn to develop these natural resources ourselves, so that our people may supply not only semi-skilled workers and coolies but technicians and scientists —men trained in our own schools and in the university we dream of building in Tauling." He smiled. "I myself plan, in a modest way, to undertake the training of nurses and laboratory technicians in the hospital. One day, if all my plans come to fruition, we shall have a properly constituted medical school, where we shall train our own doctors."

In spite of his depressed state of mind, John was interested. He asked several questions and Kim Myint replied to them frankly. He spoke of the King's support and encouragement, which had been given whole-heartedly, and of the great new temple that was even now being built in the capital.

"He too has dreams, our King. The Temple is his dream. It is dedicated to Ram, and when it is finished it will be one of the finest in the East. The Royal Family, as well as a large percentage of the ruling class in Gaupal, are, as I imagine you know, Hindu. The bulk of the common people, like the Burmese, are Buddhist, and amongst them we have a sprinkling of professional men and intellectuals. Somewhat naturally, these are opposed to His Majesty's plans for the temple, so, in fairness, he is devoting a comparable sum from his private exchequer to the restoration of the Buddhist Pagoda, which stands on the opposite side of the river to the temple site. The Peacock Pagoda . . ." he paused and his gaze rested for a moment on John's face. When John said nothing, he continued quietly, "from which the new oil company has taken its name. An intended compliment which has, I am informed, misfired a little. There's talk of dropping the Peacock from the title."

"Do you think that will help?" John asked.

Kim Myint raised his slim shoulders in an elaborate shrug. "Who knows? We practise a high degree of religious tolerance in Gaupal. We have our Muslim minority and several thousand Sikhs in the capital. We have also a very fine Christian school and orphanage, with its own church, run by a delightful man whom you will come to admire very much when you know him —Father Delarge. He is a Frenchman."

"And a friend of yours?" John hazarded.

"Oh, yes." Kim's smile widened. "More than that, really. I am one of his converts. Rose and I"—he glanced over to where Rose's dark head could just be seen above the top of her seat—"Rose and I share the same faith."

John was silent, considering this. For Rose's sake, he was glad. They had everything in common, Rose and Kim, he thought—their faith, their work, their interests. So much more, when he came to think about it, than most affianced couples had. If they weren't in love with each other, there was time for that to come. They were to work together in the new hospital, Kim had told him last night: they would have dreams to share, splendid, far-sighted plans to put into practice, a future in which both could believe.

They had so much more, really, than he and Sandra had or ever would have. His mouth twisted into a bitter line, as he recalled his recent parting with Sandra.

Kim Myint leaned towards him. He said, almost as if he had read John's thoughts, "I believe that Rose is satisfied with her father's choice of me as her future husband. We shall have a great many things in common."

"Yes, indeed you will," John agreed,

with as much enthusiasm as he could muster. "A great many."

"And you, my friend . . ." Kim hesitated, his expression guarded, as if what he were about to say required a moment of premeditation. "I saw your Miss Beauchamp yesterday evening at the reception and glimpsed her again this morning, at the airport. She is a very beautiful woman. I think you are most fortunate."

"Thank you," John managed. He was certain, studying the other's face, that this wasn't what he had intended to say, or else it was the prelude to something. else, perhaps, to which Kim Myint was cautiously leading up. He waited, holding his companion's eyes with his own, willing him to speak, to put into words whatever might be on his mind.

There was a brief silence. Finally Kim Myint said softly, "She came last night with Mr. Garrison, I believe."

"Yes," John admitted, his voice deliberately flat and non-committal, "she did, Kim. Why do you ask?"

"I have a number of reasons for asking. Is he—is Mr. Garrison a friend of yours?"

"I met him for the first time yesterday evening."

"Ah! Then you will scarcely have had time to form an opinion about him."

"Well . . . I suppose one shouldn't judge a man on so superficial an acquaintance, but I confess I didn't exactly take to him."

Kim Myint's face relaxed in obvious relief. "I am glad you feel like that, John, old man, very glad. It saves me the—the embarrassment of warning you to be careful of him." He beckoned to a passing stewardess. "Let's have a drink, shall we? What will you have?"

"Oh—a peg, I think. With water."

Kim Myint gave his order. When the stewardess had gone he changed the subject. He spoke of the house John would occupy, explaining that, while within the outer walls of the Palace, it was unlikely to be part of the Palace itself.

"You will need a staff, of course. Most important of all, you will need a good Number One boy. I believe that I know just the man, if he's free or can be persuaded to change his employment. He was my orderly for a time in Malaya and has had seven years with the Rifles. He speaks English after a fashion and his name is Karen, Bo Tin Karen. Shall I try to get hold of him for you?"

"I wish you would. But—about Garrison, Kim, I—"

"I think, if you do not mind," Kim evaded politely, "we will refrain from further mention of Garrison. The reason I brought his name up at all was because I was afraid that he might, by some unhappy chance, be a friend of yours. Since he is not and since you have formed what is, in my judgment, the right opinion concerning him, there is really no more to be said. And there are much pleasanter topics for us to discuss, are there not? Sport, for example . . . polo, shooting, tennis. We have facilities for all these in Tauling. Excellent duck shooting a few miles out which will delight your heart, and big game in the hills . . . you've brought guns with you, I imagine?"

Over the drinks the stewardess served them, Kim continued to extol the merits of the various opportunities for sport he would find in Gaupal, and John, after one or two unsuccessful attempts to bring him back to the subject of Charles Garrison, was forced to give him best and abandon the topic. His own uneasiness persisted, however, and to anxiety on Sandra's account were added the gravest doubts concerning Garrison that he ever remembered feeling in his life.

The airliner landed at Beirut and the passengers were given just over an hour in which to eat their evening meal. In spite of rumours of fighting and unrest in the capital, the atmosphere at the airport seemed normal enough.

It was a hot, sultry evening, with an electric storm hovering somewhere not far off, to contribute to the general oppressiveness. But the restaurant in which they dined was air-conditioned and the food of a high quality. John enjoyed his meal, finding Rose Lian, who seated herself on his right, a charming and entertaining table companion. She told him of the work she had been doing in England and he returned to the aircraft with his admiration for her and for all she had achieved immeasurably increased. She was a rare person, he thought, watching her as she preceded him across the tarmac, both beautiful and talented. And possessing something else too, some indefinable quality which set her apart from all the women he had ever known. A beauty of the spirit was the nearest he could come to a definition of what this was, a calm serenity which must stem only from a steadfast heart. He hoped, with a fervour that surprised himself, that Kim Myint would recognize this quality in his bride and that he would bring her happiness.

And then, filled with a strange, inexplicable anger, he put the thought of her marriage out of his mind. But the anger haunted his sleep. As the huge airliner winged its way steadily eastwards, John slept restlessly, disturbed by nightmare visions in which Rose, white-faced and terrified, pleaded with him to aid her in escaping from her betrothed, and Sandra, who was his own betrothed, laughed at his puny efforts and, pointing to a great white pagoda which towered shimmering in the sunshine above them both, called to him triumphantly, *"This is the Peacock Pagoda and Charles built it for me."*

The visions made no sense, but, waking in the throbbing dimness of the air-conditioned cabin, hours later, John found his brow beaded with sweat and his heart beating wildly. Swearing under his breath, he lit a cigarette and smoked it through before settling down to sleep again. This time he slept dreamlessly and only woke half an hour before the airliner began to descend for the landing at Karachi.

They breakfasted at the airport restaurant and took off again, ninety minutes later, into a blue, cloudless sky.

The next stop was a short one, just over half an hour, at Calcutta. John had known the city well in wartime, and the brief sight of it, as the aircraft came in to land, revived many memories for himself and Kim.

They were still deep in reminiscence when, a little after five in the afternoon, the signal went on over the door to the flight deck, requesting passengers to fasten their seat belts for landing.

John peered down, through the tilting window of the passenger cabin, as the runway came racing to meet them. They had reached Rangoon, the first stage of the long journey over. He breathed a deep sigh. Over the head of Major Aung, he met Rose Lian's gaze. Her expression was grave and pensive, her eyes, in that unguarded instant, full of a haunting sadness that made his heart contract, for it was exactly how she had looked at him in his dream.

And then, quite unexpectedly, she smiled, and the spell was broken.

The airliner taxied slowly down the runway and came to a standstill in front of the airport buildings.

"You'll find Rangoon has changed a good deal since the last time you were here, John," Kim Myint told him. If he had seen Rose's face, if he had noticed the look she had turned on his friend, he gave no sign of having done so. He went on eagerly, "There used to be a canteen here, after we recaptured Rangoon . . . do you remember it? Staffed by British and Burmese girls, Wasbies they called themselves. They had very little in the way of equipment, they had come down through Burma with the fighting divisions, all of them, and they had nothing but their pluck and their cheerfulness and a cracked old urn which never kept the tea hot. But their tea was wonderful. Do you remember it, John?"

"Yes," John agreed briefly, "I remember it."

He found himself remembering other things too, as, the Customs formalities dealt with, an airline coach took them into the city. Rangoon, as Kim said, had changed . . .

The scars of war had all been erased, the broken streets long since repaired, the rusting skeletons of bombed-out railway engines and Japanese tanks and lorries long since removed, but he saw them again in memory, saw also the blackened wrecks, and the bomb-scarred docks littered with the débris of the Japanese retreat, which had met his eyes all those years ago. He saw the prisoners, released at last from their terrible captivity, under inhuman conditions, in Rangoon Jail— emaciated, gaunt-faced ghosts of men who had once been soldiers and who had managed, somehow, to raise a cheer for their liberators. Remembering, John shivered in the warm evening air.

The coach rounded a bend and the vast shining golden dome of the Shwe Dragon

Pagoda came into sight. John saw again in memory the jewel-encrusted htee or umbrella, hung with gold and silver bells, which crowned it, and the white-crested Burmese lions which guarded its main entrance. As always, he saw, when they drew nearer, throngs of worshippers clustered about the steps leading up to it. He wasn't near enough to make them out as individuals, but he caught a flash of colour here and there and, in imagination, pictured the shaven-headed Buddhist priests in their saffron robes amongst the slowly moving concourse of cheerful, chattering Burmese in brightly coloured longyis and short jackets, smiling as the rays of the setting sun touched their upturned faces.

This was the same, it hadn't changed. He glanced across at Kim Myint and saw him nod in understanding.

The coach drove on down a wide avenue lined with trees, past prosperous looking houses with pleasant, flower-bordered gardens. The traffic thickened, the houses gave place to shops and tall office buildings, bearing British as well as Burmese names on their fronts. The people crowding the pavements were well dressed, the surface of the street was smooth and well kept, the cars modern and expensive, gleaming with chromium plate. A young woman, in a gay check tamain and embroidered jacket, with a flower in her smooth dark hair, offered cheroots for sale at the pavement edge: an old man, dignified in a green silk pasoe of elaborate design, paused to bargain with her for her wares, both arguing good-naturedly and beaming at each other with the greatest friendliness, happy and care-free as children.

John recalled the fact that the name Rangoon meant "The End of War" and his mouth compressed. It had seemed a bad joke at the time when he had heard it, but now, it seemed, it was true . . .

The coach drew up outside the shaded portico of a large hotel and Major Aung announced unnecessarily, "We are here."

Feeling suddenly very tired, John got to his feet.

7

IT wanted almost an hour to dawn when Prince Maung Saw alighted from his car at the foot of the steep track leading up to Lake Tachindaw.

The young heir apparent to the throne of Gaupal was dressed for shooting in jodhpurs and a shirt, and his boyish face, beneath the small, tight-fitting Gaupali cap, was eager and excited. He was accompanied, according to long established custom, by a captain and two havildars of the Palace Guard, but these he bade, in a tone which brooked no argument, remain by the car until he should return. Then, without a backward glance, he set off on foot up the winding pathway which led to his objective—a jheel a mile or so distant.

His personal bodyguard and present mentor, the Sikh Narain Singh, fell in at his heels, bearing his own twelve-bore and the prince's smaller, specially made Purdey.

This, too, was according to custom. Narain Singh was under strict orders never to leave his master's side and, whoever else of his guardians he might—and frequently did—shake off, the prince was forced to suffer Narain Singh's company, waking or sleeping. He was used to it and, a warm-hearted boy, was devoted to the tall, fierce old man who had been his constant companion ever since, at the age of seven, he had been released from the care of his mother and her women to take his place in the man's world of his father's court.

Narain Singh was a warrior of proven courage, who had served the British Raj and been decorated by them, rising to the rank of subadar-major in the last war, where he had seen action in the Middle East, as well as in Burma. While he presumed at times, by virtue of his age and long service, to run counter to many of his charge's more adventurous enterprises and freely spoke his mind when Maung Saw had no desire for his counsel and did not welcome it, he was, nevertheless, a loyal friend, who wielded the authority vested in him very lightly.

They had shared many adventures

together, he and Narain Singh, the boy thought as he plodded along, they understood each other and, up to a point, Narain Singh let him do as he pleased. It would be different when his new tutor arrived—the Englishman who his father had insisted must take over the Sikh's duties. Englishmen, from what he had heard of them, were stiff and formal: they did not know how to laugh and, themselves sternly disciplined, they were never happy unless they were imposing a similar measure of discipline on those about them.

Of course, Maung Saw had had other tutors, learned pundits who had taught him to read and write in three languages, others who had guided him in religious matters and still others who had introduced him to the complexities of court ceremonial. But these had frequently been changed, none had been permitted to exercise more than transient authority over him, and all had given him the respect to which his rank entitled him. So long as he behaved with reasonable attentiveness during their lessons, they asked no more —not even that he should learn what they went to such pains to teach him, since it was considered that a prince must be subjected neither to coercion nor punishment.

He wondered, glumly, whether the English colonel who was to succeed Narain Singh and the pundits held similar views or whether, in his stiff English way, he would choose to ignore his pupil's rank and treat him like a schoolboy from an English public school. It was exciting, in a way, to think that a man of his importance should travel all the way to Gaupal in order to become his tutor, but . . . it was also more than a little alarming.

And—he bit his lip . . . it was sad that he must, on the Englishman's account, part with Narain Singh after almost nine years.

"Narain Singh," he said, over his shoulder, "when the English Colonel Sahib comes, are you to be sent away?"

Narain Singh did not slacken his pace. "Your Highness knows that I am," he replied woodenly. In the dim light, it was impossible to see his face, but Maung Saw knew, from his voice, that the loyal old man was deeply moved. He halted, motioning to him to walk at his side, but

Narain Singh shook his head. "This is no time for talk, Highness," he objected, "if we are to reach the jheel before it becomes light."

"We can talk as we go."

"It is better not to talk, lest the duck hear our voices," Narain Singh told him obstinately. "In any case"—he swung on up the track—"I have no heart for such talk as you would give me now. I am to go, and that is all that can be said."

"*I* do not want you to go," Maung Saw cried angrily. "I want you to stay with me."

The Sikh did not deign to answer him and they toiled on in silence. Two shikaris were waiting, with a boat, at the jheel. They salaamed respectfully as Maung Saw entered the boat, indicating, with gestures, the route they proposed to take through the thick reeds. The boy nodded indifferently and the boat was pushed off, the two small, dark-skinned shikaris plying their paddles with the skill and soundlessness of long practice. Maung Saw held out his hand to Narain Singh for his gun. Usually the old man gave it to him smiling, the smile a reminder of some small wager they

156

had laid as to which of them should bag the greater number of duck. But today there had been no wager and the Sikh's bearded face was a grim silhouette in the darkness, his hand cold as it brushed the boy's. Nothing, Maung Saw thought bitterly, nothing was the same, all had changed because of the coming of the English colonel. He grabbed the gun impatiently and hugged it to him, anger filling his heart. It was cruel of Narain Singh to treat him thus, when the colonel's coming was not his fault and the decision to send his old servant away not his but his father's, against whose commands there was no appeal.

The boat grounded and Maung Saw stepped out. He covered the few yards to the hide in two swift, furious paces and flung himself down with scant heed for the noise he made, hearing, as he did so, the unmistakable scuttering sound as a bird took off from close at hand to make for the safety of the centre of the jheel. Disturbed, no doubt, by his clumsiness, but he did not care. Fortunately no others took fright, and faintly across the water was borne the quiet, clucking croak of feeding mallard. Narain Singh lay down some distance from him and they waited as, so many times in the past they had waited together, for dawn to break.

It came suddenly, as it always did in the East. One moment there was darkness, the next a faint grey lightening of the sky and then, swiftly and beautifully, the dawn had come. As if in response to a prearranged signal, the feeding duck took wing, flight after flight of them from every corner of the reed-grown jheel, rising skywards in a cloud, the beat of their wings a heady, intoxicating sound to the hidden watchers in the reeds. Maung Saw raised his gun to his shoulder, but he did not fire, Narain Singh, usually so eager to out-shoot him, lay motionless, not even troubling to lift his own weapon as the duck wheeled above their heads, took up formation and made off, gaining height as they went, until their bodies were small black dots against the pearl-grey vault of the sky. Soon there was not a single one in sight, and the sun rose, touching the snow-capped peaks of the distant mountains to pink and crimson and gold.

Across the few feet of intervening

distance, Maung Saw's gaze met the dark, reproachful eyes of his old servant.

"You shall not go, Narain Singh," the boy whispered, his heart breaking. "I will not let you go. If I have to kill the English colonel with my own hands, I will keep you beside me, as you have always been. I vow it, Narain-ji! Here is my hand on it."

"That is wild and foolish talk, my prince," the old Sikh warned. But, after a long moment of hesitation, he took the boy's outstretched hand and, kneeling before him in the damp reeds, held it ceremoniously between both his own, his turbaned head bowed.

8

THE Air-India Dakota banked steeply and began to lose height as the pilot throttled back his engines, preparatory to landing at Tauling.

Through the port windows of the passenger cabin could be seen the awe-inspiring peaks of the Tauling mountains knifing wickedly skyward, their snow-crowned summits reaching a height of over eighteen thousand feet. Taulai, the famous Rainbow Mountain of song and legend, lay to the east, dwarfing the rest of the range but, as always, shrouded in the weird, rainbow-hued mist from which it derived its name.

Rose looked down, suppressing a shudder. They had flown over the range, passing within a few miles of Taulai, but until she knew that they were safely across, she hadn't dared to look down. Which was absurd, of course, since aircraft frequently flew over Gaupal's mountain barrier and came to no harm, but . . . she couldn't help her tiny shiver of revulsion.

In the days before aeroplanes had been thought of as a means of transport, the mountains had been a formidable barrier and had taken full and terrible toll of those travellers who had sought to cross them without a guide. In Gaupal they were regarded with superstitious fear even today, Rose knew, and Taulai was believed by the natives to be the home of the sacred Peacock Deity from whom, according to an old legend, the ruling family could claim direct descent. Half bird, half human, the Peacock god was said to have been a favourite of the great Lord Buddha and granted by him the power, once in every generation, to assume human form and reign as King of Gaupal.

The curious anomaly which had arisen in consequence of the Royal Family's adherence to the Hindu faith was explained by the fact that, five hundred years ago, the Spirit of the Peacock had descended upon a Hindu warrior prince from the borders of Nepal, whom chance and the desire for conquest had brought to Tauling at the head of a marauding army.

From the seat immediately in front of her own, Rose heard Kim Myint repeating the story to Colonel Anson. She had heard it many times before, as a child, but it still held an odd, compelling fascination for her and she leaned forward, listening, her eyes bright. Kim Myint was a practised raconteur. He told the familiar story well, illustrating it with many eloquent gestures of his slim brown hands in the direction of the massive, rainbow-crowned peak, now gradually receding into the distance as the aircraft dropped lower into the valley.

"There was an ancient prophecy, John, one which had been passed on from generation to generation, its origin lost in the mists of time. This warned the people of Gaupal that *'One from afar, fair of face and decked in all the glory and splendour of the peacock's hue'* should come down from the high mountains and make the whole kingdom his own, without striking a blow and without the shedding of a single drop of blood . . . I think we can safely assume that the wording of this prophecy became known to King Laotse Dah when he entered the country. At all events, he fulfilled it to the letter. He had the reputation of an astute, as well as a brave and ambitious man, and obviously the idea of conquering Gaupal without striking a blow and without bloodshed must have appealed to him strongly. He possessed one of the attributes the ancient soothsayers had forecast—he was an albino. The others he interpreted in his own way. Decked in a cloak made from the feathers of a score of slaughtered peacocks, he climbed to within a few thousand feet of the summit of Mount Taulai with a picked band of his warriors—a feat which had never previously been accomplished, according to our historians —and there he lit fires, which could be seen for hundreds of miles, to give warning of his approach. After that, he simply came down the eastern slope, and when he entered Tauling he did so in triumph, with the populace bowing down before him and hailing him as king. Not a blow had to be struck, and, according to the legend, the only casualties were two of his soldiers, who lost their lives during the difficult and dangerous ascent of the mountain." Kim Myint's hand described another expressive gesture in front of the cabin window. He added dryly, "And, of course, the unfortunate boy king whom Laotse Dah deposed—a child of ten, at the time—he and his entire family disappeared without trace."

"What a fantastic story," Rose heard John Anson say.

"Isn't it? King Laotse's descendants have ruled in Gaupal ever since. They have adopted Gaupali names and customs and dress, but have retained their own religion. So have the descendants of the invading army, with the result—as you will see in a moment or two, when we sight Tauling —that Hindu temples and Buddhist pagodas are built side by side everywhere in the city. There are, I think, more shrines of one kind or another in Tauling than in any other city of comparable size in the Far East. And while I may be swayed by a natural but, I trust, excusable pride in the city of my birth, I am confident that when you see it, you will agree that Tauling is the most beautiful of them all. When men build shrines to the glory of their gods—no matter which god they serve—they build with inspired imagination and without thought for the cost or the labour involved. Look, John, now! We are coming in sight of the city . . . there is the first bridge, which is called the Bridge of the Dragon. The Royal Palace stands on the east bank of the river . . . that vast collection of towers and terraced buildings behind an encircling wall—can you make it out? Directly ahead of us now. And opposite the Palace is the Peacock Pagoda, of which I told you yesterday. It is built of turquoise blue tiles —you will see when the sun touches it . . . there!"

Rose, too, affected by Kim Myint's excitement, looked down eagerly at the city she knew so well, seeing it as if for the first time through the eyes of a stranger.

Certainly it was a lovely sight, spread out below them, the setting sun bathing it in a crimson glow and touching the tapering pagoda spires and bell-shaped domes to molten fire. They rose, hundreds of them, tall and graceful, high above the roofs of the humbler dwellings which neighboured them, each set in a garden and bordered by shade-trees, symmetrical, receding terraces rising to a central dome. The spires and rooftops were in a profusion of colours—white, red, saffron and blue, mixed by the alchemy of sunlight and by the speed of the aircraft's approach into a rainbow vista that defied description.

The Peacock Pagoda, standing by itself on the west bank of the wide, swirling waters of the river, was perhaps the most impressive sight of all. Scores of small, carved wooden boats and sailing craft had gathered, like so many richly hued butterflies, at the foot of its lowest terrace, which rose on stone piles out of the river. Their reflections, mingled with the reflection of the pagoda itself, made the water seem alive. Rose knew that the height of the slender pagoda spire was over a hundred and seventy feet from the ground, but, seen from the air, it looked minute and toylike, a delicately fashioned structure of quite incredible and unearthly beauty, too fine and ethereal in construction to owe its existence to the hand of man. She heard John Anson's swift, amazed intake of breath as he caught his first glimpse of it and then they had passed it by, the aircraft banked again, very steeply, and, leaving the river behind, headed for the thin white ribbon of the airfield runway, engines throttled right back.

They touched down smoothly, their speed slowly decreasing as the end of the runway came in sight and the pilot applied his brakes. Then they were taxiing sedately up to the new, shining white reception building, with its squat concrete control tower which, the last time Rose had landed here, had still been uncompleted. She breathed a little sigh and, rising, found Kim Myint at her side. He said, smiling down at her, "How long is it since you were here, Rose?" and she had to pause to consider before answering him. It had been a long time.

"Three years," she said at last. "Yes, almost three years."

"You saw the hospital?" he questioned eagerly, and his face fell when she shook her head.

"I didn't notice it," she confessed.

"Well, you will soon be inside it which, I suppose, is the view any doctor would prefer." His smile returned, warm and friendly and admiring as his gaze rested on her face. Rose lowered her own gaze, feeling the colour rush to her cheeks. This was the man to whom she was betrothed, she reminded herself, the man to whom, in a few months' time, she would be married. Yet he was a stranger, his mind and his thoughts and feelings a closed book to her, and she was curiously shy of him, inexplicably reluctant to take any step which would put her on terms of intimacy with him. It was not, of course, that she disliked him—rather the reverse, for even on this short acquaintance he had revealed himself as a man of charm and culture, widely travelled and at ease in any company, with a gay, attractive personality. Yet there was something, some barrier between them which even she could not have explained and for which she could find no reasonable excuse. She bit her lower lip, very conscious of the fact that his eyes were still on her bent head.

"I am very much looking forward to my first visit to the hospital," she told him politely, and felt his hand close gently over hers.

"It will be my privilege to take you on a tour of inspection, Rose," Kim Myint returned. He released her hand. "But now

I see that we are about to disembark. If you will forgive me, I think I should see that Colonel Anson is properly received and introduced. No doubt they will have sent a car from the Palace for him, but I had better, perhaps, make sure. May I expect you tomorrow morning, at the hospital?"

Rose inclined her head. "Thank you. I shall be there."

He left her and she went to join Major Aung and his wife, with whom she had been sitting, and to collect her hand baggage in readiness for unloading.

The cabin door was open when she reached it and she saw Colonel Anson descending the steps with Kim Myint at his heels. A small group of officials, most of them in uniform, had emerged from the airport administration building and were walking towards the aircraft. Rose did not recognize any of them, but she saw Kim Myint greeting them, exchanging salutes and handshakes and then formally introducing each in turn to his companion. Behind the official reception party, a second and smaller group had gathered, amongst whom she saw her father's major-domo and a uniformed native chauffeur who had, presumably, been sent to meet her. She waved to them and both men hurried over to her, relieving the steward of her baggage. His Excellency's car was waiting for her, the major-domo announced, indicating it, and he would attend to the collection of her heavy luggage and await her in the car. Rose thanked him and turned to make her farewell to the Aungs.

It was then that she noticed a European standing at the edge of the circle of officials to whom Kim and Colonel Anson were speaking. He was a short, broad-shouldered man, dressed in a white tussore suit of obviously English cut, and his face, which was pink and a trifle flabby, was shaded by the brim of a worn panama hat. Rose had never, to the best of her recollection, set eyes on him before, but the fact that he was there with the official reception party suggested that he must be a person of some importance, and she studied him, from where she stood, with considerable interest.

He was, she imagined, in his middle forties or thereabouts. His pink and white complexion and general plumpness contrasted strongly with the tanned faces and slim, sinewy bodies of the men about him, and she put him down, for this reason, as one engaged in a sedentary occupation. An assistant secretary from the British Embassy, perhaps, or—she saw Kim Myint shake hands with him and turn to introduce John Anson—one of the new oil company's representatives. His greeting of the new arrivals was cordial, the round pink face wreathed in smiles, and his handshake, when John Anson reached his side, was prolonged and effusive. Talking volubly, he grasped the younger man's arm and started to lead him towards the airport buildings, pointing, as he did so, in the direction of a large, silver-grey touring car which was drawn up just behind the one into which her father's major-domo was now loading her own suit-cases. Rose stared at it, puzzled, and from it to John Anson's face which, lit by a smile barely an instant before, was suddenly white with controlled anger. She was too far away to hear more than a word or two that was being said, but it was not difficult to guess from John Anson's voice that he was as angry as his expression suggested.

The man in the tussore suit stepped back a pace, obviously surprised, two bright spots of resentful colour rising to burn in his plump cheeks as he glared back at his fellow-countryman. John Anson came to a standstill, drawing himself up to his full, impressive height. He waited, saying nothing, for the other to speak.

The Gaupali officers, Kim Myint and Major Aung with them, halted too, their faces blank but their eyes curiously alert and watchful. It was as if, Rose thought, sensitive to the sudden tension which had seized the hitherto amicable little party, it was as if they were waiting for some issue to be decided between the two Englishmen and reserving judgment until it should be decided, one way or the other. That the issue was important she could have no doubt, but she was completely at a loss to understand what it was or why it should be of importance to any of them.

She hesitated, her heart quickening its beat, but the decision never came. At that moment two horsemen galloped at breathtaking speed from the perimeter of the airfield, bringing the eyes of everyone in the group to watch their progress as they thundered down towards the concrete apron.

The leading rider was a slim boy, mounted on a magnificent, pure-bred grey Arab, which he handled with such superbly reckless skill that Rose, despite the fact that it was more than three years since she had last seen him, knew at once who he was. Prince Maung Saw, her mind registered, it could be no one else, with the tall Sikh at his back and the flying Arab stallion beneath him. The young heir apparent to the throne of Gaupal had come to greet his new tutor in characteristically dramatic fashion, seeking perhaps, by this arrogant display, to take his measure as, a few minutes before, the officers had sought, less dramatically, to take it. She wondered, watching him anxiously, whether John Anson was aware of the identity of the newcomer and, if he was, how he would react to the prince's swift, unheralded arrival and the informality of their introduction.

The official reception party came stiffly

to attention. Hands flew to the salute as the two horsemen reached the edge of the concrete. The Sikh prudently drew rein, pulling his horse back into a trot, but the boy on the Arab came on, scarcely breaking stride as his animal's hoofs struck the treacherous, unyielding surface of the apron. It was only when he was within half a dozen yards of the man he had come to see that he pulled up, jerking the beautifully trained grey back on its haunches with calculated brutality. Colonel Anson, Rose saw, had not moved. He stood his ground, eyeing the boy dispassionately from beneath lowered brows. He was in civilian clothes and so, of course, could not salute, but when Maung Saw bowed to him, he removed his hat, bringing his heels quietly together.

The prince opened his mouth as if to address him and then, thinking better of it, closed his teeth on his lower lip.

They stood looking at each other in a strange, pregnant silence for fully a minute, while around them the small circle of officers stood rigidly to attention, their faces as blank and inscrutable as they had been before. Etiquette demanded that the prince speak first, and since he uttered no word they all remained silent. No one moved, and the only sound was the hum of an aircraft's engines, muted by distance as it circled the field. Even the porters and the servants standing by the parked cars seemed, for that moment, to have been frozen into immobility.

Rose let out her breath in a long-drawn sigh. Almost as if he had heard it and had taken it as the signal for his departure, Prince Maung Saw jerked the grey's near rein and, wheeling abruptly, was away in the direction from which he had come, breaking into an extended canter the instant he was clear of the concrete.

The Sikh did not immediately follow him. His eyes, too, had been fixed on John Anson's face throughout the strange little scene, and in them, suddenly, dawned an unwilling recognition so swiftly suppressed that Rose, watching him, wondered afterwards if she had imagined it. To her astonishment, she saw the Englishman step forward with outstretched hand. His voice held a deep note of pleasure and surprise as he addressed the Sikh in his own tongue. "Subadar-sahib! It is good to see you again. How are you, after all these years?"

The Sikh saluted, but he ignored the outstretched hand. Sitting very erect in his saddle, he said in careful, deliberate English, "I am sorry, Sahib, but you mistake me for someone else. I have not the honour of the Sahib's acquaintance. Salaam, Sahib!" He saluted again, the brown hand punctiliously raised to the immaculately wound turban, the bearded face shuttered and unsmiling. Then, before the Englishman could say a word in answer, he swung his horse round in a tight circle and set off in pursuit of his royal charge, now almost out of sight on the far side of the airfield.

Rose watched him go. When she turned, she found John Anson beside her and realized that he had come to bid her farewell. She gave him her hand. "I am so sorry" —she spoke impulsively—"for what happened just now, Colonel Anson. You must think us rather—rather uncivilized. But His Highness is—"

"His Highness is a boy, Dr. Lian. I expect he thought it would be an amusing idea to come and look me over." He smiled, his voice quite even, his manner completely normal and unruffled. But it was typical of him, Rose thought, not to pretend to misunderstand the implications of her apology, for he added, his smile fading, "I didn't expect that I should find my task here an easy one, you know."

"Didn't you?"

"No." He shook his head. "Scarcely that. Although when a man with whom I served for over a year refuses to admit that he's ever seen me before in his life, it . . . makes me wonder a bit, I must confess."

"You mean His Highness's body-guard?" Rose asked.

"Yes, I do. Subadar-major Narain Singh —that *is* his name, isn't it?"

"Yes, I believe it is." She hesitated. "Colonel Anson, he *did* recognize you! I was watching his face and I'm certain he did."

"I thought so too," John Anson agreed flatly. "Well, no doubt there is an explanation. Your father warned me that I should probably meet with opposition from certain quarters, but he also gave me the hope that I might count on your friendship and Colonel Myint's. May I presume to do so?"

"Of course you may." Again on impulse, she put out her hand. "At any time."

"Then"—he retained her hand in his and stood smiling down at her—"we shall meet again, shan't we, before very long?"

"I shall be very happy to see you, Colonel Anson," Rose assured him with sincerity. "You will find me at the hospital or in my father's house. That is—you will find me and Colonel Myint also at the hospital. He is in charge of it, as I expect you know."

"Thank you, Dr. Lian." His fingers tightened gently about hers before he let them go. "I'll say au revoir then and— good luck to you in your new appointment."

"And to you in yours."

He bowed. Rose watched him take leave of the rest of the party and then stride over to the car that had been sent from the Palace to meet him, Kim Myint at his side.

Of the man in the tussore suit there was now no sign, and as she made her way across the apron to her own car, she saw that the big grey tourer had also vanished. For some reason, she felt pleased that it had . . . pleased and oddly relieved. She got into her own car, the driver closed the door on her and slid behind the wheel, looking back at her enquiringly.

"Don't wait," she bade him, suddenly impatient and eager to be home. Obediently the man let in his clutch.

As the car gathered speed, Rose leaned forward in her seat. In the distance she glimpsed the great Tauling mountains, a hazy outline now as the light began to fade abruptly into darkness. Borne faintly on the evening breeze, she could hear the curious tinkling sound of temple bells, ringing out as if in welcome, and she caught her breath, feeling tears ache in her throat as the familiar sound reached her, like a nostalgic echo from her childhood.

She was coming home, Rose told herself, coming home, at last, to Tauling. And suddenly she was glad that she had come . . .

9

JOHN ANSON looked round the large, luxuriously appointed room and stifled a sigh as he settled himself at the desk, picking up his pen and pulling a block of flimsy airmail paper towards him. He had been almost a fortnight in Tauling and knew that he could no longer put off writing his promised letter to Sandra. Beyond a brief announcement of his safe arrival, hastily scribbled ten days ago, and an equally brief note to his father, he hadn't written to anyone. Yet a curious reluctance to write possessed him now, and—more in order to delay the actual moment of starting on his task than because he really wanted to smoke—he reached for his pipe. Having lit it, he sat back, drawing on it absent-mindedly and gazing out over the veranda rail to where, in the beautifully laid out garden which surrounded his house, a flock of peacocks preened themselves in the muted rays of the setting sun.

Peacocks were sacred in Gaupal and they were everywhere. At first John had found the sight of them a pleasingly unusual one, but they were so many and their noisy screeching so disturbing that now he was beginning to view them with more annoyance than pleasure.

He sighed again and, setting down his pipe, made an effort to collect his thoughts. There was so much to say to Sandra, so much to tell her that it wasn't easy to decide where he should begin. And, of course, there was the question of her feelings for him to be discussed . . . their parting at London Airport had been, to say the least of it, miserably discouraging, and it had left him uncertain of where he stood, lacking confidence in himself and faith in her, and wretchedly afraid of what the future might hold for both of them.

He pulled the single sheet of airmail paper on which he had written "Sandra my darling" from the pad, tore it impatiently into shreds and began again.

Sandra darling—I am writing this in my quarters at the Royal Palace in Tauling. I gave you my first impressions of the Palace and the city in my earlier letter, which should have reached you by now, so I won't repeat myself.

Suffice it to say that, on a closer inspection, both are even more beautiful than I imagined. The city of Tauling stands on a Plateau some six thousand feet above sea level, which means that the climate is extremely pleasant by European standards —days of brilliant sunshine, followed by cool nights, and there is always a breeze coming, fresh and invigorating, from the mountains.

The city is surrounded on three sides by mountains—we flew over the range on the Burmese frontier, as I told you, a magnificent sight—and it is bisected by the River Htun Yee which flows south, through the narrow corridor of Gaupal Treaty territory between Burma and Thailand, to the Gulf of Martaban. It is this river which makes it possible for the oil company—in which your friend Charles Garrison is interested—to consider . . .

John stopped writing. The thought of Charles Garrison was a disquieting one and, frowning, he put his pen through the final sentence. It would be wiser not to mention Garrison's name to Sandra—yet. Time enough for it, time for her to bring Garrison's name up, if she wanted to and if she thought it necessary to tell him anything about the man. Perhaps she wasn't seeing him, perhaps his anxiety on Garrison's account was merely the result of his own imagination—his own jealous imagination, his own mistrust. He was aware, by this time, of course, that his mistrust of Charles Garrison had been justified, for the episode at the airfield had more than confirmed his suspicions.

The attempted gift of a large and expensive car had been a very clumsy attempt at bribery—a trap, calculated to bring about his downfall if he fell into it. And it had been unexpected; he had supposed that his refusal of the first offer had put an end to the idea. Garrison must have worked fast, to bring it about so swiftly—to have the infernal car at the airfield, awaiting his arrival. His frown deepened. Garrison *had* worked fast, although the lord only knew to what purpose—unless it were to discredit him. However limited his experience of the East, he couldn't possibly have failed to realize the effect on the Oriental mind of an open offer and the open acceptance of such a gift, made to a man who was about to take up a position of trust. And made to an Englishman, whose position of trust was under an Eastern ruler—whose integrity was as precious to him in Gaupal, as life itself . . . more so, perhaps, if he cared about his country's good name.

John's hand clenched about his pen gripping it so fiercely that the knuckles gleamed white beneath the tautly stretched skin. Seen in this light Garrison's scheme was the act of a madman or, at best, a fool. And yet the man hadn't struck him as a fool, very far from it, which made his behaviour the more puzzling . . . for he wasn't a madman either, if his reputation were anything to go by. He was a clever, calculating, ruthless businessman, and he obviously hadn't got where he was now by being clumsy.

Well, it wasn't the slightest use wasting time on fruitless speculation concerning Garrison's motives at this early stage. Probably, in time, they would become clear and comprehensible, together with all the other problems which, at the moment, seemed to be hemming him in behind a cloud of uncertainty and doubt. John smiled wryly to himself. Previous experience of the East had taught him to be patient and to accept procrastination and delay with resignation, if not with enjoyment, and at least he could put this lesson to good effect, if he did nothing else. He could wait.

He returned to his letter, going to some pains to describe in detail the house he had been allotted. It was a delightful bungalow, built of seasoned teak and richly carved and ornamented, standing in its own small garden beneath a grove of tamarind trees, within the outer wall of the Palace. He waxed enthusiastic in his description, for the place had appealed to him strongly from the minute he had set eyes on it, and he wondered, reading his letter through, whether he had managed to convey a picture of it to Sandra. Perhaps he hadn't, but he had done his best: she would sense his delight in his new surroundings and, he hoped, would sense also his longing to share them with her . . . that, surely, she couldn't doubt.

He went on, writing swiftly now: In this

area, which is outside the moat that encircles the Palace proper, live those officials of the court whose duties require their daily attendance on the king. The Prime Minister lives—in much greater state than I, needless to remark—almost opposite. I can see the gateway to his house from my bedroom window. He received me in private and quite informal audience the day after my arrival: he is a charming old man, who speaks perfect English and is widely travelled, and he made himself extremely pleasant to me.

So far I have not been received by the King. His Majesty, so the Prime Minister informed me, is away, staying at his shooting lodge in the mountains for a few days, but I am to be summoned to an audience when he returns. This means, of course, that—apart from our somewhat melodramatic meeting on the airfield, when the young gentleman appeared at full gallop on a very handsome Arab stallion and did his best to ride me down—I haven't yet been introduced to my royal pupil. I gather that he's with his father in the mountains. From what I hear he is a keen sportsman and a very fine shot:

certainly he can handle a horse—I was able to see that much for myself.

By one of those strange and very unlikely coincidences that do sometimes happen, his personal bodyguard is a Sikh, Subadar-major Narain Singh, who was in 231 Brigade with me in Burma—an exceptionally good type of native officer for whom I always had the greatest respect. Unfortunately, however, the respect doesn't seem to have been mutual, since he failed to recognize me when he came with the Prince to look me over the day I arrived . . .

John paused, and once more his brows came together in a puzzled frown. He was still at a loss to account for Narain Singh's strange behaviour on the day of his arrival. But—perhaps this was another of the things which time would make clear. He had gone over all the possible explanations in his mind and had been unable to find one that could be called logical. If it had been anyone but Narain Singh, he might have understood: as it was, he simply did not understand.

He picked up his pipe and relit it, glancing through his letter for the second time. As a commentary to a travel film, it might pass muster, he decided wryly, but as a letter to a woman from the man who loved her, it was a poor effort, and Sandra would be bewildered and probably hurt by it. He tore off the last page and began afresh, finding it hard, in spite of his longing to do so, to put his feelings into words. His feelings were conflicting, his emotions muddled and inexplicable, even to himself, and after a while, as he continued to write, the image of Sandra's face faded into a nebulous blur and he could no longer distinguish her features. His words became more stilted than ever and finally the flow, even of these, ceased altogether, and he found himself staring down helplessly at a blank sheet of paper.

How could he write of love and of hope and of longing to a woman from whom he had parted on such terms as those on which he had parted from Sandra? How banish the hideous fear that tore at him, how escape from the conviction that it was Charles Garrison who mattered to Sandra, rather than himself? How—without asking her, without accusing her . . . without losing her?

In despair, John returned to his original letter. Better a travelogue, he thought grimly, than what he had just so unsuccessfully attempted to put on to paper. He could only hope that Sandra would understand and that, understanding, she would resolve his doubts when she wrote to him, that she would answer and refute the accusations he had not made and could not bring himself to utter now. It was, he knew, a faint hope, but it was the only hope he had.

He finished the letter with a description of the Royal Palace, which made up in length for what it lacked in artistry and ended:

Darling, I think you will know why it is that I have written to you in this vein. I can't write in any other until you tell me that what happened at the airport didn't mean what I'm so afraid it did.

I want to know if you love me, Sandra. That's about the long and short of it, and however much it may hurt you to say it or me to hear it—the truth is what I want, plain and unvarnished. If you don't love me enough to come out here to marry me, then tell me, Sandra, please, without trying to spare my feelings. They're pretty chaotic now, as you can probably imagine. But I want to know—it's not knowing that is so unbearable.

If you do still love me, then, as always, I'm yours to command—I think you know that too, don't you?

Whatever you decide and whatever is the truth, I intend to stay here for the year I've agreed to and to do everything in my power to make a success of the job I've taken on . . .

John signed his name, folded the half-dozen pages he had written and put them carefully into an envelope. Then he addressed it to Sandra, stamped it with the gaudy blue peacock that was the symbol of Gaupal and laid it beside the envelope he had already addressed to his father.

It was done, he thought dully. If Sandra wrote at once, on receipt of his letter, he might expect to receive her reply within about a week or ten days, depending on whether or not she missed the bi-weekly mail.

He knocked out his pipe and, suddenly weary and at the end of his tether, called out to his boy for a drink.

There was a soft tap on the door and it opened, in response to his shouted command, to disclose the round, smiling face of his Number One boy, Bo Tin Karen.

"Thakin call?" he suggested, the smile spreading.

"Yes, Bo Tin. Bring me a peg, will you?"

The boy pattered over to his side, setting a silver salver in front of him on which were placed a bottle of whisky, two glasses, water in a cut glass jug and a bowl of ice. He poured the peg deftly, adding just the right amount of water and, looking up into John's face in mute question, an ice cube in the tongs he held in his hand. John nodded, and the ice tinkled into his glass.

"Thanks, Bo Tin."

Bo Tin grinned back cheerfully. The boy had only been with him for just over a week, but already he had made his capable presence felt in the small household, as Kim Myint, when sending him, had promised that he would. Besides being a most efficient servant, he possessed a happy, extremely likeable personality and the gay, uninhibited sense of humour that distinguished his race from any other. He was neat and clean in person, always immaculately turned out, and he spoke a little English while understanding considerably more. John was finding him a useful guide, for he knew every nook and cranny of the vast, rambling palace, and could be relied upon not only to reel off the names and titles of the various court officials with whom his master might have dealings but also to produce a helpful list of their habits and customs.

He did everything that could be expected of a well-trained Number One, and more. The house ran like clockwork, meals appeared on time and were appetizing and plentiful, and whoever John required, from a tailor to make his uniforms to a dhobi to wash them, Bo Tin conjured up, as if by magic, the instant he was asked to do so.

The inactivity of the past fortnight, due to the absence of the King and his family, had begun to prove irksome, but Bo Tin, from the moment he had set foot in the bungalow, had found ways and means to keep his master profitably occupied.

There was this one and that one, on whom John should call: Bo Tin was acquainted with their Number Ones—there was no need to wait for introductions, Bo Tin would see that his Thakin was expected. The Prime Minister's private secretary would be deeply honoured if permitted to give him tea. By the same token, although the Army Commander was regrettably absent from the capital, his Chief of Staff was not, and he too, according to his Number One, was anxious to entertain Bo Tin's new master.

Bo Tin, in fact, John reflected, eyeing the little man affectionately, was rapidly making himself quite indispensable and, even in so short a time, was friend as well as servant to him. Thanks to his Number One, he had made many very useful contacts and his social life, at first so barren, was now becoming busy and interesting. So much so, indeed, that he hadn't yet paid his promised call on Kim Myint and Rose Lian at the hospital, although both had dined with him earlier in the week. He finished his whisky and began to relax.

"Master," ventured Bo Tin, coming to take his glass. "Excuse, please."

"Well, what is it?" John asked.

"Evening time, His Majesty come back."

"Is that so?" John sat up. "Are you sure?"

The boy nodded. "Yes, Master, sure. Morning time, come messenger, saying His Majesty hold durbar."

John was silent, considering this. If the King had returned, then his duties would begin. He would be presented officially to Prince Maung Saw, at a big, formal reception of which the Prime Minister's secretary had warned him.

"Thakin," said Bo Tin, fiddling with the glass in his hand, "there is one man waiting. He ask audience of Colonel Anson Sahib."

"Who?" John demanded. "Who is the man, Bo Tin? What's his name?"

Bo Tin hesitated for a moment before replying. Then he said, his eyes on the ground, "He is Subadar-major Narain Singh, Master."

John's brows came together in a puzzled frown. Finally he said, his tone flat and uncompromising, "Very well, Bo Tin, I will see the Subadar-sahib. Show him in here, will you?"

"As you command, Thakin." The boy spoke in his native tongue, as if thus to imply disapproval of his master's visitor. He added in English, so as to be quite certain that John understood his warning, "This man your enemy, Master. He mean you harm."

"Does he? Well, we shall see about that. Show him in, please. At once," as the boy hesitated. "Don't keep him waiting."

Bo Tin pressed the palms of his hands together and bowed. He left the room and returned a few moments later, to admit the tall Sikh in ominous silence. Narain Singh was in uniform. He came smartly to attention and saluted, his bearded face as expressionless as if it had been carved from a piece of solid teak. Only his eyes, dark and watchful, gave any hint of his feelings.

"So you have remembered me after all, Subadar-sahib?" John suggested. He indicated a chair in front of his desk, making no move, this time, to offer the man his hand. "Sit down, won't you?"

"If the Colonel Sahib will permit, I

prefer to stand," the Sikh answered with dignity.

"Certainly, if you wish it. What is your business with me, Subadar-sahib?"

"It can be simply stated," Narain Singh told him. "First, I wish to offer my apologies to the Colonel Sahib for not having acknowledged him on the day of his arrival."

"Very well, I accept your apology. No doubt you had a reason for refusing to shake my hand."

"That is so," the Sikh conceded.

"May I ask for your reason, Subadar-sahib?"

"That, too, is a simple one, Sahib. According to the Sikh code, a man must not shake the hand of one to whom he intends enmity."

John met the level, dark gaze, his own surprised and questioning. "So you intend me enmity, Narain Singh?"

The dark eyes flashed. "Yes, Colonel Sahib, I do. That is why I am here, that I may warn you. In the past, in the days when I served the British Raj as a soldier, you were one of my officers and I respected you."

"As I respected you, Subadar-ji."

"Sahib!" The Sikh stiffened, but a faint smile curved his lips. John regarded him in frank and unconcealed bewilderment. He was a fine looking old man, proud and dignified, the bright medal ribbons on his chest telling the story of his years of loyal service to the British Raj, on the Frontier, in the Middle East and Burma and in South-East Asia, hundreds of miles from his homeland. Yet now, it seemed, on his own admission, he had come not as a friend and comrade in arms but as an enemy. The dark eyes, beneath their grizzled brows, held anger and hatred and a bitter, sullen resentment for which John was unable to account. He said, honestly seeking an explanation for it, "Subadar-sahib, you surely don't imagine, do you, that I have come to take your place?"

"Have you not, Sahib?" the old man challenged. He was no longer smiling. "Is it not on your account that I am to be sent away? I, who for nine years have been my prince's shadow, am to yield his care to you! . . . I am to retire, on a pension . . . to be dismissed from my service and sent back to Lahore!"

So that was it, John thought. No wonder the old man resented his coming so bitterly. No wonder he had refused to shake his hand . . .

"Narain Singh," he said quickly, "on whose authority have you been dismissed? Surely there is work for both of us? My duties with His Highness are those of tutor —I am not his bodyguard."

"Nay, Sahib, I know. Another body-guard has been appointed, one of commissioned rank, closer to your own. It was thought that this would be more suitable. And as to whose authority has brought about my dismissal, why"—the broad, khaki-clad shoulders rose in an expressive shrug—"I had it from the officer who commands the Palace Guard. But the orders came from a higher source, Sahib."

"You mean—"

"I mean from His Majesty the King, Sahib. From His Highness's illustrious father."

John was silent. He felt deeply sorry for the fine old soldier who eyed him so reproachfully from across the desk, but he knew—as, no doubt, Narain Singh knew even better than he—that the King's orders, once given, were unlikely to be countermanded. While he himself had been, in all probability, the reason for the King's decision to appoint a new, higher ranking bodyguard in Narain Singh's place, it was doubtful whether, with the best will in the world, he would have sufficient influence to obtain the old Sikh's reinstatement. Certainly not yet, when he hadn't even taken up his appointment as the prince's tutor and was still, in a sense, himself on trial.

"I don't know," he began sympathetically, "what I can do to help you, Subadar-sahib. You understand, of course, that I should like to help you if I could, but—"

"I am not asking for your help, Colonel Anson Sahib," the Sikh put in, with a flash of anger. He drew himself up to his full height. "It was not in order to ask for it that I came here to speak with you this evening. I came rather for another purpose."

"Well? And that is . . . ?"

"If you were to go," the old Sikh said tonelessly, "there is a chance that all might be again as it was in the past. Therefore, Sahib, I came to tell you that I should use every endeavour to *make* you go, in the short time that is left to me. I am an honest man, Sahib, and I wish that you should know the truth, that you should not imagine that I am going behind your back, as is the way of cowards, with a knife hidden in my hand. I stand here before you, as your foe, giving you warning of my intention. If you refuse to heed my warning, I cannot answer for the consequences. Sahib"—again he came to attention and again his hand rose in an impeccable, parade-ground salute—"I ask your permission to dismiss."

John got to his feet. He said, quite evenly, "All right, Subadar-sahib. Thank you for your warning. You know, of course, that I can't heed it, don't you? But I'm grateful to you, nevertheless, for giving it to me. Your action was the action of an honourable man whose hand, were it not for these unfortunate circumstances, I should be proud to shake, as I did in the past. Salaam, Subadar-ji!"

"Salaam, Sahib."

They faced each other for a second or

two, and then Narain Singh turned on his heel without another word. Bo Tin, in response to John's shouted command, showed him out into the gathering darkness of the courtyard.

When the houseboy returned, he made no mention of the visitor. His master's bath, he announced prosaically, was prepared, if his master would care to bathe himself. John sighed, gave him the letters to take to the Palace mailbox and went into his sleeping quarters to divest himself of his clothes.

He lay in the tin tub which served him for a bath until the water grew cold, lost in his own troubled thoughts and only roused from them when the light faded completely and he heard Bo Tin moving about in his bedroom, lighting the lamps and laying out his evening clothes. The bedroom was empty when he entered it, but his evening dress trousers, together with the white sharkskin dinner jacket and the cummerbund he wore in place of a waistcoat, lay neatly folded on the bed, waiting for him. Usually Bo Tin assisted him to dress: this evening, however, he failed to put in an appearance.

He was absent at dinner also. The Number Two boy, a round-faced, earnest young Gaupali, served his solitary meal. The boy stood behind John's chair, plying him with course after course of perfectly cooked, appetizing food and attentive to his smallest need, but in spite of this, John missed Bo Tin.

After dinner he repaired to the veranda to smoke a pipe and watch the moon rise, and it was here, at last, that Bo Tin came to him, a letter in his hand. The envelope was large and it bore on the back flap the gorgeously coloured peacock, with crowned head and tail erect and spread, which was the emblem of the ruling house of Gaupal. His summons to the King's presence had come, John thought, as he slit open the envelope. The invitation it contained was written in English and stamped with the King's seal: it requested his attendance at a durbar, to be held the following morning in the Palace, and the secretary who had so painstakingly penned it, in a beautiful, copperplate hand, had thoughtfully added the information that uniform, with decorations, should be worn.

John looked up to find Bo Tin's eyes on him.

"Well," he said, "I imagine you know what this is."

Bo Tin's smile reappeared. "Indeed, Thakin, I know. The Thakin's uniforms are now ready for inspection." He waved a hand in the direction of the bedroom. "May I have the Thakin's medals, that I may clean them?"

"But I didn't think the uniforms were to be ready until next week," John demurred, and the boy's smile widened.

"I stand over tailor with big stick," he returned, and led the way, triumphantly, to where the uniforms had been laid out to await his master's approval.

Despite the haste with which they had been completed, they were extremely well made, and a critical inspection could detect no flaws. The full dress uniform, which he would have to wear at the durbar, was made of a very good quality rifle-green cloth, John saw, and, with its scarlet facings, looked exceptionally smart. The others were of khaki drill, tailored to the British pattern but with the badges and buttons bearing the distinctive Gaupali crown. All the uniforms fitted, when he tried them on, better even than those his military tailor in Aldershot had made for him in the past, after numerous fittings.

"Well done," he said to Bo Tin, and the boy beamed as he presented the tailor's modest bill, all trace of his former resentment vanishing as if it had never existed. Neither he nor John, as if by common consent, referred to the Sikh's visit again, but instead, talked of other things.

At ten, Kim Myint's big American car drew up outside and, hearing it, John went out to meet him, conscious of a faint disappointment when he saw that Kim had come by himself. There was no reason, of course, why he should have brought Rose Lian with him, but in spite of reason John's disappointment persisted. He enquired for her when greetings had been exchanged and they were sitting together on the veranda, a tray of drinks between them.

Kim smiled. "Oh, she is in excellent health, and asked me to give you her best regards. You will be seeing her tomorrow, I imagine. You've been summoned to the durbar, of course?"

John nodded. "Yes, I have. Bo Tin has performed a minor miracle, getting my uniform finished in time for it."

"He's managed to get you full dress? Excellent. He's a good boy, that one."

"He is indeed. I'm very pleased with him."

"I will call for you tomorrow, if you like," Kim offered, "before the durbar starts. I shall be expected to present you to His Majesty, so it would be easier if we arrived at the Palace together. The presentations will be made in the Throne Room and we shall have to take our places there before the King comes in. Rose won't be with us until later."

"Won't she?"

"No." Kim shook his head. "In Gaupal, a durbar is never attended by women, it's always an exclusively male affair. While we are paying our respects to His Majesty, Rose will call on the Senior Queen to pay hers. Afterwards, there will be a less formal reception in the garden, at which a mixed company will be present. That will probably last for an hour or so and be followed by lunch, but we needn't stay for that—Rose thought you might care to come back for lunch with us, at His Excellency's house. It will be less formal and we shall be able to relax."

"Thank you, I should like to lunch with you and Dr. Lian very much."

"Good, then that's arranged. Have you bought a car yet?"

"No," John confessed, "not yet. I intend to, of course"—he met Kim's dark, searching eyes and grinned at him—"a more modest one, though, than the one I was offered when I arrived."

Kim Myint echoed his smile. "You are wise, my friend . . . thanks . . ." He accepted a cheroot from the box John passed him, and when it was lit he leaned back in his chair with a little sigh. "It's good to relax. We have been busy at the hospital and I'm tired."

"Are you?" Lighting his own cheroot, John studied the face of his guest. Kim looked tired, he thought. His eyes, usually so bright and interested, were dull and lacklustre, and there were lines of strain about his mouth and criss-crossing his brow which John did not remember having seen there before. But he brightened as he launched into a description of the work he had been doing and the wonders of his new, splendidly equipped hospital.

"We're hampered, of course, as I feared we would be, by lack of trained staff. Besides Rose and myself, we have only three other doctors—all of them physicians and all of them young—so that the bulk of the work and all the surgery falls to us. Rose has been wonderful, quite wonderful . . . she is a very fine surgeon, you know. Better than I am, for her technique is more up to date and mine is rusty from disuse. But obviously it is going to be far too much for her to cope with, virtually single-handed, when the hospital really gets going and all our beds are occupied. Then, you see, as Director, I shall have a great deal of organizing and office work to do and I shall not be able to assist her. Mine is an administrative appointment and is intended to be purely supervisory—I have, in addition, my Army duties, you understand."

"What will you do then?" John wanted to know. "About staff, I mean?"

Kim Myint inhaled smoke from his cheroot. "We shall have to increase our staff," he said slowly, "it's quite essential. I can manage temporarily if I can persuade the Minister to let me have two of our Army surgeons, men I know well, who have been compulsorily retired during my absence. For"—he hesitated, and then added bluntly—"for political reasons."

John stared at him. "Surely their politics shouldn't affect their medical work?"

"No, they should and will not, if I have my way." Kim Myint's expression hardened. "Both are experienced surgeons and have been trained in England and India. At present they are forbidden even to work in private practice, and we haven't so many doctors in Gaupal that we can afford to lose them."

"The hospital is a civilian one, isn't it?"

"Primarily civilian, yes. But a section of it is intended as a military unit and reserved for military patients. Hence my own appointment, which is due less to my merit than to the fact that so few of our medical officers have administrative experience. I, as you know, gained mine in the British service. And I was in command of a military hospital in Malaya for two years at the end of the war."

"Yes, I heard you were." Without asking whether or not he wanted it, John refilled Kim Myint's glass.

"Thank you." Kim sipped gratefully at his drink. "I must go, I only came in order to arrange things for tomorrow and to pass on Rose's luncheon invitation." But he made no move. After a short silence, he went on, "As Director of the Army Medical Service, I ought to be able to call on any Army personnel that I require, both medical officers and trained orderlies, for work in the hospital." He broke off, frowning down at the glowing tip of his cheroot.

"Aren't you able to call on them?" John questioned, sensing more behind the words than they implied.

Kim's scowl deepened, etching a maze of tiny lines across his smooth brown face. "I would say this to nobody but you, John, and it's confidential, you understand. Frankly, the answer to your question is no . . . I'm not. I have been away too long. My appointment as Director of the Army Medical Service appears to be considered a more or less nominal one, my deputy is well established and on the best possible terms with the Minister. Between them, they control all regimental medical units and field hospitals, and it has been made clear to me that they intend to go on controlling them. I am supposed to be merely a figurehead so far as the Army is concerned, and they think that I shall occupy myself with the hospital, leaving the Army to its own devices."

"And will you?" John asked curiously. The reply was the one he expected. "No," exploded Kim Myint, "I will not! I have never been a figurehead in my life. And —again this is strictly between ourselves, John, my friend—I believe with all my heart that both medicine and the Army should be free from any sort of political influence. I have returned to find that here they are not. But"—his face relaxed suddenly—"this is no time to burden you with my troubles, is it?"

"I don't mind," John assured him, "if it helps you to talk of them, Kim. I don't pretend to understand all you've told me, but at least you know that I won't betray your confidence."

Kim Myint put out a hand to grasp his. "I know that, my friend. Perhaps I haven't made things very clear to you, but I've told you a little of what I am up against, and even telling you so little has helped me more than you can imagine. I've got one or two things off my chest, which is always a help, isn't it? Like the good old British soldier, I've had a grumble and feel the better for it. You've been kindness itself to listen to me."

"Nonsense. I'm interested. And as a soldier, I share your views about political influence."

Kim rose. "I must get back. Thank you for your hospitality, John. We'll meet again in the morning."

"We will. What time will you be here?"

"Oh, soon after nine. About nine-thirty, let's say." They walked together to the door, Kim with a hand on John's shoulder. "I shall have Rose with me— you won't mind if we drop her on our way?"

"Of course not. I shall be delighted to see her."

Bo Tin appeared from the rear of the house, like a genie spirited there by magic, as John opened the door. He bowed and went over to Kim Myint's car to rouse his sleeping driver.

Kim halted and turned to offer his hand. "Talking of influence," he said thoughtfully, "you will soon be one of the most influential men in this State, John. You realize that, don't you?"

John laughed. "How so?"

"You will have the ear of the future King, my friend. When that happens, I shall have to guard my tongue more closely than I have this evening, perhaps."

"I hope you'll never find that necessary with me."

Kim Myint smiled. "I hope I shan't. Good night, John, and—thank you again."

"Good night," John echoed. He stood in the moonlit courtyard, watching until the twin rear lights of the big car receded into tiny red pinpoints and then vanished from sight at a bend in the road.

Behind him, a ghostly silhouette against the backcloth of purple, star-bright sky, the Royal Palace of Tauling stood, silent and mysterious, behind its ancient moated walls, apparently deserted. But as he watched, a sentry moved, high up on the ramparts, the metallic scrape as he grounded his rifle a strange, incongruous breaking of the prevailing quiet and a reminder that the walls were guarded.

John stared back in the direction of the sound. Tomorrow, for the first time, he would enter the Palace and it would seem mysterious no longer. Tomorrow he would see and swear allegiance to the King he had come to serve.

And after tomorrow he, and not Narain Singh, would assume responsibility for the King's son . . .

10

PUNCTUALLY at nine-thirty next morning, Kim Myint's car drew up outside John's gate. Bo Tin hurried to the door, and John, already in full dress uniform, tucked his helmet under his arm and went to receive his callers.

Rose Lian came first. She was wearing Gaupali dress, and John caught his breath at the sight of her. He had never seen her in any but European clothes before, and in the graceful blue and silver tamain with its short, stiffly starched white jacket, she looked lovelier than he had ever imagined any woman could look. And yet, despite the flowers in her hair and the natural grace and dignity of her carriage, she looked more European than ever. By contrast, Kim Myint in his resplendent uniform seemed alien and out of place at her side and, going forward to greet them, John was forced to exercise stern self-control to prevent his thoughts revealing themselves in eyes or voice as he spoke their names.

But it was wrong, he thought despairingly, so terribly, horribly wrong to couple these two together. They did not belong together. The racial barriers between them had never seemed to him so noticeable or so insurmountable.

He forced a smile as Rose gave him her small white hand. With an effort, he raised his eyes from their linked fingers and looked into her face, shocked by the pain and the sadness he saw in it and by the wan parody of a smile with which she responded to his greeting. But their words were prosaic enough. Rose said, "Good morning, Colonel Anson," politely, and he, releasing her hand with inexplicable reluctance, enquired whether she would like coffee or tea.

She glanced quickly at Kim Myint. "Tea, I think, if you will be so kind, Colonel Anson," and Kim confirmed her choice. They went into John's living-room and he gave the order to Bo Tin.

Kim announced, looking at his watch, "We haven't a great deal of time, you know . . . I wonder . . ." He looked again at his watch. "Perhaps, while you are having tea, I should go and have a word with the Prime Minister's secretary. It won't take me long and there are one or two points of etiquette that I'd like to discuss with him. You will not mind, will you, John, if I leave Rose in your care?"

John shook his head. "No, indeed. I'll do my best to entertain her, if you feel you ought to go." To his own surprise, he found that he was looking forward to this unexpected opportunity of talking to Rose alone, but when Kim had left them alone together, he could think of nothing to say to her.

Bo Tin brought their tea and poured it for them, while John answered the polite questions Rose put to him concerning his doings since his arrival and his impressions of Tauling. He told her of Narain Singh's visit, and saw her brows come together in a worried pucker.

"He did remember you, then?"

"Yes," John confirmed, "he did remember me."

"Did he offer any explanation of why he failed to do so at the airfield?"

"Well, he seems to have the impression that my appointment as His Highness's tutor has led to the termination of his own.

He is to be retired, he tells me, and sent back to his home in Lahore. I hope, if the opportunity should arise, to plead his cause for him—he doesn't want to retire."

Rose considered this, her brow still furrowed.

"And that was why he refused to shake hands with you? Because he blames you for superseding him?"

"It appears to be, yes."

"He didn't . . . threaten you, Colonel Anson?"

"Well, in a way he did. He was very honest and straightforward about it. But I could scarcely take him seriously. After all—"

Rose Lian put in gravely, "I think you should take him seriously, Colonel Anson. I have been making enquiries about him since the incident on the airfield, and it seems he is deeply attached to the prince —quite fanatically so, in fact. Please be careful in your dealings with him. Fanatics can be dangerous."

Her evident concern for him touched John's heart. He said warmly, losing his constraint, "It was good of you to take the trouble to make enquiries on my behalf,

Dr. Lian," and then, seeing her flush, realized that he had said too much.

She answered with a hint of impatience, "My father asked me to help you in any way I could, Colonel Anson."

Feeling absurdly as if she had struck him, John got to his feet. "Then thank you for your advice. I won't forget it if I have any dealings with Narain Singh. But, as I told you, I knew him well in the past —we served together during the war. He is naturally upset at losing his job and, like many old soldiers, bitterly resents the fact that he has reached retirement age. I don't think it goes further than that, quite honestly."

Rose Lian set down her untasted cup of tea. Across the tray, with its beautiful, eggshell-thin Gaupali china, he met her gaze and was astonished to see that her eyes were full of tears. "You don't understand, Colonel Anson," she told him, in a strained, unhappy whisper, "you don't understand . . ."

"What should I understand?" John asked gently.

She, too, got to her feet and came to

stand beside him, looking up into his face, her own very serious and unsmiling.

"There is so much," she told him earnestly. "Some of it I do not yet understand myself. But things have changed here, changed completely and—and horribly. It makes me afraid. I am afraid for you and for Kim and for myself."

"Why, Rose?" John caught her hands, clasping them tightly in his as he felt them tremble. He used her Christian name without realizing it. "Why are you afraid? Of whom or of what are you afraid? Won't you tell me?"

Rose hesitated for a long moment, her eyes searching his face. They were still brimming with unshed tears and the sadness in them moved him deeply. He forgot his momentary rebuff: she hadn't meant to put him in his place, a little while ago, he decided, she had been worried and upset, impatient, perhaps, with his failure to understand what she was trying to tell him. "Please," he begged urgently, "tell me what is wrong and why you are worried. Is it because of conditions at the hospital? Because I've heard about that from Kim—"

"It's not the hospital," Rose said, with flat finality, "although that is part of it— a small part of the whole. I can't tell you now, it would take too long and there isn't time. Kim will be back soon and we shall have to go to the Palace. Listen . . ." Her ears, sharper than his, had caught the sound of voices in the courtyard outside. "He's here now and will want us to go. He must not suspect that I have said anything to you."

She sought to free her hands from John's clasp, but he held them firmly, forcing her to look at him. "I *will* tell you," she promised, her voice low. "Please let me go now."

"When will you tell me?" John persisted.

"At the first opportunity. I—I will make an opportunity as soon as I can."

He released the hands he had held imprisoned. "That's a promise, Rose?"

She bowed her head in assent. "Yes, it is a promise, Colonel An . . . John." Kim's footfall sounded in the hall and Rose moved away from him, brushing the back of her hand across her eyes in an instinctive attempt to hide the traces of her tears. In the bright silk robe, with the flowers in her hair, she looked childishly young and vulnerable, a different person from the serene and competent young woman doctor John had known in London. But then Tauling wasn't London. This was a different world, a world apart, and for him at least, as Rose had told him, it was one he hadn't yet begun to understand.

Kim came in smiling, and the atmosphere, so tense an instant before, returned to normal.

"I think," Kim said, linking his arm in Rose's, "that I have arranged everything. And it's time we presented ourselves at the Palace . . ." He went into details of what he had arranged as they walked out together to the car, but John scarcely heard him. The driver slipped behind the wheel and engaged his gear. The car moved smoothly forward. A few minutes later they were crossing a bridge over the moat, the sentry on duty presenting arms smartly as they passed him. Further on, outside what was evidently the guardroom, an officer stopped them and then, recognizing their uniforms, saluted and waved them on.

In a wide, shaded courtyard, they left the car, with Rose in it, to proceed to the wing occupied by the Queen, and Kim said, gesturing to a slowly moving line of military and court officials which was approaching a vast gilded door in the wall of the building opposite, "We must join the queue, John, old man. They're all on their way to the Throne Room, so I'm afraid it's going to take some time."

They attached themselves to the rear end of the procession and John looked about him with interest. From where he stood he could see, beneath a low archway to his right, a garden, shaded by a clump of magnificent trees and with a fountain playing in its midst. Beyond it, as always in Tauling, rose a slender pagoda spire, crowned with the inevitable golden htee or umbrella, which caught the sunlight and reflected it back with dazzling fidelity.

The building they were about to enter stood by itself, forming one side of a shallow square. To the left was a second building, older than that containing the Throne Room and evidently consisting mainly of offices, for there was a constant coming and going of scarlet-uniformed messengers through its several doors. Both buildings were of wood, richly carved and gilded, but the gilding had worn in places on the older of the two and had not been replaced, giving it a faint but unmistakable air of dilapidation, so that it contrasted oddly with the splendour of its newer neighbour. On this, above the great main door towards which they were moving a pace at a time, John saw that an enormous effigy of a peacock had been set up, reproduced in all its flamboyant natural colours and carved from a single block of wood. A crown surmounted the head, and the tail, each feather of which had been intricately carved, was spread wide and proudly erect.

Kim said, interrupting his interested contemplation of the vast bird, "The British Ambassador is not to be here this morning—it seems he is unwell, which is a pity from your point of view. But you've called on him officially, have you not!"

"I signed the book," John confirmed, "the day after I got here. But Sir Edwin was unwell then, so I didn't see him."

"He is a sick man," Kim went on thoughtfully, "and has been for some time, I'm told. There's talk of his being relieved if his health does not improve. Gaupal will lose a good friend if Sir Edwin goes . . ." He talked on about the Ambassador, and then, as they reached the door at last, started, in a low voice, to indicate various notabilities as he recognized them amongst those gathered in the first ante-room. The majority were in uniform of one kind or another, but a few, obviously ministers of the government, wore brilliantly coloured silk putsoes, with short, quilted white, jackets. A single filet of white muslin bound the head of each, caught up in a tail at the nape of the neck, the number of ends left showing giving an indication, Kim explained, of the wearer's rank. Ministers of Cabinet rank were entitled to four, the Prime Minister displayed five, but only royalty might show more and only they, according to ancient custom, wore a coloured headdress.

"No one knows the origin of this custom," Kim added. "It dates back hundreds of years. But probably it is connected with the sacred peacock, which is the symbol of majesty and power in Gaupal. I think . . . ah, we are moving on at long last. Once we enter the Throne Room we shall be able to spread out a little and it will not be quite so congested and airless. Are you finding the heat very trying?"

"No, not unduly, thanks," John assured him. As they moved slowly forward, he found himself wondering what Sandra would think of this gathering if she could see it. Probably it would impress her, for the sight of so much Oriental magnificence *was* impressive, but . . . he sighed. She would regard it with disbelief, like a spectacle from a play or a scene from some imaginative, highly coloured fairy story, as she would, he felt certain, regard many other things in Gaupal. It was odd that he should suddenly feel so certain what her reaction would be. But—Sandra was part of another world now, a world he had left and from which he was cut off and remote.

He sought for her image in his mind and, for a moment, saw her face reflected back to him from a mirror on the wall. Then it faded with startling abruptness, leaving the mirror blank, reflecting nothing more substantial than a ray of sunlight from the window opposite.

Kim touched his arm and he realized that he was facing a court official who, bowing, had said something to him which he hadn't heard.

"Your name," Kim prompted, "you have to give your name for the presentation."

John supplied it, and an officer of the Palace Guard, in a gold-laced green uniform, led them to their places in a shadowy, lofty-ceilinged room. At the far end was a raised dais on which stood a massive, gold-encrusted throne; fashioned in the shape of a peacock, the spreading tail forming the back of the throne. The dais was hung with brilliant, turquoise blue velvet, and a carpet of the same colour, exquisitely woven, covered the floor, extending to the three shallow steps which led up to the foot of the throne. A gilded wooden railing enclosed the front of the dais, save for a space of about three feet immediately in front of the throne. Below this, standing as motionless as statues, were posted two of the Palace Guard, both officers with drawn swords, who waited, their faces impassive, for the coming of their ruler. The placing of the throne had been arranged cleverly, so that sunlight from the windows on either side of the roof struck and illuminated it, leaving the rest of the room in comparative dimness.

John waited, taking in all these details and looking from the throne to the assembled company, now ranged in a semi-circle about the dais. There were, he supposed, as nearly as he could judge, upwards of a hundred gathered in serried ranks round the room, apart from the guards. They were silent now, expectant, tense, as if the empty throne, with its promise of their King's coming, had over-awed them. No one spoke to his neigh-bour, and there was little movement until, evidently at some signal John didn't catch from whoever was in official charge of the proceedings, all squatted down in the curious half-sitting, half-lying posture that he had seen the Burmese adopt.

He followed their example, and under cover of the sounds of general movement Kim whispered hoarsely, "The King is coming now."

In front of the throne, the two officers raised their swords, turning to face each other, and then very slowly lowered them in salute. A door at the back of the dais was flung open, and as the waiting multitude bowed their heads in reverence, a majestic figure in blue and gold stepped forward to take his seat on the peacock throne of his ancestors.

His Majesty King Pao Shwe Dah of Gaupal was a man of about thirty-five, John knew, but in his robes of state he looked a good deal older. The robes were heavy and the King inclined to corpulence, so that the richly brocaded garments hung on him shapelessly, emphasizing both his plumpness and his lack of height.

His face too, was plump and curiously devoid of expression, the mouth firm but with a hint of cruelty in its slightly down-curving corners. The lower lip, more protuberant than its fellow, gave his face the appearance of pouting sullenness and with it a suggestion of sensuality. A small moustache adorned his upper lip and, following its line, added to the impression of petulance. The eyes, small and slanting. were not attractive, yet they held a fugitive gleam of humour to bely the pouting mouth, and as they passed swiftly over the bent heads below him, they were keen and shrewd and fearless.

He seemed, John thought, studying him covertly, at first sight, at all events, an oddly contradictory character. Years of intermarriage with the people over whom they ruled had, he was aware, rendered the Royal Family of Gaupal indistinguishable from their subjects in colouring and facial structure. The King was undeniably a Gaupali, and yet, for some indefinable reason, he was different. The difference lay, perhaps, more in manner and bearing than in any inherited ancestral characteristics, but it was there and it set him apart. He was . . . a King.

A court chamberlain, gorgeously clad, stepped from the side of the dais and, bowing very low, began to speak in a high-pitched monotone, addressing the King and reading, John saw, from a many-leafed, book-like collection of notes which he held in both hands and scanned from right to left.

"He's reading out a list of those who are to be officially presented to His Majesty,"

229

Kim explained in a whisper, his mouth close to John's ear. "Your name has just been read."

John became conscious suddenly of the King's eyes on him. He straightened and met the small, keen dark eyes across the distance that separated them, feeling his pulses quicken. Then another name was read, the King lost interest in him and, after a time, the presentations began. First a high-ranking officer in a plumed helmet advanced to the foot of the steps leading to the throne, saluted, bowed and touched the King's hand: he was succeeded by another and another, and finally John felt Kim's hand grip his arm. "Now," came the soft whisper, "walk at my side."

Together, he and Kim advanced as their predecessors had done to the foot of the steps. They both saluted. The King permitted Kim Myint to touch his hand. Then, turning to John, he said affably in English, "Colonel Anson, I am happy to welcome you to Gaupal. Later, I shall present you to my son."

John saluted and the presentation was over. With Kim beside him, he walked past the dais and out into the garden beyond.

As he turned to accept a cigarette from Kim's proffered case, a bright object flashed past his head. He jerked round, startled, and saw a knife, its handle still quivering, embed itself in the teak carving of the wall behind him.

11

ROSE was on her way to the garden, at the rear of the Chief Queen's procession, when she saw the knife flash past John Anson's head and strike the wall of the Throne Room.

A cry rose in her throat, to be swiftly stifled when she realized that he had escaped injury. But it required a great effort of will not to cry out, and her heart was beating painfully as she moved to the Englishman's side.

"John—" she began, "John, you—" and broke off, her voice a tiny whisper of sound, as she met his gaze and saw him raise a cautionary finger to his lips.

"Hush," he bade her urgently, "don't say anything, please." His warning was evidently intended for Kim Myint as well as herself, for he jerked his head and Kim nodded, his face pale beneath its deep golden tan. Rose felt his fingers close about her arm and yet, strangely, despite this tangible evidence of it, she was scarcely aware of his presence, all her attention being concentrated on the man for whose heart the knife had been aimed. Suppose the ugly little weapon had found its mark—suppose now that, instead of standing looking into John Anson's alert blue eyes, she had been bending over his slumped body, watching the life ebb from it, powerless, for all her training, to save him? A shudder convulsed her. It was an appalling thought, so appalling that she thrust it from her, horrified.

"Who," she asked shakily, "who tried to kill you? Who would *want* to?" And then, remembering, "Was it Narain Singh?"

"Narain Singh," John returned with conviction, "would never have missed me. I think I know who my would-be assassin was, though. Don't you?" He glanced significantly at Kim, who nodded again, tight-lipped, and then asked, his tone brusque, "Who else saw what happened, besides ourselves? Anyone, do you suppose?"

"Well," said Kim grimly, "no one is admitting to it, at all events. It is possible that they did not see."

"Rose did," John pointed out.

"She was behind the others. And the knife came from close at hand . . . from behind the pavilion, I imagine." Kim measured the distance with narrowed eyes, still retaining his grasp of Rose's arm. The front of the small garden pavilion, in which the two Queens were holding court, was thronged by a laughing, chattering crowd which pressed forward eagerly, apparently quite unaware that anything unusual was afoot.

Incredible as it seemed, Rose thought, the swift passage of the knife through the air had gone unobserved by everyone except herself . . . unless, equally incredibly, all those who had left the Queens' apartments with her were feigning blindness for reasons of their own. And that, surely, was unlikely? After all, as Kim had reminded her, she had been a pace or two behind the others—perhaps even she would have noticed nothing untoward, if she hadn't chanced to look in John Anson's direction at the precise instant that the knife blade had caught the sun as it flew towards him.

She said so, and both men inclined their heads gravely.

"What are you going to do, John?" Kim asked.

For answer, John Anson stepped forward and, his body masking the movement, he quickly plucked the knife from where it had lodged in the carving of the wall and held it out for Kim's inspection. It was a deadly little weapon, Rose realized, both blade and point of razor-edged keenness, but apart from this, there was nothing unusual about it. It was a cheap, bone-handled sheath knife, of the kind that could be picked up for a few taus in any of the city bazaars, and on this account its ownership would be almost impossible to establish.

"Well?" John said. He thrust the small weapon into his pocket and looked questioningly at Kim.

Kim sighed. "It could belong to anyone, of course."

"Quite," agreed the Englishman dryly, "which, no doubt, was why it was chosen. I think I shall keep it for the time being —who knows, I may find an opportunity to return it to its owner one of these days?"

"You are going to say nothing about it now?"

"I think that might be the wisest course, don't you?"

Rose felt Kim's fingers relax their grip of her arm. She sensed his relief as he said, "Yes, I think it might."

"But if you know," she put in, looking from one to the other in unconcealed astonishment, "if you *know* who threw it, why aren't you going to say anything? Why aren't you going to report it?"

They exchanged glances and Kim said quietly, "*Because* we know, Rose. For that very reason."

"But—"

John Anson added quietly, "My new pupil isn't anxious for me to commence my duties, you know, Rose. But it would, I think, be a mistake to let him imagine that he can scare me off."

The colour slowly drained from Rose's cheeks as the implication of his words sank in. It hadn't occurred to her that the hidden knife-thrower could have been Prince Maung Saw, but now she realized that, of course, it could have been no one else. She looked at Kim Myint and saw the confirmation of her fears in his concerned dark eyes.

"Then what are you going to do?" she asked, helplessly. "Treat this as—as just another boyish prank?"

"Something like that," John agreed. "It's probably not much more—that knife missed me by at least a foot. But I think it might be an idea if His Highness and I were officially introduced to each other, don't you, Kim? I see"—he gestured and Rose saw that he was smiling—"that he has returned to our midst, having, no doubt, done so by a circuitous route so that we shall suspect nothing. Well, are you ready?"

"I am ready," Kim admitted reluctantly. They excused themselves politely to Rose and she watched them threading their way through the crowd in the wake of the youthful prince, whose gorgeously robed figure had just vanished into the interior of the pavilion.

Rose waited uncertainly. She had already paid her respects to the Chief Queen and to her sister, Queen Shwe Kah, and the King had not yet left the Throne Room. It would in all probability be an hour or more before he made his appearance in front of the pavilion, for a meeting of his ministers had been arranged to follow the durbar, and that, Rose knew, would occupy some considerable time.

Her presence would not be missed if she were to leave now, and, in view of the fact that she had spent every available moment at the hospital during the past week, she could employ the next hour more usefully in her father's house than she could here. There was the luncheon party to arrange and she had letters to write—one, in particular, long overdue, to her father, who would be anxious for news. Up till now she had been able to tell him very little, but now—she sighed. Now there was much to tell and it would be a relief to write to him of the rumours she had heard and the disquieting whispers which had come to her ears . . .

She moved slowly towards the archway which gave on to the main courtyard. Kim's car would be there. She could tell the driver to take her to the city and then, when he had dropped her, she could send him back, with a message, to wait for Kim and John Anson.

She was halfway across the courtyard when she heard a familiar voice calling her. Surprised, Rose halted, to find herself looking into the bright, twinkling eyes of an old man in clerical garb whom she recognized with delight as Father Delarge. She had seen him only once since her return and then it had been very briefly, at the conclusion of the church service she had attended with Kim, for after that Father Delarge had departed on one of his periodic tours and she had not known when to expect him back. "Why," she said, when greetings had been exchanged, "I had no idea that you had returned, Father." From sheer force of habit, she addressed him in English.

"I returned last night," the old priest answered. He, too, spoke in English, but his voice was weary and there was a note of strain in it which, because in him it was so unusual, Rose heard with astonishment and concern. He offered no explanation of it, however, contenting himself with a brief description of the places he had visited and the people he had seen.

Reaching Kim's car, he looked down at her with a smile and asked, "You are going back to the city, my child? Then let me drive you. My car is here, and if, admittedly, it is not quite as comfortable as this one, it will get you to where you want to go and I shall be glad of your company. Are you on your way back to the hospital? Shall I put you down there?"

"I am on my way to my father's house," Rose told him, and he patted her arm indulgently. "To relax for a little, I hope? They tell me you are very hard at work."

"The hospital has been busy," Rose confessed, "and so have I. But today I am giving a lunch party, Father." She beckoned to Kim's driver and left word of her whereabouts with him. She and Father Delarge walked over to his shabby, old-fashioned two-seater and he helped her into it, clicking his tongue apologetically when at first it resisted his efforts to get it to start.

It did so finally, and the old man beamed.

"She is a little temperamental this morning, is she not? I fear that she is wearing out, but she is an old and faithful friend and, much as I should like to own a newer model, I should miss this old one if I were to part with her. You see"—steering a somewhat erratic course, Father Delarge negotiated. the guard-house—"she is accustomed to my bad driving and I am inured to her displays of temperament, although . . ." He broke off abruptly as they approached the bridge and the sentry on duty there raised his rifle, making urgent signals to them to halt. "*Mais qu'est-ce qu'il fait, cet homme-là?*" the old priest demanded, relapsing into a torrent of indignant French as his engine stalled in protest against the harshly applied brakes. "*Qu'y a-t-il, alors . . .*" The rest of his tirade was drowned by the blare of a motor horn, sounding imperiously behind them as they skidded to a standstill.

The guard sprang to attention as a large black car, flying the Royal Peacock of Gaupal on its bonnet, came hurtling past, taking the corner on two wheels and raising a dense cloud of dust in its impatient wake. It was gone before Rose could catch more than a glimpse of its occupants, but she saw enough to recognize Prince Maung Saw at the wheel.

Beside him, crouched low, she thought she saw Narain Singh, the Sikh, but his face was in shadow and she could not be certain.

She looked at Father Delarge, who shrugged expressively and attempted to re-start his recalcitrant engine. He said dryly, when it again woke to noisy life, "His Highness would seem to be in an even greater hurry then we are to leave the festive scene. Did you notice, Rose, that his usual escort was not with him?"

"He had his bodyguard, hadn't he, Father? He had Narain Singh."

"Had he? I thought not, myself, but I could be wrong. Certainly there was only one man with him, instead of the usual three or four. They were moving very fast, so I did not really see them at all clearly, but I wondered if the man seated beside him could be his new tutor, the Englishman, Colonel Anson? You know him, do you not?"

"Oh, yes, I know him," Rose affirmed. "We travelled out together, Father. But I hardly think that *he* would be with the prince so soon after—" She hesitated, and Father Delarge glanced at her from under lowered brows. "After what, my child? You sound very mysterious."

Rose told him of the knife-throwing episode and his brows lifted. "That was a pity. The boy is behaving very foolishly . . . Tell me, what is he like, this Englishman? Will he be able to control his impulsive young Highness, do you think?"

"I'm sure he will," Rose answered emphatically. "Colonel Anson is—oh, he is an exceptional person, Father. He . . ." She launched into an enthusiastic description of John Anson's sterling qualities, to break off, reddening a little, as she became aware of the old priest's eyes on her face. There was an odd, questioning expression in them, as if he had read more into her words than she had intended him to guess, and her colour deepened and spread when he said thoughtfully, "You seem to approve of him very highly, my child."

"I—yes, I do. He really is an exceptional man, Father. I think, when you meet him, that you will approve of him as —as highly as I do."

Father Delarge was silent. They had entered the teeming main street of the city and he had, perforce, to give all his attention to his driving, for the street was narrow and very steep and, at this hour, thronged with people, both afoot and awheel.

Rose stirred uneasily at his side, wondering if she had said too much. Father Delarge had been her mother's confessor and she had known and loved him all her life, yet even to him she was reluctant to admit the growing warmth of her feelings for John Anson. She had no right to have such feelings, in any case, when Kim Myint was her father's choice for her and her affianced husband. She had no right to them, but . . . she bit her lip, feeling its sudden tremor. When, a little under half an hour ago, she had seen the knife so narrowly miss him, she had become conscious of the fact that she was not and never could be indifferent to anything that threatened John Anson's safety or his well-being.

Was she, Rose asked herself miserably, really a good deal fonder of him than she had realized or admitted, even to herself? Could she be in danger of falling in love with him? It would be disastrous if she were. Worse than that, it would be wicked and wrong—it would be madness, utter madness. Quite apart from any question of race, he was bound, just as she herself was bound, in honour to someone else. His engagement to Sandra Beauchamp had been announced in the newspapers before he left London—hadn't she seen it, with her own eyes, in *The Times*? Hadn't he introduced Miss Beauchamp to her as his fiancée at the Embassy reception, the night before they began the long flight to Gaupal? The night that *she* had been betrothed to Kim . . .

Rose clenched her hands at her sides, closing her eyes as she felt the tears fill them. She respected Kim Myint and admired him, but she didn't love him. He knew this, of course—she had never pretended to feel otherwise about him. How could she, when they were virtually strangers? In Gaupal, love was not considered an essential prelude to a marriage, which was invariably arranged by the parents of the young couple. After marriage, it might come or it might not: if it did not, there were the ties of marital duty which were as binding as any ties that love might fashion—as binding and as unbreakable. Had she been so long in the Western world that she had allowed herself to forget this? Was she not thinking and feeling now as a Western woman might think and feel, putting emotion before duty, seeking to follow the dictates of her unruly heart, instead of obeying the stern injunctions of her conscience?

She drew a deep, painful breath. Of course she was, it was useless to deny it. Ever since she had first set eyes on him, she had been attracted to John Anson, finding a bitter-sweet pleasure in his company and a delight she had never before experienced in such small things as the sound of his voice and the touch of his hand, in his smile and in the way he spoke her name. She had simply been afraid, until this moment, to admit to the strong attraction he had for her, to face up to it and to the possible consequences it might have for them both.

But, having admitted it, what now? Must she avoid him in the future, deny him—for both their sakes—the friendship she had promised him? She did not know how he felt about her, he had never given any hint of his feelings, had always behaved towards her with kindness and courtesy but nothing more. She knew him for a man of staunch loyalty and high principles, to whom a promise meant fulfilment and to whom his word, once given, was sacred. His long friendship with Kim Myint was yet another barrier between herself and him, perhaps the most impossible of all to break down—even if she had wanted to break it down.

And did she? Rose sighed again, aware that she did not. The qualities which made John Anson so exceptional a man, in her eyes, were those which must preclude any attempt on his part to betray Kim's friendship. Had she not, only this morning, been about to seek his help on Kim's behalf, quite certain that he would not refuse it? And . . .

"You are very quiet, Rose my child," Father Delarge said gently. They were leaving the city behind them now, climbing steadily in the direction of her father's great, rambling palace on its outskirts, and he turned in his seat to look at her, his eyes very kind and understanding as he asked, "You are glad to be back in Tauling, are you not?"

"Oh, yes, Father," Rose assured him. "Very glad."

"And yet," he accused, "you look unhappy. Is not your work here of satisfaction to you?"

"It is of great satisfaction, Father. Even in the short time that I've been working here in the new hospital, I have found it so. There is much to be done, and I am needed here as I never could have been in England."

"I am pleased to know that . . . *Doctor Rose* . . ." The old man smiled, savouring the title. "To be needed is a great thing. You have done well to have achieved as much as you have in so short a time. It has meant a great deal of study and much hard work for you, has it not?"

"I don't regret any of it. I love my work, Father."

"Well, then, child, why are you unhappy? Why do you sit there, thinking such long, sad thoughts? Are you worried about your forthcoming marriage to Kim? Is that, perhaps, what is wrong?"

"I . . ." She could not lie to him, Rose knew. Reluctantly, she bowed her head. "Yes, Father, that is it. I am not sure if I shall be doing the right thing if I marry Kim. He is of Gaupal, while I. . . ." She broke off, feeling tears come to ache in her throat.

"While you are not?" the old priest pursued. "Is that what you mean?"

"Perhaps I have been away from Gaupal for too long, Father. I don't know. In my heart I can't be certain that Kim and I are right for each other."

"You will have time to search your heart and your conscience on that point," Father Delarge reminded her. "I understand from Kim that there is no question of your being married immediately."

"No, not for some months. We are to work together for a time. I scarcely know him, Father, we . . . we are still strangers to each other."

"Kim is a fine young man, Rose."

"I know that, Father. He's fine and good, he's everything that is admirable. Perhaps that is why I'm—why I'm afraid."

Father Delarge slowed down for the familiar turning into the drive entrance. He said kindly, "Any guidance I can offer you—and my prayers—are yours, Rose, always and at any time you feel in need of them. The matter is one for you to think over carefully and decide only after you have given it careful thought. Kim is, I know, devoted to you—he has told me so. But remember it would not be right to marry him if, for any reason, you could not give him the same devotion as he is prepared to give you. If"—his thin old hand came out to clasp hers gently—"if, for example, your emotions were involved elsewhere, it would be very wrong indeed to become his wife, would it not? More especially if, now that you have returned to Gaupal, you feel yourself alien and unable to settle here. Your mother, remember, was not of Gaupal either. It may be that a man of her race or an Englishman would bring you happiness and fulfilment, if Kim cannot do so."

"That"—Rose flushed—"that isn't likely, Father. It isn't possible, in the circumstances. Not for me. I. . . ."

Father Delarge drew up outside the imposing portico of the Lian residence. A servant came running to open the door of the car, but the old man waved him away.

"Do not make up your mind on that

point yet, Rose, my child," he said, smiling at her. "And do not forget that, if you need me, I am here."

Rose, thanked him gratefully, as much for his kindness and sympathy as for the tact he had shown in not probing deeper into her confused state of mind. "Won't you stay for lunch?" she invited, but he shook his head.

"I must go back. I am expected at the Palace this afternoon for"—he frowned—"an interview with His Excellency the Prime Minister. I tried to see him this morning, but it was not possible, owing to the durbar—about which I had forgotten."

"You didn't attend the durbar, then, Father?"

He shook his head. "No, I was not invited to attend. I returned, in any case, a week sooner than I had expected to, owing to . . . well, owing to something I learned when I was on tour." His smile vanished, to be replaced by the lines of strain and weariness Rose had noticed when she had first encountered him in the courtyard of the Palace. Preoccupation with her own worries had blinded her to his, she thought contritely, and, leaning towards him, she asked in a low voice "Father, *you* are worried about something, aren't you? We have talked only of my problems, but you too have something on your mind, I feel sure."

Father Delarge inclined his head. "I have, yes, Rose. That is why I have asked for an inteview with the Prime Minister."

"It is . . . something serious, then?"

"I am afraid it may be. Rose"—he looked up with a sigh, gravely searching her face—"you have not been back for very long in Tauling, so perhaps you have not heard the whispers—"

"I have heard some of them, Father. The city is alive with rumours, it is impossible not to hear them."

The old priest sighed. "There is trouble brewing," he stated, "serious trouble; the rumours have that much foundation. My tour took me to the site of the proposed new oil wells, and that is where the trouble, if it comes, will start. The oil company is at the root of the trouble."

"Is it? But"—Rose stared at him—"how, Father?"

"The King wants to grant concessions

to the company, but there are those who are against him in this. It is a long and complex story, but briefly, the whisper that all profit from these concessions will go to the King has been started and is gaining credence amongst the simple country folk. Agitators are going amongst them, spreading the lie and stirring up trouble—agitators whose allegiance is to a foreign Power, dangerous men, who do not want to see Gaupal happy and prosperous. They are being helped by a small minority of our own people, who seek personal advancement and the power they can only have at the expense of the monarchy. One man in particular—a man who is in a position of trust in the government—is working against the King and organizing the agitators, using his official position to conceal his treachery. Quite by chance, Rose, I have found out who this man is, and it is my intention to inform the Prime Minister of his identity."

"But, Father"—Rose was shocked—"can you prove anything against him?"

"Yes," the old man assured her, "I can, child."

"Your knowledge could be dangerous."

Rose's fingers closed about his arm. "Dangerous for you, I mean. Father, you will take care, won't you?"

"Of course I will take care. Once I have told what I know to the Prime Minister, then the matter is out of my hands. I am a priest of God, Rose—politics are not my province, any more than they are yours. I am seeking out the Prime Minister for one reason and one only—it is my duty to prevent bloodshed and strife. By putting the civil power in possession of the facts as I know them, I hope to enable them to act in time to avoid trouble. That, as I see it, is the limit of my responsibility."

"Would you like to take one of my father's servants with you?" Rose offered. "I don't think you ought to go alone, Father. After all—"

"Child, I have worked alone all my life." Father Delarge leaned across and opened the door of his ramshackle old car. "Off you go now and attend to your lunch party. I shall come to no harm. No one is aware of the knowledge I possess—I have spoken of it to no one but you." He smiled. "And you, I know, will not divulge anything that I have said. In any case, I have added little to what you have already heard and what everyone else has heard. I do not propose to share the rest of my burden with you. I have named no names to you."

"No, but . . . if you would like to, I—"

"I think not, Rose," Father Delarge said firmly. He watched her get out of the car and raised a hand in benediction. The old car chugged explosively down the drive, its worn engine backfiring at regular intervals, so that Rose could still hear it for a considerable time after it had vanished from sight. But at last even this sound faded and she turned, with furrowed brows, to enter the house. The major-domo, who had been waiting for her in the hall, came forward respectfully to ascertain what orders she had for him. Rose gave him instructions for luncheon and, having inspected the table and seen that everything was as she wanted it, she went into the small, pleasant room her father used as his study and settled down to the writing of her letter.

It took a good deal of thought. She could not repeat, in a letter, what Father Delarge had told her: for one thing he had asked her not to divulge it and, for another, she could not be sure to what degree of censorship her letter might, in the circumstances, be subjected. Yet her father, she knew, must be warned. He had spoken, before she left London, of the possibility of his own early return to Gaupal, so—aware that he would read between the lines—she contented herself with a brief and carefully worded résumé of the disquieting rumours she had heard and ended by urging him not to delay his return for any longer than absolutely necessary.

She was finishing the letter when the Number One boy announced John Anson. Rose turned, surprised to see that he was alone. "Oh, didn't Kim come with you? I thought—"

"He was called to the hospital," John answered, "and asked me to tell you that he would be here as soon as he possibly could. He suggested that you shouldn't wait lunch for him, but so far as I'm concerned there's no hurry, Rose, if you'd prefer to wait."

"Well, perhaps for half an hour, then

. . . if you are sure you do not mind?" She waved him to a chair. "Do sit down."

"Could I possibly mind, when it gives me the opportunity to talk to you? We didn't finish our conversation this morning, did we?" He took the chair she had indicated, watching her face.

"No," Rose admitted, "we didn't. But I"—she avoided his gaze, her own fixed on the envelope she had just addressed, feeling suddenly ill at ease with him and at a loss for words. She asked, more in order to avoid the personal topic he had sought to introduce than because she wanted information, "Do you know why Kim was called to the hospital? Did he tell you?"

"It was an accident, I believe. Rather a serious one, judging by the urgency of the summons he received. But I don't know who was involved, I'm afraid. Kim didn't say. However"—John smiled—"he did tell me that I shouldn't let you worry about it and that I mustn't let you go dashing off to the hospital without your lunch."

"Oh—oh, I see. Well, we—we could

257

have a drink, couldn't we? What would you like, Colonel Anson? That is—"

"It was John this morning, Rose," he reminded her. "Aren't we friends any more?"

"Of course we are. I'm sorry, I forgot."

"Don't forget that we are friends, Rose —don't ever forget that. Your friendship means"—John's voice was warm and vibrant and it set Rose's heart pounding in her breast—"it means a great deal to me, you know."

"Does it?" She got to her feet, feeling the hot, betraying colour rush to her cheeks, flooding them with a scarlet tide. She went blindly over to the tray of drinks the boy had brought in and busied herself with it, scarcely aware of what she was doing, intent only on hiding her face from him.

"If that's for me," John protested, "it's rather more whisky than I'm accustomed to in the middle of the day." He had come to stand behind her, and now he took the glass from her with a murmured apology. "I'll do it, shall I?" He added quietly, as if there had been no interruption, "Of course your friendship means a lot to me—yours and Kim's. You've both been more than good to me, and it's made all the difference, I promise you. I'm a stranger in a strange land, and not, it seems, a very welcome one, judging by this morning's incident."

His words, the fact that he was speaking of her friendship in conjunction with Kim's, steadied Rose. She was behaving absurdly, she chided herself. Like a child, like a half-grown girl, in love for the first time, instead of what she really was—an adult woman of twenty-five, a qualified doctor and . . . a woman of Gaupal, honourably betrothed to a man of her own race. She turned to face him, her own glass in her hand. "You saw the prince, after I left? You were presented to him?" Her voice, to her relief, sounded quite normal and her hand clasped the glass without a tremor.

John nodded, his mouth wryly compressed. "I was presented to His Highness, yes. But rather than remain in conversation with me, he invented some urgent business and left the Palace."

"Yes, I saw him. That is, he passed the car I was in, driving very fast. Did he—

did he mention anything about the knife or offer any apology for what he tried to do?"

"I hardly expected him to do that," John answered with a rueful shrug. "But if you mean, did he show any signs of contrition, then the answer is—no, he did not, I'm afraid. He appeared anything but contrite to me. Well"—he sipped his whisky appreciatively—"no doubt we shall have to have a showdown sooner or later. I commence my duties officially tomorrow, you know."

She looked up at him. There was no fear in his eyes, no anger, only a strange, compelling purposefulness which defied any possibility of defeat. He knew what he was going to do, this tall Englishman, knew and was determined to do it, no matter what the cost might be to himself. And he wasn't afraid . . . Rose caught her breath. She said, as a little while before she had said to Father Delarge, "You will take care, won't you?"

"Good lord, yes!" He was smiling. "Of course I'll take care. Although I don't honestly think, where His Highness is concerned, that it will be necessary. He's spoilt and wilful, but he's only a boy. Given half a chance, I'll be able to handle him. I had quite an illuminating talk with his father before I left, and he assured me of his backing. That's really all I need, Rose."

"Is it?" In spite of his confidence, she was afraid for him, but dared not show it. Her fingers played nervously with the stem of her glass and a tense little silence fell between them which was broken abruptly by the arrival of Kim Myint.

He came striding into the room, brushing aside the boy's attempt to announce him. One glance at his face was enough to warn Rose that something was wrong. It was the colour of parchment, and the pain in his eyes brought her running to meet him. "Kim! What is it? What has happened?"

He took both her hands in his and stood looking down at her. "You're needed at the hospital, Rose. That accident I was called to . . . it's pretty serious and we're going to have to operate at once."

"All right," she promised readily, "I'll come. But"—the expression in his eyes alarmed her—"what is it? Why are you looking like this? Who is the patient and what is wrong with him?"

Kim hesitated for a moment. Finally he said, "The patient is Father Delarge, and he has a fractured skull, Rose. He crashed in his car after leaving you here, and I wouldn't like to give him a better than even chance of survival. If you are ready, I think we had better go."

Rose followed him, her heart a stone in her breast and fear rising in her throat so that it seemed almost as if it would choke her. "Was it," she asked, as Kim helped her into his car, "Kim, was it an accident? Are you sure it was?"

Kim flashed her a puzzled glance. "He was in a head-on collision with another car. The good Father is nearly a saint, I know, but he was never a good driver—it's a wonder he hasn't been involved in an accident before now. Why do you ask, Rose? Have you any reason to imagine that it was *not* an accident?"

Ought she to tell him? Rose wondered —ought she to pass on to him at least as much as Father Delarge had confided to her, just before they had parted? While she still hesitated, Kim went on, his voice flat and devoid of emotion, "Rose, the poor old Father believes that he is dying. He had a brief moment of consciousness a few minutes before I left the hospital to fetch you, and he confided a secret to me which, in the circumstances, I believe that I have no right to keep from you—it has been kept from you, God knows, for a long time."

"A . . . secret?" Rose turned in her seat to gaze at him in open bewilderment. "A secret that has been kept from *me*? But—"

"A secret that has been kept from you," Kim repeated tonelessly, "by all those to whom it was known."

"You don't mean the purpose of Father Delarge's interview with the Prime Minister? The—the one he was going to, when he met with his accident?"

Kim shook his head emphatically. "I know nothing of that, nothing at all. I had no idea that he was seeing the Prime Minister, Rose. Do you know why?"

"I know part of the reason—"

Kim interrupted her. "That does not matter now, does it? He did not see the Prime Minister."

"No." Rose stifled a sob. "No, he did not see him."

Kim's free hand left the wheel and closed, very gently, over hers. "The secret Father Delarge told me concerns *you*, Rose . . . not the Prime Minister. And, indirectly, I suppose, it concerns me too, since we are betrothed to each other."

Rose waited, bracing herself, for him to continue. But he was silent, letting his foot come hard down on the accelerator. They entered the city, driving through one of the bazaars, Kim using his horn vigorously but scarcely slackening speed.

He said suddenly, his voice loud and harsh, raised above the wail of the horn, "Rose, if you were wholly French—if you had no Gaupali blood in you at all, would you still, in spite of this, consent to become my wife? Would you remain betrothed to me?"

Rose's heart missed a beat and then began frantically to pound. For one moment she found herself wondering whether his grief over Father Delarge could possibly have turned Kim's brain, and then, glancing at him, she ceased to wonder. Kim Myint was in deadly earnest, his dark face paler than its wont and set in gravely resolute lines.

"I don't know," she managed at last. "I don't know, Kim. Don't you see, it's not a question I can answer? And it—it doesn't arise, it can't . . . ever! I'm not wholly French. You know who my father is. Why do you ask me such a question?"

"Because it has arisen," Kim assured her emphatically. "That is the secret Father Delarge told me, less than half an hour ago. He said he could not die with it on his conscience. Your father was a Frenchman, Rose—his name was Jean Philippe Renoir and he was a Lieutenant in the French Foreign Legion. He was your mother's first husband, with whom she eloped when she was seventeen—"

"But he was killed!" Rose cried. "Kim, he was killed in Indo-China . . . I know the story, my father told me."

"Nevertheless," Kim said, "you were his child. He was killed before you were born, but you were his child. The man you know as father bears you no blood relationship. Father Delarge received a letter from him in which he admitted this."

Rose stared in front of her through tear-blinded eyes, desperately fighting for control. She did not doubt the truth of what Kim had told her, after the first shock of it had passed—she could not, for telling her had cost him so much pain. And, if he had learnt it from Father Delarge, then it must be the truth.

They turned into the hospital gates and drew up outside its main door. "Well?" Kim asked very gently, "I put a question to you, Rose. Are you going to answer it?"

She shivered. "Not yet, Kim. I—I can't."

He opened the door of the car. "Very well," he said, "I will wait until you feel able to answer me. Come"—he offered her his hand—"we have work to do, a life to save, with God's help, Rose. I think we are going to need that help."

Rose took his outstretched hand. Breathing a silent, inarticulate little prayer, she went with him into the hospital.

12

IT was with somewhat mixed feelings that John presented himself at the Royal Palace the following morning at the appointed hour.

He had seen nothing of either Rose or Kim Myint since they had left him so precipitately in order to return to the hospital, and all he knew of the outcome of the emergency operation they had gone to perform had been gleaned from Bo Tin, whom he had sent to make enquiries. The patient had come through the operation, the boy told him, but was still unconscious and critically ill. This was as much as he could find out, short of telephoning or calling in person at the hospital, which, for fear of intruding where he wasn't wanted, John was loth to do. Kim, he felt sure, would let him know if and when there was any news.

He had received no letter from Sandra either, and this worried him a good deal. She had had time to write since he left

England, ample time, and the fact that she hadn't written added immeasurably to his feeling of frustration and uncertainty. As he paced up and down the anteroom, waiting for the Prince's chamberlain to announce him, his restlessness grew. It only wanted Maung Saw to refuse to see him, he thought bitterly, to provide the last straw. But, to his surprise, the chamberlain returned almost immediately to tell him, in hesitant English, that his royal pupil was awaiting him.

Prince Maung Saw was, indeed, waiting with every appearance of docility. Simply dressed, in jodhpurs and a silk shirt, the boy received him in a room which had obviously been designed as a study, for books and maps lined the walls. Smiling, he waved a hand to the table which occupied the centre of the room, on which books and writing materials had been set out, and after bidding his tutor a polite good morning, announced cheerfully, "You see, Colonel Anson, I am ready for my first lesson. Shall we be seated?"

A trifle taken aback, John sat down at the table and glanced at the pile of textbooks which had been neatly arranged according to subject matter and placed conveniently in front of him. All the books were in English and the subjects they covered ranged from mathematics and chemistry to geography and a history of the British political system.

"I thought," Maung Saw said, still smiling, "that you would want to see what books I have before working out a curriculum of study for us to follow." John hid his amazement. Yesterday, this strange, unpredictable young autocrat had attempted to murder him: today he apparently expected their lessons to begin as if their relationship were completely normal. He sighed. "If Your Highness has no objection," he said formally, "I am of the opinion that we should devote our first hour together to getting to know each other."

The boy's bright, intelligent dark eyes met his without flinching. "Certainly, Colonel, if you wish. What is it that you want to know about me?"

"Your interests, your hobbies, which subjects you most enjoy studying . . . that will do, for a start."

"Very well. My interests are wide. I am interested in people, in human psychology, in every aspect of government, in current affairs, in the atom bomb and its effects—oh, in a host of things. My hobbies are, for the most part, sporting. I like to ride, play polo, shoot—both birds and big game—and I enjoy falconry, too. I like to climb amongst our mountains, to camp out, living on what I can bring in myself for food, with rod or rifle. I play tennis, of course, but not well, so I do not enjoy it as much as the other activities I have mentioned. And as for study, I think with me it depends on who is teaching me . . . I like to learn French because my teacher makes it seem amusing and easy. But I made little progress in mathematics because the good pundit who has endeavoured to instruct me until now is old and boring and his lessons are as dull as he is himself. I fall asleep while he is explaining his problems and never remember a word of what he has said."

"I see. I'll take that as a warning, shall I?" John found himself echoing the boy's smile. His crisp, concise reply to the question he had been asked was revealing, to say the least.

Choosing his words carefully, John

continued to ask questions, gradually drawing the boy out until he had gained a fairly clear picture of Prince Maung Saw's character and achievements, his likes and dislikes and the way in which his mind worked. That he had, in many ways, been over-indulged and spoilt was very evident, yet, in spite of this, he had much more good in him than John had expected to find. He was extremely intelligent and possessed a mature sense of humour for one of his age. He was proud but not vain, endearingly boyish in his enthusiasms and loyalties and yet, at the same time, surprisingly adult in his outlook and in many of the views he held.

For a boy of sixteen, he was remarkably well read on the subjects that appealed to him and strikingly ignorant where those which did not were concerned. A readiness to laugh was offset by a readiness to indulge his temper, which appeared to be equally easy to provoke. But the youthful prince had courage and charm, and long before he had come to the end of his questioning, John was conscious of a bond of mutual liking and sympathy which had begun slowly to grow up between them.

271

The boy talked so frankly to him, of his family, of his mother and father and of the numerous brothers and sisters he possessed and his relations with them, that John was tempted to see if he would carry his frankness a step further and admit to having attempted yesterday to injure him.

He took the small knife from his pocket and laid it on the table between them, the blade catching the sunlight and gleaming back at him wickedly.

"Tell me, Your Highness," he said, his tone deliberately casual, "have you ever seen this before?"

"This? This knife, you mean?" Maung Saw picked it up and subjected it to a minute inspection. He shook his head as he returned the knife, holding it by the tip and offering John the handle. "I do not think so, Colonel Anson, but it is a common type of weapon here, you see— there are hundreds of such daggers on sale in the bazaars." He lifted his eyes, which appeared innocent of guile, to those of his interrogator. "Why, Colonel? *Should* I recognize it? Has it, perhaps, some particular significance?"

John accepted the ugly little weapon and

replaced it in his pocket. "No, it has no significance, since Your Highness has failed to recognize it," he replied cryptically. "Well"—he picked up the treatise on British political development and opened it—"shall we see how much you know about the British political system?"

"Certainly," the prince agreed good-humouredly. "I have studied that book very carefully. Ask me any questions you wish."

His boast proved to be no idle one. He had, indeed, absorbed the contents of the book from cover to cover, and John was able to find no gaps in his knowledge. Furthermore, warming to his subject, the boy drew comparisons between the British system of government and that of his own country, his remarks as illuminating as his replies to the earlier questions had been.

"When I succeed my father as King of Gaupal," he announced gravely, "I shall institute many reforms that he is afraid to institute—I shall bring Gaupal closer to the West and I shall not cut myself off from my people, as my father does. I shall, of course, be an absolute monarch, but I shall not rest until I have destroyed the

273

absurd, out-dated legend that I am a god as well as a king. I shall go among the people, talk to them and hear what they have to say and show them that I am a man and human, just as they are. What do you think, Colonel Anson? As an Englishman, don't you agree with me?"

John smiled. What a curious contradiction the boy was! He answered mildly, "I agree with you in principle, Your Highness, yes. But reforms cannot be over-hastily brought into being, you know—people must be educated before they will accept Western ideas. They must be taught to understand before they are able to make use of them. And a legend which has endured for hundreds of years is not easily destroyed—it might not be wise to attempt prematurely to put an end to it. Your father has more experience than you have yet acquired in such matters."

Maung Saw's face fell. "I thought that you would be the one man who *would* agree with me," he said, with a hint of sullenness. "Is not your purpose here to teach me of the West?"

"Yes, Your Highness, it is. I shall teach you all I can of the West, but my object in doing so will be in order that you may form your own judgment of the ideas I shall put before you. Try to understand . . ." He talked on, and the boy listened with rapt attention, his dark eyes never leaving John's face.

An hour passed and still they talked, the bond of sympathy between them now so strong that, when it was over and they both rose, Maung Saw extended his hand to his new tutor and, when John took it, he held it to his forehead. The gesture was the Gaupali token of respectful submission and obedience, and John felt oddly moved because his pupil had offered it.

"I do not know," Maung Saw told him, "why it was that I resented and dreaded your coming. Perhaps it was because I did not know what manner of man you would be. But now I am glad that you have come, Colonel Anson. You are a man after my own heart and there is much that I can learn from you, now that I can look upon you, not as a stranger but as a friend."

"I hope you will always do so," John acknowledged. "I should like to give you friendship, Your Highness, as well as education."

"I have not many friends," the boy admitted, his tone wistful. "Until now only Narain Singh has been a real friend —he is my bodyguard and you knew him, I think, in Burma during the war. The others who companion me are not my friends—they are afraid of me, they treat me with too much reverence, so that I cannot talk to them as equals. But old Narain-ji was never afraid of me. Perhaps that is why my father intends to send him back to India."

"Has he gone yet?" John asked curiously.

Prince Maung Saw shook his head. "Not yet. But he will. My father has commanded it. This afternoon—" He hesitated, eyeing John uncertainly. Then, evidently reaching a decision, he went on, "This afternoon I go with Narain to fly a new goshawk after hare. We shall go out by car; the horses have been sent to await us at the village of Saiyawah. It is quite entertaining, Colonel Anson, if you would care to accompany us. The goshawk is new and I cannot promise that she will kill, since this will be the first time that I have handled her, but it might interest you to see how we train our birds to hunt in Gaupal. Have you ever seen a good falconer at work?"

"No, Your Highness, I haven't."

"Then this would be your opportunity. Narain Singh is an expert with the pursuit hawks, it is a joy to watch him. As today will be our last expedition together, I decided that we would go to Saiyawah so that he might exercise his skill in the art which he loves best. Would you like to come with us?"

It was John's turn to hesitate. Finally he declined the invitation with regret. The proud old Sikh would undoubtedly resent his presence, since the expedition had been arranged for his benefit and might, as Maung Saw had said, be the last he would make with his young master.

"I think not," he said. "Let Narain Singh go on his own with you. He will not want me with you on his last day."

"He will not mind," Maung Saw returned cheerfully, "if I tell him it is my wish that you come, Colonel. In any case you will not be taking part, you will be a spectator and that he will enjoy. See, I will send a car for you. Do not decide until after you have eaten. If you do not want to come with us, then send the car away. But I should like you to come and bring anyone you wish with you." He waved John's thanks aside and bowed with dignity. "The lesson is over," he announced formally, his raised hand now a gesture of regal dismissal. "It is time that I present myself to my father. Thank you, Colonel Anson."

"Thank you, Your Highness." John came to attention and the prince's chamberlain appeared in response to his call, to bow his master from the room and then escort John himself to the door of the royal apartments.

It was in a thoughtful mood that the Englishman returned to his own small bungalow at the Palace gates. The morning had gone a good deal better than he had dared to hope it would. If the prince's attitude towards him continued as it had begun, then he might not meet with the difficulties he had anticipated in dealing with his new pupil. After so inauspicious a start to their acquaintance he hadn't expected to find the boy either likeable or intelligent, but he was both and, in addition, he was sensitive . . . it would be a delight to teach him, not a hardship. It would be, John decided, the most rewarding task he had ever undertaken, if he succeeded in accomplishing it. And the first step towards success would be if he could make the prince trust him sufficiently to admit to having thrown the knife at him yesterday—such an admission, in the face of his denial this morning, would set the seal on their future relationship. Without trust, there could be no real or lasting friendship between them, he knew. While for Maung Saw, as for any Oriental, prince or peasant, a lie was of small account, to climb down and confess to having lied would mean loss of face. Would the boy, John wondered, consider his friendship worth the price he intended to set on it?

He fingered the small dagger in his pocket. It would be necessary to move slowly. To rush things would be to lose the confidence he had managed to inspire in his pupil this morning. To demand a confession of guilt might be fatal. The confession, if it came, must come from the boy himself, without prompting. The heir to the throne of Gaupal had yet to learn his first lesson from the West. He must be made to understand and accept the fact that, to an Englishman, the truth was of greater value than all the fabulous wealth of Gaupal . . .

John entered his own house and found Bo Tin waiting for him with the English mail. He took the little pile of letters the boy gave him and retired to the veranda to read them. Outside in the garden a small, brown-faced garden-boy laboured industriously, the noonday sun hot on his bent back and the peacocks keeping up their incessant squawking as he moved among them. John glanced through the unopened envelopes in his hand, noticing with an odd sense of resignation that one of them —a very thin one—bore his name and address in Sandra's unmistakably large, flowing hand.

So it had come, he thought. The envelope could only contain a single sheet of writing paper, even if it were the light airmail stuff. And what could a single sheet mean, save his dismissal? What could Sandra have to say to him so briefly, except goodbye? Possibly she would offer some excuse or other, but it would be the end, all the same—the end of his dreams and his plans, the end of his hopes. The end of his uncertainty . . .

He sighed. Perhaps it was better to be certain, to know. False hopes were the devil, a dream that could never be realized must only be torment. And, surprisingly, the loss of his dream of Sandra did not hurt nearly as much as, a little while ago, he had believed it would. Memory was a queer thing—his had been playing him tricks ever since his arrival in Tauling. He hadn't been able to remember Sandra's face clearly, for one thing: each time he conjured up a mental vision of her, the vision had faded, as it had the other morning—yesterday—on his way to attend the King's durbar. He had seen her, and then, quite suddenly, she had gone. He . . .

"Master . . ." Bo Tin's voice broke into his thoughts and with an effort he turned to the boy.

"Well?"

"Master, lunch ready."

"I don't want any lunch, Bo Tin. Tell the cook I'm sorry, I'm just not hungry."

Bo Tin looked visibly taken aback. He said, distressed, "It is curry for lunch. Very good, Gaupal curry."

"I'm sorry, Bo Tin. Honestly, I can't eat, whatever it is—I'm not hungry."

The boy shuffled his feet. Finally he padded away, to return, a few minutes later, with a tray on which he had placed whisky and ice and a single glass. He set this down at John's elbow in silence and then, as silently, left him alone. Grateful for his tact, John helped himself to a liberal peg, drank it quickly and refilled his glass. He sat for a long time, the glass in one hand, Sandra's letter, still unopened, in the other. He was curiously reluctant to read the letter, and in order to postpone the necessity for doing so, he opened and read the rest of his mail, leaving her envelope at the bottom of the pile.

His other letters were uninteresting, except for one from his father, which gave him a good deal of news. He read the first page through twice without really taking more than half of it in. The second time he read it, he noticed a paragraph which he had evidently overlooked on his first reading.

I hear, his father wrote, that it is expected in diplomatic circles that the Gaupali Ambassador is shortly to be recalled to Gaupal for talks concerning the proposed oil concessions. Pagoda Oils have been fluctuating wildly on unconfirmed rumours of a bid from a rival company, which have now reached the London Stock Exchange . . . but I imagine you are better informed on this point than I am . . .

Better informed? John smiled to himself at his father's assumption that, because he happened to be on the spot, he knew what was going on. And then, as the final paragraph of the letter caught his eye, he lost interest in the oil company and its rumoured rival. I lunched with your fiancée yesterday, his father ended, but again, you'll probably have heard from her yourself that she's decided to sell up. I think, from all points of view, her decision is a wise one. She has been overworking for far too long and, as a doctor, I deplore the toll this has taken of her health. I hope it may mean that, when she has disposed of Sandra et Cie, she will be able to join you in Tauling sooner than either of you originally planned. Not, of course, that she confided any such intention to me, but you will no doubt urge it upon her the moment you are settled.

His father had lunched with Sandra the day before he had written the letter? John looked at the date under the embossed Harley Street address and from this to the postmark on Sandra's envelope. Sandra had written three days later than his father. His fingers not quite steady, John tore open the envelope. Could he, after all, have been wrong? Was Sandra writing to tell him that she hoped to come out to him, instead of, as he had imagined, giving him his congé?

The envelope contained the single sheet of airmail paper he had expected. It began, John, my dear, and, in a few lines, it resolved all his doubts. Sandra did not want to marry him. She begged him, in the stilted words that were all she could find for him, to try to understand. I'm not in love with you, John . . . Perhaps I never was, I don't know. I only know that it wouldn't work and there's no sense in pretending or fooling myself that it would.

Ever since you went away, I've been trying to bring myself to tell you how I felt. Well, now it's done—I've told you the truth. I hope it won't hurt you too much.

The words blurred before John's eyes. What she had told him didn't hurt. He had been waiting for her to tell him just this, nerving himself to take it, expecting it. But it made him angry. Why had she lunched with his father, and why, when she had, hadn't she told *him*? Because, three days before, she hadn't made up her mind not to marry John? Yet she had made up her mind to sell the shop, to give up Sandra et Cie—she had told his father that and let him believe that her reason for giving up her work was connected with himself!

He lit his pipe, cramming tobacco into it impatiently. Then, forcing himself to do so calmly, he picked up the letter again and went on reading.

There's someone else, John, Sandra continued . . . Garrison, John thought savagely, Charles Garrison! She didn't say so, in so many words, but he knew from all she had left unsaid, that it must be Garrison. I knew him a long time ago and now he's come back into my life. I don't know yet if I shall marry him, but it's on the cards . . . so I want you to release me from our engagement. Whatever happens, it would be wrong to marry you, feeling as I do.

I'll see to publishing the 'marriage will not now take place' thing in the necessary papers here and I'll return your ring. I'm sorry, John, my dear. I can only ask you not to think too badly of me. Oh, and I will write to your father. I saw him the other day, he gave me lunch, but I said nothing to him about this then. But perhaps seeing him provided the spur I needed to write this . . . you're very like him, you know, and—I'm not your kind of woman, any more than I'm his. I saw it very clearly when I tried to talk to him. I've never really been able to speak your language either, John. I wasn't brought up to it, you see. Or do you? Well, perhaps I'll explain one day, if you're interested. Suffice it now to say that it's the most terrific relief not to have to pretend any more about anything.

Goodbye, John, my dear. Please try to

find it in your heart to forgive me, if you can.

The signature was simply *Sandra*.

John let the letter slip from his hand. It fell on to the table and lay there, the faint breeze from the garden stirring one corner of it, so that it made a tiny rustling sound in the stillness. The garden-boy had departed for his midday meal, even the peacocks seemed to have taken themselves off and it was absolutely quiet.

John sat where he was, the pipe, dead now, still clamped between his teeth. He was conscious neither of pain nor fatigue and yet he could not move, it was too great an effort even to think of getting up from his chair.

Bo Tin squatted in the room behind, out of sight, watching him anxiously. It was a relief to both of them when the silence was broken by a brisk, purposeful knock on the front door. Bo Tin jumped up and hurried to open it. He returned, a few seconds later, beaming.

"Master," he announced softly, "Master, you have a visitor, please."

John got to his feet. His earlier lethargy left him when he saw who the visitor was.

Rose Lian, looking cool and charming in a soft blue linen dress, came smiling to meet him. His own pleasure at the sight of her surprised even himself. "Why, Rose!" His voice was warm and eager. "Come in, won't you? I'm simply delighted to see you. What can I get for you—you've lunched, I suppose? Then some coffee, perhaps, or a cold drink?"

Rose shook her head. "I'm afraid," she told him, flushing a little under his scrutiny, "I've come in my professional capacity this afternoon." She indicated the small leather bag she carried, and John laughed. "What is this—a public health check or something? Do you want to immunize me against some epidemic?"

Again she shook her head. "No, not that either. I have come to ask a very great favour of you."

He relieved her of the bag and led her to a chair.

"Anything at all I can do," he assured her, "you've only to ask, you know. What is it, Rose?"

"Do you know what blood group you are?"

The question was so unexpected that

John stared at her. "Good heavens! But as it happens, I *do* know. It's considered comparatively rare, I believe. I'm—" He named the group and Rose sighed in unconcealed relief.

"Oh, I hoped you might be. It is rare, you see, and we need some blood of your group rather urgently. The only two donors we have listed in Tauling are both away and I was at my wits' end how to get them back when I remembered a conversation I'd had with your father a few weeks ago. He mentioned that his blood was in this group, so I took a chance and came to see if yours was too. It was a fifty-fifty chance, of course—you might not have been in the right group."

"Well," John assured her, "I'm glad I am. How much blood do you need and when? Do you want me to come along to the hospital right away?"

"If you don't mind, I'll make a test first. I've got all the apparatus I need here." She was opening her bag, taking out a flat white square of china and some bottles and pipettes. "This is called cross-matching," she explained. "Here"—she expelled a small drop of a colourless fluid on to the plate—"is a drop of the patient's blood serum. I'm going to take a drop of your blood—just a prick with a needle—and then I'll test it against the serum. It's only a rough check, just to find out if it's worthwhile dragging you down to the hospital at all. You see, even if you are the right group, your blood may react against the patient's for various reasons and so it would be no use. Now, do you mind if I prick your thumb?"

John held out his hand to her. He had never seen her at work before and he found himself admiring her brisk competence. Her fingers closed about his hand and he was conscious of a little thrill, like an electric impulse, running up his arm at her touch. Then she was swabbing his thumb with a piece of cotton wool and he felt a sharp prick as the needle pierced the skin.

"Who," he asked curiously, as she drew a drop of blood carefully into a pipette, which hung from a short length of rubber tubing held between her lips, "is the patient? Not the one on whom you operated yesterday, is it? The priest who was hurt in the car smash—Father Delarge?"

Rose nodded, watching the level in the pipette.

"Yes," she said, removing the stem from her mouth. Her voice was bleak and unhappy. "I'm sorry to say it is Father Delarge. He came through the operation quite well, but there are other complications besides the head injuries, and he has lost a great deal of blood. That is why I came to ask you if you would act as donor—a transfusion is the only thing that might save him. A transfusion of whole blood, I mean. We've tried everything else we can try."

"Then I hope my blood will be right," John said soberly, infected by her gravity. "He means a lot to you, doesn't he, Rose?"

"Yes," she answered simply. "Father Delarge is one of the finest men I have ever known, you see. Perhaps the finest. He is very much loved in Gaupal. I *can't* let him die." He caught the glint of tears in her eyes as she spoke and his heart went out to her. Beneath the calm, competent, professional façade, she was desperately worried, he realized, and she looked worn out when she allowed her smile to relax.

She had probably had no sleep the previous night. He imagined that she would have sat up with her patient and—since Kim had told him that she was doing the major part of the surgery at the new hospital—she had probably operated on him too. It was bad enough when the patient was a stranger . . .

She busied herself with the bottles and the white china plate and John went to stand behind her, watching the swift movements of her hands. "How soon shall we know about my blood?" he asked.

"In a few minutes," she returned tonelessly, "if it doesn't agglutinate."

They waited in silence, both watching the tiny drops of fluid on the plate. There appeared to be no change in these and, after a while, he heard Rose expel her breath in a deep sigh. "Is it going to be all right?" he demanded.

"I think so. We'll have to do another test at the hospital, just to make sure. It's all going to take rather a lot of your time—I do hope you don't mind? What were you going to do this afternoon?"

"Nothing more important than this, I promise you. His Highness did suggest that I go hunting with him, but we left it open. I can send Bo Tin with a message to explain where I am and why I can't join him."

"Oh, I'm glad. But"—Rose's glance went to the small pile of letters on the table—"you've just got your mail, haven't you? And you were reading it—I do apologize for having disturbed you, John. I hope you've had good news from home. Of your father and of—of your fiancée, of Miss Beachamp. She must be missing you. Has she made any plans to come out here yet? Because—"

"Miss Beauchamp," John interrupted, with bitterness, "has just written to tell me she's thinking of marrying someone else. So I can assure you, she has made no plans to follow me to Gaupal. For this reason, I would much rather spend the next few hours at your hospital, helping you, if I can, to save a life, than remain here by myself, with no better companionship than that of my own not very pleasant thoughts."

Her question had struck him on the raw, but the instant he had told her of his break with Sandra, John regretted it. The colour leapt to Rose's neck and cheeks, suffusing them with scarlet and then, very slowly, drained away, leaving her pale with shock. Almost, he thought, appalled by what he had done, almost as if he had struck her.

"I'm very sorry," she said, before he could think of anything to say in mitigation of his thoughtless outburst, "that is . . . very bad news. You must be upset. I —I really do apologize for coming here at such a moment. I wouldn't have come if it hadn't been so urgent. Please forgive me, I didn't know."

"Of course you didn't know," John put in quickly, embarrassed by her sympathy. "How could you possibly have known? There's absolutely nothing to forgive, and, in any case, Father Delarge's life is of a great deal more importance than my broken engagement."

Rose bent over the table and began re-packing the apparatus she had used in her bag. She didn't speak, and John went on, forcing a lighter note into his voice, "Well, at least you and Kim are together. You're working together and—"

"Yes," Rose agreed flatly, "we are

working together. And we are to be married sooner than we had planned."

"Sooner?" He gazed down at her, shocked by the wave of fury that swept over him at her words. The idea of her marrying Kim Myint had always been repugnant to him: now, suddenly, it was intolerable. With a tremendous effort, he controlled himself and repeated dully, "Sooner? Why sooner, Rose? Surely there's no hurry? I thought you were going to wait until your father returned?"

Rose raised her eyes to his face. They met his gaze stonily and her voice was flat and cold as she answered, "It is to be sooner because Kim wishes it and because I have given him my promise. That is why." She closed her bag with a little click. "Shall we go? If we hurry you may still have time to join the prince at his hunting."

John hesitated, struck by something odd about her manner. But she moved towards the door and finally, with a shrug, he followed her.

They went in silence to her waiting car. He gave Bo Tin a message to take to the Palace and then got in beside Rose. She did not speak as the car gathered speed, but the colour gradually returned to her cheeks.

By the time they reached the hospital, she was her normal quiet, serene self, talking to him as she usually did.

He ascended the steps of the tall white building at her heels and Kim came, smiling, to meet them.

13

NARAIN SINGH sat his horse and watched proudly as Prince Maung Saw trotted ahead of him, the new goshawk perched on his gloved hand.

Truly, the old man thought, his prince was a pupil to be proud of—why, he handled the hawks now like a veteran, so that even his teacher must look to his laurels if he were not to be outshone. The goshawk was young, but the boy managed her admirably. She was a fine bird, the sunlight glinting on her slate-grey feathers and folded wings. Perched there, hooded and docile, she gave no hint of the speed and power of those splendid wings, and her talons, gripping the leather-clad hand of her master's right arm, looked harmless enough . . . now. But in a little while . . . the Sikh's bearded lips parted in a mirthless smile. In a little while, when the beaters running beside his stirrup should fan out and drive towards them, a hare or a tiny Tautin gazelle would leap from cover and make off, seeking escape. Then the goshawk should have her chance. Then his master should see that Narain Singh's parting gift to him was one of value. Then . . .

"Narain-ji! Here, man, and ride beside me."

It was the prince's voice, and Narain eagerly put spurs to his lagging horse. "What dost thou want of me, my prince?" he asked, adding a soothing word to the falcon he carried on his own hand, which had been disturbed by his sudden change of pace.

"Let us have a wager," Maung Saw suggested mischievously.

"Well? Name it, Highness. Make such terms as thou wilt."

Grinning, the boy outlined the wager he proposed. It was flagrantly unfair to the falcon, but Narain Singh refrained from argument. "Very well," he agreed, "so shall it be. Thy bird against mine—the hawk of the hand against the hawk of the lure, each to make one flight only and thine to fly first. I will order the beaters to set forth." He flung commands imperiously to the men on foot, and obediently they started to fan out as they approached a belt of thick woodland. Both riders drew rein to await the outcome, watching tensely.

At first nothing happened and then, with startling suddenness, a big, sleek, bluish-grey hare broke cover and sped off at right angles to the motionless horsemen. Maung Saw released the jesses from between his fingers, plucked the hood from his hawk and raised his arm aloft. The bird remained for a moment on his hand and then, sighting the quarry, sprang from her perch with a whirr of her broad wings. Rising only a few feet into the air, she set off in pursuit, her pinions spread wide and beating the air with swift, powerful strokes.

"Ai, ai!" shouted the prince, in breathless excitement. He gave his horse its head and tore after the goshawk at breakneck speed as the first of the beaters emerged from the wood. The man shouted something, but Maung Saw ignored him. Narain Singh, following more slowly at his master's heels, paused to wave the beater to silence.

Hare and hawk, seemingly joined to each other by invisible strings, tore on, the goshawk gaining slowly but surely on the running hare. Thus for another fifty yards they continued, with the boy after them, crouched low on his horse's neck and urging it forward with hands and heels.

Then Narain Singh saw the hare change direction and plunge into a second clump of trees, desperately seeking the cover that would hide it from its relentless pursuer overhead. The goshawk struck, but Narain Singh had dropped too far back to see if she had killed her prey. He quickened speed, but by the time he gained the wood, Maung Saw was out of sight.

"Your Highness!" he called, cupping his hands about his mouth. "My prince! Where art thou?"

There was no answer. Worried, the Sikh drew rein, looking about him with narrowed eyes for some sign of the boy's passing. He saw a little circle of torn fur which showed him where the goshawk had struck, but, he decided, if she had killed, she had carried her prey, and the boy, his master, angered by this failure to adhere to her training, must undoubtedly have gone after her.

But where? The Sikh hesitated. Should

he call up the beaters, wait until they joined him and then quarter the wood, in case Maung Saw had fallen somewhere amongst the trees? It was possible that he might have. Or perhaps he had ridden round the edge of the trees, looking for a clearing so that he might enter the wood without dismounting. The car in which they had driven from Tauling was a long way back, waiting on the outskirts of the village, with the guards, on the prince's orders, until they should return . . . and Narain Singh alone was responsible for the prince's safety. He alone, and—he had let his master out of his sight. For the first time, he had failed in his duty. He, on the last day of his service, had allowed his attention to stray. He . . .

A single shot rang out, echoing eerily through the closegrowing trees. A . . . *shot*. And from a rifle. But the prince carried no rifle, he was unarmed. The blood ran suddenly cold in Narain Singh's veins. He leapt from his horse and flung himself into the undergrowth with a despairing cry.

14

DRIVING along the steep, curving road to Saiyawah with Rose Lian at his side, John felt curiously elated and filled with a keen sense of anticipation.

Their expedition to join the prince had been arranged quite fortuitously. Rose had mentioned Prince Maung Saw's invitation to Kim while the final blood tests were being made in the hospital laboratory, and Kim had urged them both to go, even offering them the loan of his car if they wanted it.

"Rose has been working much too hard," he had stated, waving aside Rose's objections. "It will be good for her to get right away from this place for a few hours. And Saiyawah is a lovely spot, John—translated, its name means 'Valley of the Ten Villages.' It stands high up, at the head of the valley, in magnificent country which abounds with game, with the River Htun Yee running below and the eastern edge of the teak forest just visible from the road. You ought to see it. In any case, you won't be feeling particularly energetic after we've taken your blood for Father Delarge. A quiet drive out into the country will be a restorative. Off you go, both of you, and trust the good Father to me. I shall not leave his side until he improves, and I am confident that he *will* improve once we've given him this transfusion."

So they had set off—Rose with obvious reluctance, himself with an eagerness that he found a trifle surprising—as soon as the transfusion had been started. He had been permitted a glimpse of the injured priest and, after this, had understood Rose's anxiety for her beloved old teacher and even begun to share it in no small measure, for it was evident to him, although he was a layman, that Father Delarge was hovering very close to the Valley of the Shadow now.

At first, as they drove through the busy, crowded streets of Tauling, John was at pains not to speak of the desperately sick man they were leaving behind them, seeking instead to distract his companion's thoughts, but after a while, Rose interrupted him. "I wish Kim had let me stay," she said miserably. "I'm sorry, since this drive was originally your idea, but—I hate leaving Father Delarge."

"I know you do, Rose." John put out a hand to clasp hers in wordless sympathy. The gesture was impulsive and thoughtless, and for a moment Rose let her hand lie in his without comment. Then, flushing slightly, she withdrew it.

"He is such a dear old man." Her voice was a faint whisper of sound above the hum of the car's engine. "Such a dear *good* old man . . ."

"Yes. But you've done all you can. And Kim is with him."

"Oh, I know. But—" She broke off and, glancing down at her, John saw that she was fighting against the tears which had come to fill her dark eyes.

"But what?" he prompted gently.

She looked up at him. "You know, of course, that he was injured in a car smash —that he was in collision with another car? It happened just after he had left me at my father's house yesterday morning. John, I ought not to have let him go by himself. I should have sent someone with him, I—"

"From what I can gather," John pointed out, in an attempt to console her, "Father Delarge wasn't a very good driver. It could not, by any stretch of the imagination, have been your fault that he met with an accident, Rose . . . accidents happen here, as they happen in England, on the roads. If you had sent anyone with him yesterday —even if you'd gone with him yourself— do you suppose that the accident could have been avoided?"

"You don't understand," Rose protested.

"Don't I?"

She shook her head. "No. You see, I can't be certain that it *was* an accident. Father Delarge was on his way to an audience with the Prime Minister yesterday. John, he had found out something, something important and . . . and dangerous. He . . ."

Her expression grave, she recounted all that Father Delarge had told her the previous day. John listened with furrowed brows and for the most part in silence, only occasionally interposing a question when the implication of her words did not seem quite clear to him. He heard with growing alarm that the good Father had given it as his opinion that the new oil company was at the root of the trouble that was brewing. He realized, from what he knew of the King, that the lying rumours which had been started, concerning his seizure of the profits from a sale of the oil concessions, might well gain credence as they went from ear to ear. Such whispers were all too readily believed and, where there was unrest and organized agitation, they could do an incalculable amount of harm. A remote, god-like King who held himself aloof, behind the high, closely guarded walls of a splendid palace few of his humbler subjects were permitted to enter, must—in the very nature of things —inspire a superstitious awe. But awe wasn't trust: it wasn't love or popularity, for it came too close to fear. And if one of his own privileged ministers should be— as Father Delarge seemed to think—the fount from whom the whispers sprang, then the King's position might be a far from happy one. He would suspect no treachery from such a man; why should he dream of its existence? But the minister's pronouncements, no matter how little truth they might contain, must carry weight by reason of the fact that he held a trusted position in the government and was present at meetings of the King's Council. In the absence of an official denial, they would be accepted without question by illiterate peasants and with little doubt by the better educated, upon whose minds the agitators had already been at work.

Remembering what Kim had told him of the building of a temple within the palace walls, John's mouth compressed. Grimly, he asked, "Father Delarge gave you no idea who the traitor might be, I suppose? He gave you nothing to go on?"

Again Rose shook her head. "He told me that he did not propose to share the burden of his knowledge with me. He was aware of how dangerous it was, of course —he couldn't fail to be."

"Have you talked to Kim about this?"

"I tried to, but—oh, we've been so busy and so upset. Kim had other things on his mind. Father Delarge told him something else, something more . . . more personal."

"Father Delarge was conscious, then?" John suggested.

"Yes," Rose confirmed, "he was. But very briefly, after he was admitted to the hospital. He has not recovered consciousness since I took over his care."

"He's under guard, of course?"

Her brows lifted in surprise. "In the hospital? Oh, no, it isn't necessary."

"I see. And this other matter—the personal matter about which he told Kim. Could that have any bearing on what he said to you?"

"None whatsoever," Rose answered emphatically. To his astonishment, John saw her redden. "That," she went on, "concerned only me. For—for various reasons, I'd rather not tell you what it was now. You see, it has been settled between Kim and myself. Our decision to marry at once is"—she lowered her gaze and her voice was muffled as she finished— "because of the secret which Father Delarge revealed to Kim about me. I don't suppose you will understand, but . . . that is how it is, John. I made what I believed was the right decision, in the circumstances."

John studied the little he could see of her face in perplexity. He had not the remotest idea of what she meant, but clearly it was no use asking her for an explanation: her last words had held a curious finality. She and Kim had decided to advance the date of their wedding because of something Father Delarge had told them—or told Kim, rather.

He had no right to question their decisions, no conceivable right, and yet, for some utterly inexplicable reason, he did question it. Despite the flat lack of emotion in her voice, he knew that Rose was unhappy and that her unhappiness went deeper even than her anxiety for Father Delarge or her concern for the treachery which the old priest had apparently uncovered. It was personal and it stemmed from the very depths of her being. Sensing it, he was deeply moved, and suddenly he, who, all his life, had been reticent and controlled and sternly disciplined, felt anger overwhelm him. His anger wasn't reasoned, it was instinctive and primitive and he had experienced it before—though never quite so strongly— whenever mention had been made in his presence of Rose's betrothal to Kim Myint.

His foot came down violently on the brake pedal and the big car skidded to a halt so abruptly that Rose, startled out of her abstraction, lifted her face to his, her eyes wide with alarm.

"What is it?" she asked, catching at his arm. "John, what is wrong? Why have you stopped?"

"Because," John answered fiercely, scarcely recognizing his own voice as he said it, "I've got to talk to you, Rose. That's why I've stopped." He turned in his seat to face her, reaching for her hand. This time, although it trembled perceptibly at his touch, she didn't attempt to withdraw it but sat looking up at him in silence, her lower lip quivering and her eyes bright with unshed tears.

"We've . . . we've been talking," she managed at last. "Haven't we? What else is there to—to talk about?"

"We've never talked about the one thing that matters, Rose. We've never talked about your marriage or about you or why you're unhappy. I know you aren't happy,

I can feel it. But I've never asked you why, until now, have I?"

"No." Every vestige of colour had drained from her cheeks. John saw this and his anger faded. "I made a mistake," he said gently. "I almost married the wrong woman," and knew, as he made the admission, that it was the truth. The memory of Sandra was faint and far away and it no longer possessed the power to hurt or move him. It was no longer real, it was part of another life, part of the past, dead and gone and all but forgotten. Perhaps it had never been quite real . . .

"Are you trying to tell me," Rose asked, with strange, quiet dignity, "that I am in danger of making a similar mistake? Are you suggesting that I should be making a mistake if I married Kim?"

Was he, John wondered, *was* he? Yes, of course he was. It was wrong. She could not marry Kim Myint, he could not stand by and let her do it, he *would* not . . . "Are you in love with him?" he countered. "Tell me the truth, Rose—are you?" A great deal, everything perhaps, hung on her answer, he knew.

She sighed. "That isn't a question one asks in Gaupal, John."

"Perhaps it isn't, if one asks it of a woman of Gaupal. But I'm"—anger rose again in John's throat, so intense that it almost choked him—"I'm asking you, Rose."

"You think I am different from—from the other women of Gaupal?"

"I know you are—and so do you! Tell me the truth, Rose, please. Are you in love with Kim Myint?"

"No." Her voice broke on a sob. "I am not. But I—I am betrothed to him."

"That isn't irrevocable."

"No, perhaps not, in England." John felt the hand he held tremble violently in his, a small, cold, frightened hand that seemed suddenly to have no strength. "Here it is . . . *almost* irrevocable. And there is Kim, you see. He is a fine person, he has always been good to me—generous and kind and honourable. Yesterday . . ." She hesitated and then, looking up very directly into John's eyes, asked him, in an oddly strained voice, "Why are you speaking to me like this, why are you asking me these questions? Kim is your friend."

He drew a quick, uncertain breath. As she had reminded him, Kim was his friend, but he had ignored the claims of friendship. Worse, he had forgotten them. Kim had trusted him, had sent him out this afternoon with Rose, who was his betrothed, secure in the belief that his friend would not betray him. But what else, in heaven's name, was he doing?

It was borne on him suddenly, in that moment, as he sat in the car with Rose's small hand imprisoned in his own and her tear-filled eyes looking into his, that what he had already done was betrayal. A betrayal as base and cruel as that of the traitor whom Father Delarge had tracked down—for it was motivated by selfishness, by envy, by desire. He did not want Kim to marry Rose Lian because . . . *because he wanted her for himself*. Because he loved her. This—this and nothing else— was the explanation of his bitter, futile anger, this the reason for his outburst.

He had fallen in love with Rose and had been too blind to see it. From the first moment he had set eyes on her, getting out of her car at the door of the Gaupali Embassy in London, he had been aware of the attraction she had for him. But he had deceived himself. There had been his engagement to Sandra, for one thing, and, for another, there had been the barrier which he had imagined that Rose's race must set between them.

Now, gazing down at her, he knew that whatever the barriers, real or imagined, of race and creed and blood, he would ignore them, for they simply did not matter to him and never would. There was only one barrier that he could not ignore, if he were ever to be able to look himself in the face again, and of this Rose herself had reminded him—Kim was his friend . . .

John found his voice at last. "Rose," he said humbly, "I owe you an apology. I shouldn't have said what I did to you. Forgive me."

"But why," she whispered, "*did* you say it?" Her mouth trembled. "You asked me for the truth just now and I didn't withhold it from you. Please tell me why."

Her gaze met his and he read in her eyes that which set his pulses racing and his heart beating wildly. For Rose, too, this was the moment of revelation, of decision. She had lowered her guard: he knew, as he looked at her, that he had to tell her the truth. He owed her that, whatever he owed Kim, for her feelings were the echo, at this moment, of his own. Her eyes told him that, his every instinct told him, beyond the smallest possibility of doubt, since the pain and the heartbreak he glimpsed in her face might have been the reflection of that which he was himself enduring.

"I am in love with you, Rose," he said, and had to exert all the self-control he possessed not to take her in his arms and crush her to him. "That is the simple truth. I've been a fool, a crazy, witless imbecile not to have realized it before, but I promise you, I did not realize it until now—until this moment. No, wait, please"—as she opened her mouth to speak—"hear me out. I would ask you to become my wife, if it were not for Kim— that is what I want to do. Because of Kim I can't ask you, at least until I have seen him and told him how I feel about you. But I won't even do that, if you tell me you don't want me to, Rose. All I shall ask is that you will not marry Kim if it's going to make you unhappy. Please, my dear, don't do that, for your own sake, if not for mine. Postpone your decision, wait a little. Wait until your father returns. You—"

"My . . . father. Yes." A strange expression, that was half pity and half pain, flickered across her white, tense face. Then her mouth compressed and he heard her stifle a sob. "I gave my word to Kim," she told him miserably. "I promised him. I promised him again . . . *yesterday*."

John's fingers tightened their pressure on hers. The emphasis she had put on the single word reached his ears, but he attached no particular significance to it. From the depths of his own misery he demanded, with bitterness, "Am I to take it that you don't want me to say anything to Kim at all, then?"

Rose ignored the question. It seemed to John, watching her, that she could not have heard it, for she smiled at him suddenly through her tears, a warm, lovely smile that wrenched at his heartstrings and made him long, quite desperately, to put out his arms and draw her to him, never

316

to let her go. But he controlled the impulse and she said, her voice low and charged with some emotion he couldn't analyse, "You would have asked me to become your wife, if I were not betrothed to Kim? You would marry me, if it were not for that, in spite of—in spite of . . . John, you would marry a—a woman of Gaupal?"

"If she is you." His throat ached with longing and his voice was harsh with the effort he had to make in order to control it. "I love you, Rose. Whether or not I have the right to—I love you and that is all that matters to me. But I wish with all my heart that Kim had never been my friend."

Rose was silent for a long time. She had withdrawn her hand from his and sat with her back half turned towards him, her face hidden and her slim body very stiff and erect. Although she made no sound, John knew that she was crying and his longing to comfort her grew until it became almost unbearable. He clenched his hands at his sides and fought against it and, after a while, she said, without turning round, "Shall we . . . shall we go on?"

"If you want to," he agreed tonelessly. "Do you? We'll go back if you'd rather."

"Oh, no." She shivered. "Not yet. I can't go back yet, John, I—I can't."

He leaned forward, fumbling for the starter switch. The car moved slowly forward. A flock of small green parrots rose in a screeching cloud from a tree at the roadside, disturbed by the sound of the car's engine, as John's foot touched the accelerator. He saw them out of the tail of his eye and then, as the car picked up speed, forgot them, giving all his attention to his driving. The road, narrow and steeply cambered, climbed in a series of hairpin bends towards the foothills, and, a mile or so beyond the spot at which they had halted, he glimpsed the vast, snow-capped peak of Taulai through a gap in the clouds.

Rose sat silently beside him, staring ahead of her with unseeing eyes. Her face, seen in profile, was pale and set, still bearing the traces of her tears. But she had ceased to weep, and gradually the tension that had been between them lifted.

John did not attempt to intrude on her

thoughts and, at last, she turned to look at him.

"You have made me very proud," she told him, a catch in her voice. "To know that you love me, even if it can lead to nothing more for either of us, is a very wonderful thing—the most wonderful thing that ever happened to me in all my life, I think. And you loved me, in spite of believing that I was a woman of Gaupal. I"—he felt her fingers brush his arm— "there is something that I must tell you about that, about my birth—something I have only just learnt myself. But first— John, you know that I feel as you do, don't you? You know that I love you, with all my heart, with everything that is in me . . . I love you. I don't have to tell you that."

He could not trust himself to answer her. Gripping the wheel hard, he nodded, his gaze on the steep white ribbon of the road ahead. He knew, she didn't have to tell him, but, aware that she was about to ask him to renounce their love, a wave of bitterness surged over him. Was this to be the end of it all—this and nothing more? Must loyalty to Kim and the reluctance to go back on a promise be carried to such lengths? And then, refusing to yield to his own bitter resentment, he admitted to himself that it must. For his sake and hers, Kim must suffer no betrayal. Their future —his as tutor to Prince Maung Saw, Rose's in her profession—would be placed in jeopardy if they betrayed Kim Myint. He loved this girl who sat beside him, but he must not touch her, must not even kiss her, for they had learnt of their love for each other too late. The betrayal had been only in words . . . He said, from between stiff lips, "You want it to end, here and now?" He changed gear clumsily, with a harsh grating of metal on metal. "May I not go to Kim and tell him what has happened—*how* it happened? Neither of us meant it to happen, Rose—he will understand that and believe it, surely?"

"Was that how your—was that how Miss Beachamp ended her betrothal to you? Did she simply tell you that she was in love with someone else and no longer wished to marry you?"

"Yes, that was . . . more or less how it ended."

"And you did not mind?"

"I think I expected it. I do not think she ever really cared about me, and—" He hesitated and then went on, his voice not quite steady, "I believed I was in love with her, Rose. But that was before I met you. Now I know what it is to love a woman, to want her, to . . . I have learnt what love means by loving you."

Again the warm, lovely smile lit her face. "I too, John," she confessed. "I too have learnt what it means by loving you."

"Well, then," he urged eagerly, "if I tell Kim—"

Very slowly, Rose shook her head and the smile faded as swiftly as if it had never been. "In Gaupal," she said, "if a man should rob another of his betrothed, the honour of both becomes involved. You would insult Kim in a manner which he could never forgive—he would have to avenge the insult, his honour would demand it. I could not let that happen, John."

"But surely Kim is sufficiently Westernized to understand? Surely he—"

Her hand closed gently over his. "No one is sufficiently Westernized in Gaupal to accept the loss of his honour, my love.

The only way in which I could obtain my freedom would be if Kim were to give it to me, freely and of his own choice, and that I fear he will not do. Yesterday he offered to and I—I refused it."

"I see." He did not ask her why she had refused it, the words stuck in his throat, and Rose offered no explanation. As they drove on, silence again fell between them. Several times, John sensed that she was about to speak, but although her lips parted, no sound came from them. Whatever it was that she wanted to tell him was evidently difficult to put into words, so he waited, hoping that she might voice her thoughts aloud.

They reached the village of Saiyawah and saw the prince's car drawn up at the side of the road, the guards grouped about it. They were whiling away the time with some game of chance which they played, squatting in a semi-circle beneath the fragrant shade of a gungau tree. They got to their feet when John pulled up beside them and the officer in charge gave him a courteous salute. Prince Maung Saw and the Sikh, Narain Singh, had gone ahead on horseback, he explained, in answer to

Rose's question. They had taken two birds with them, a goshawk and a falcon, and intended to hunt on the far side of the valley. He indicated the direction they had taken and added, smiling, that probably they had found good sport, since neither had yet returned. The light would last for another two hours at least: he did not expect his master to call a halt until just before dusk, for there was plenty of game in this place and the prince was trying out a new bird.

"If you are wishing to follow and watch them," he added, "it is possible to do so by car. The road runs to within a few hundred yards of their hunting ground. But that covers a large area. You would perhaps be well advised to drive to the top of the pass and look down from there, in the hope of seeing them. There are, of course, horses here, if you would prefer to go on horseback, but I think it is now too late to catch them up by such means. A car is faster."

John glanced at Rose. She inclined her head.

"We might as well go on in the car, John. If you want to go on."

For answer, he engaged his gear. There might be very little chance of finding the prince, but at least, if they tried to do so, they would have a little longer together. He too was loth to return to Tauling before he need. These few precious hours in Rose's company might be all he would have of her, all he would have to remember in the barren years that stretched ahead of him.

He nodded his thanks to the young officer and they drove on down the narrow village street, past a small bazaar backed by one-storey wooden houses of primitive construction, and skirting a temple on which stood four of the crested peacocks of Gaupal, on guard at its entrance. A priest in a saffron robe turned in the act of mounting the steps of the temple to stare after them, and the temple bells, ringing softly, followed them like a melodious echo, long after the temple itself had been lost to sight. It was a peaceful, pleasant sound, and John sighed as he listened to it. How happy this moment might have been for Rose and himself, bemused by the wonder of their new-found love for each other, if circumstances had been

different, if Kim had not been involved—
if they had not been in Gaupal.

They crossed the river by a slender
wooden bridge and the road resumed its
steeply curving climb, passing now
between lines of giant trees, their trunks
half-hidden by the luxuriant jungle creeper
which twined about them. A jungle cock
called noisily from the undergrowth, and
a flight of duck, in wedge formation, rose
from the marshy bank of the river and
made off to the eastward, their small
bodies black against the sunlit blue of the
sky. John's gaze followed them momen-
tarily, and then, as the surface of the road
began to deteriorate, he was compelled to
slow down and give it his undivided
attention.

Rose said suddenly, breaking the
silence, "Is it Mr. Garrison whom your—
whom Miss Beauchamp intends to marry,
John?"

Taken by surprise, John's mouth
tightened grimly.

"I imagine it is," he admitted,
"although she didn't tell me so."

"He is not a good man, this Garrison,"
Rose stated. "From what I have heard my

father say, he is the cause of much of the trouble over the oil company. He gave bribes, lavish bribes, when he was out here—corrupting many people who might otherwise have remained loyal. I think it is a pity for Gaupal that he ever came here."

"Well," John told her, "it would seem that he has run up against something in the way of competition. *My* father said, in his last letter, that the shares of Pagoda Oils were fluctuating wildly, on rumours of a bid from a rival company for the Gaupal concessions. The rumours were unconfirmed, but—who knows? They might easily be true."

"Yes. I am sorry to say this, John, but I hope they are. Because I am certain that the minister of whom Father Delarge spoke to me yesterday must have been one . . ." She broke off and John heard her give a little, startled gasp.

"What is it?" he demanded in quick alarm.

"John, look!" There was a note of bewilderment in her voice. "Isn't that a man, lying there at the edge of those trees? A man and—a horse. Oh, yes, it is . . . it's Narain Singh, and . . . he seems to be hurt. John, stop, would you? I think he must have had a fall."

As he applied the brakes, John followed the direction of her pointing finger and saw that the prostrate form at the roadside was, indeed, that of the prince's Sikh bodyguard. Narain Singh lay slumped at the foot of a creeper-grown tree, his head resting in a strangely unnatural way on his outstretched arms and his face turned from them. His horse, grazing quietly a few yards beyond him, pricked its ears as the car pulled up and came whinnying towards it, limping badly.

John stifled an exclamation and dived for the door of the car. "Wait, Rose," he said warningly. "Let me see what's wrong first. Stay in the car until I call you."

He got out and knelt beside the still figure, the horse nuzzling his shoulder as if in dumb enquiry. The Sikh was unconscious, his bearded face pale and deeply lacerated and a livid bruise just visible beneath the lower edge of the tightly wound pugaree. Judging by the state of his uniform, which was torn and mudstained and dark with sweat, he had evidently been travelling at some speed through the undergrowth, probably on foot, since it was too dense to permit a horse and rider to penetrate it. And yet . . . John looked up at the horse, frowning. The Sikh appeared to have fallen from his mount and the animal was lame, dragging its near hind, the joint swollen and painful, which would suggest that he had been riding it when disaster overtook him—no doubt as the result of a hole or a tree root, into which he had unwittingly galloped.

Galloped? But no man in his senses would have attempted to gallop through such close-growing jungle, least of all a horseman as expert as Narain Singh. There was something wrong, something that did not fit in with the picture of a fall. The horse, a pure-bred black Arab, was not a weight-carrier, such as he would have expected the Sikh to choose, John's mind registered: it was a fast, mettlesome young animal more suited to Narain Singh's master, the youthful Prince Maung Saw. And there was a hawk of some kind, hooded, perched motionless on the saddle-bow . . .

"John"—it was Rose's voice, calling to him from the car—"hadn't I better look at him and see if there's anything I can do? I have my bag with me and some dressings—"

John got to his feet, and went to open the door of the car for her. As she, in her turn, knelt beside the injured Sikh, he walked over to examine horse and bird, his brows still furrowed and the first premonition of danger sending small, icy prickles of fear to contract his heart. If this were the prince's horse, then where was the prince? His guards, patiently waiting for him by the parked car in the village, several miles away, had not set eyes on him since he had left them, at least two hours ago, on their own admission. And if Narain Singh were hurt, then . . .

"Here, boy," he called, "here." The Arab came to him with a low whinny and he bent, a hand on the bridle, to feel gently for the cause of the animal's lameness. When he withdrew his hand, it was wet with blood. Shocked, he went down on his knees, the better to ascertain the nature of the wound, murmuring softly to the frightened horse to stand still. It obeyed him, but the leg was obviously very tender so that, for a moment or two, he was unable to examine it properly. Then he saw, faint but unmistakable, the trace a bullet makes when it grazes the skin. This horse had been fired on, at close range.

He glanced across at Rose, but she was busy with the unconscious Sikh, absorbed in the task of bandaging his head, and did not look up. John straightened himself and started to examine the saddle and the bird perched on it, seeking for some means of positive identification of their owner. The hooded hawk did not move, it seemed scarcely to be breathing, and he left it alone, uncertain of how it would react if he touched it. But the saddle yielded the proof he sought, putting an end to any lingering doubts to which he might cling. Of beautifully polished, hand-tooled leather, it bore the prince's personal monogram on the flap and—this discovery causing his heart to sink—a further search revealed traces of a second bullet embedded in the leather.

He went to join Rose, a prey to the worst forebodings he could ever remember, and one look at her face was enough to tell him that she, too, was alarmed.

"John," she said, her voice low and shaken, "the Sikh didn't hurt himself in a fall from his horse. He was shot—shot and wounded. There's a bullet wound in his chest, which fortunately is slight, and I'm almost certain that his head injury is from the same cause. Although it isn't much more than skin deep, it was enough to give him concussion."

John met her gaze without flinching. "The horse has been shot too, Rose," he told her quietly.

"Yes, but—"

"It's Maung Saw's horse, darling"—the endearment came easily and naturally to his tongue, and Rose gave no sign that she had heard it—"and he seems to have disappeared."

"The prince—disappeared? Oh, no!" There was agony in her voice. "But of course, the guards said they hadn't seen him, didn't they? And he was *with* Narain Singh."

"Yes."

"What—John, in heaven's name, what are we going to do?"

"I'm going to look for him," John said decisively. "But before I go, I'll lift the

Sikh into the car. Can you drive back with him to the village and send His Highness's guard up here to join me? I'll keep close to the road, so that I'll hear them when they get here. It's just possible, if Maung Saw has fallen by the edge of the trees, that I may find him quite quickly. But if not, we shall have to organize search parties—get people from the village and probably the beaters and shikaris, if they're still in the locality, which they ought to be. Come to think of it, it's odd that they haven't turned up. They must have heard the shots, surely?"

"Not if the prince and Narain Singh rode after a hare," Rose pointed out. "They could be miles behind, and the sound of the shots would be deadened by the trees, wouldn't it?"

"Shots carry a long way. Well"—John gestured to the khaki-clad form at their feet—"shall I put him into the car? Is there any particular way you want me to lift him?"

"If you could be careful of his right arm, please. See, I will help you."

Between them, not without difficulty, they placed the wounded Sikh in the back of the car. He stirred uneasily as John laid him down, and Rose said, coming to stand beside him and feeling for his pulse, "I think he is recovering consciousness. Wait a little, John. He may be able to give us an account of what happened, even to tell us where to look for the prince. It would be easier for you if you knew in which direction to begin your search, wouldn't it? Easier and"—she suppressed a shudder—"perhaps safer."

"Safer?"

"Someone fired those shots, someone who intended harm to the prince. You might run into an ambush. Please, John, if you must go—be careful. I cannot bear the thought that you may be in danger."

John's expression relaxed. Briefly, he put his arm about her shoulders. "I'll take care, don't worry. If there was an ambush, those who laid it will have fled for their lives by this time, darling—they won't hang around, waiting to see what we're going to do. They—"

Rose lifted a finger for silence. "Narain Singh is coming round, I think. Listen . . . he's trying to speak, to tell us something."

333

The Sikh's eyes opened. They gazed up blankly into Rose's face, without recognition, and his lips moved feebly.

"He's asking for water," John said, catching a word. He leaned closer to the bearded face. "You shall have water, Narain Singh," he promised, "as soon as we get you down to the village. Try to stick it till then, if you can. Are you in pain?"

At the sound of his voice, recognition dawned in the dark eyes, to be followed swiftly by a look of shocked apprehension. "Anson Sahib! You!"

"Yes," John acknowledged, "I'm here, Subadar-sahib. Now listen to me, will you? I want to know exactly what's been happening. Where is His Highness? And who fired on you?"

"His Highness?" There was incredulity in the faint voice. "His Highness is hunting, Sahib. He is flying the new goshawk I gave him, as a parting present. Sahib"—the old man attempted to raise himself on one elbow, but John gently restrained him—"Sahib, I am going away from Gaupal. I am to leave my prince, and you—"

"Don't speak of that now," John bade him sternly. "Try to tell me what occurred here a little while ago. Try to remember. You were with His Highness, hunting with the hawks, and somebody fired a shot. He fired at you, Subadar-sahib—once and then again. Two shots, three . . . try to remember. I must find the prince, and you are the only one who can help me—you are the only one who could have seen what happened."

"I did not see," Narain Singh said. He closed his eyes as if to emphasize the denial. "I saw nothing, Sahib, nothing. Or if I did, I do not now remember it. All is blank in my mind, as if a cloud were hanging over it."

"It's hopeless," John said, in a whisper, to Rose. "I'd better go. Maung Saw may be badly hurt and—"

"Let me come with you. Please, John" —her eyes pleaded with him—"I am a doctor. If the prince is hurt, you may need me, don't you see? I think—"

He took her hand and bore it to his lips. "Darling, I'll move faster alone. And I need you to fetch the guards. You can come back with them. If I find the prince,

I'll get him to the road. And I do know something about first aid. I won't move him if there's the least risk, I promise you. But every minute may count and it's my duty to go and look for him. I'm his tutor and it's my responsibility now that Narain Singh is out of the fight. Look—I'll turn the car for you, shall I? And then will you do as I ask?"

Rose capitulated. "All right," she said. "But don't worry about the car, I can manage to turn it myself. You'll take care, won't you, John?"

He hesitated and then bent his head, his lips gently brushing her cheek. "I'll take care," he promised. "Au revoir, darling, and—"

Narain Singh's voice, stronger now, broke into their farewells. "Sahib!"

"What is it, Subadar-ji?"

"Sahib—" Wide-eyed with terror, the old Sikh dragged himself into a sitting position, clutching at John's sleeve. "Sahib, I have remembered now what happened. It is coming back to me. They who fired the shots . . . Sahib, they were many. They lay in ambush for us—for the prince first and then for me, when, hearing the shots, I went after him. They had a car waiting here by the roadside, a big car, into which they forced him. Sahib, these are wicked men! They have abducted my prince and carried him off in the big black car. Sahib, you must go after them."

"But where, Narain Singh? Where have they taken him? Do you know?"

The Sikh's face was contorted, tears running down his bearded cheeks which he did not attempt to conceal. "I do not know, Sahib—how should I know? I saw them but for the space of a few seconds, long enough to recognize but two of them." He sank back on the cushions of the car, exhausted.

John exchanged an anxious glance with Rose. He saw her nod. "Narain Singh," he pleaded urgently, "who were the men you recognized? Think, man, think! Your prince's life may depend on it." The dark eyes were already glazing, resuming their blank look of semi-consciousness, but hearing the urgent note in his questioner's voice, the old man made a last courageous effort to respond to it. "One of them was Thakin Maw Shwe, Minister of the King, Sahib—he who rebuilds the Peacock

Pagoda in Tauling. And the other . . . the other was Garrison Sahib of the Oil Company." The slurred words faded into silence as Narain Singh's head slumped down once more on to his chest.

"But Garrison isn't here!" John exploded. Rose met his gaze across the still form of the prince's bodyguard.

"He arrived in Tauling this morning," she said quietly.

15

KIM MYINT glanced at the transfusion apparatus suspended over Father Delarge's bed and breathed a heart-felt sigh of gratitude and relief as he watched the slow drip of the life-giving blood flowing into his patient's frail body.

Already the good Father's colour had improved and his breathing was easier. In a little while, Kim thought, two fingers on the steadying pulse at the old priest's wrist, he would be out of danger. He was showing signs of a return to consciousness now, but it was too soon to rouse him, too soon to permit him to talk, as he so obviously wanted to . . . Kim motioned to the small, dark-skinned nurse who stood beside the instrument trolley. She placed a hypodermic syringe in his outstretched hand, swabbed an area of exposed skin and looked up at him expectantly. He gave the injection with swift competence and stood up.

"Stay with him, nurse," he ordered. "I

shall be back again to see him in an hour, but call me at once if there should be any change in his condition."

The nurse inclined her head and took her place obediently in the chair beside the bed. "He is better, sir, is he not?" she ventured, looking down at the still white face with pity in her eyes. "A little better, at least."

"Yes," Kim confirmed. "He is improving. In an hour's time you will see a great difference in him, nurse. This transfusion is what he needed. I am thankful that we were able to find a donor in time. This blood is of a rare group and not easy to come by in an emergency."

Rose had made an excellent job of Father Delarge's difficult and delicate operation, he reflected, as he left the ward. She was a brilliant surgeon, gifted and skilful and, in the theatre, so serene and calm that it was hard, at times, to remember she was a woman. Very few women were natural surgeons, but Rose was just that, and she was a tower of strength at his side, as far as the running of the new hospital was concerned. Kim wondered, looking back, what he would have done without her, and he was thoughtful when he returned to his office and saw the pile of paperwork awaiting him.

The volume of administrative detail connected with the hospital was steadily increasing, and he was finding that, coupled with a shortage of experienced staff, he was left with little leisure to spend with his betrothed and scarcely saw her, except when they were both on duty. It would have been pleasant if he could have gone to Saiyawah this afternoon, for instance, with Rose and John Anson, but —Kim sighed. His letter to the Minister, Thakin Maw Shwe, had met with no response, in spite of the fact that it had contained a most urgently worded request for the allocation of at least two more doctors from the military reserve. The two he had asked for temporarily were, it seemed, still under a cloud—for reasons best known to the Minister—and his earlier request for their reappointment had been bluntly refused. And without apology or explanation, which made it harder to accept. The tour of the military medical units under his command, which he had been trying to arrange ever since his return to Tauling, could not be undertaken while he was so fully occupied with and in the hospital—he could not thrust the burden of responsibility on to Rose.

He could and would not, and there was no one else on his staff capable of bearing it. The situation had exceeded the limits of absurdity, he thought, when he, newly appointed to command of the Army Medical Service, was not only unable to inspect his command but, owing to lack of co-operation on the part of the Minister for War, could not even obtain the temporary services of any of the officers he was supposed to be commanding.

Angrily thrusting to one side the small mountain of documents requiring his signature, Kim rang for his secretary and set to work to compose another letter to the man who appeared so determined to frustrate him in his efforts to staff the hospital and attend to his military duties. In this he set out his requirements in terms that could not possibly be misunderstood or ignored and, when it was done, he dictated a second letter to his deputy in the Army Medical Service, informing him that he might expect a visit from his superior within the next twenty-four hours.

"I intend," Kim said, and his voice shook with the intensity of his feelings, "to make a tour of all the medical establishments under my command at the first possible opportunity. But in the meantime, until that opportunity shall arise, I require a full and complete report from you—a report which, I need hardly remind you, should have been, by this time, in my hands. In my opinion . . ." he was interrupted in midsentence by a knock on the door. "Wait," he ordered sharply and completed the letter before telling his caller to come in. "Well?" It was the nurse he had left in charge of Father Delarge, he realized, and his anger subsided. "Is the good Father conscious?"

The nurse bowed her smooth dark head. "Yes, Duwa, he is conscious and asking for you by name. He would not rest until I promised him that I would come in search of you. He said that I was to tell you that he had a matter of vital importance to discuss with you and to beg you to come to him at once."

"Then go back to him and say that I am coming at once," Kim bade her. He turned to his secretary. "You have taken down all that I have said, Ma Kyaw? You have understood it?"

The girl looked at him shyly, her brown eyes grave and a little frightened. "Yes, Colonel Myint, I have everything down. Is it your wish that I should transcribe these letters at once?"

He nodded. "At once. And have the letters delivered by hand as soon as they are ready. You may bring them to the ward for my signature if I am not back by the time you have finished them."

She hesitated, and Kim knew that, child though she was, she was afraid for his sake and would have advised caution had she dared. Maw Shwe was a powerful man who had made himself feared in Gaupal, but—Kim smiled, a trifle grimly, to himself. "Both letters are to go, Ma Kyaw," knowing, as he said it, that he had burned his boats behind him. But his patience was at an end and he no longer cared if the Minister took exception to the tone of his letter, so long as it stirred him into action. The hospital had to be staffed and he was prepared to risk a great deal in order that it should be—his career, if necessary. Although that, even if matters should come to a trial of strength between himself and the Minister, was unlikely. There were few doctors of his calibre in Gaupal, none with his military experience. If not completely indispensable, he would be extremely hard to replace, he was aware, and his political integrity was beyond question.

He was, however, thinking of Rose again when he re-entered Father Delarge's ward. The prospect of his marriage to her was one that occupied much of his thoughts, but he wondered, as he approached the old priest's bed, whether or not they had made the right decision yesterday. From his point of view, it was one thing to marry the daughter of Gaupal's Ambassador to Great Britain, even if her mother had been French: it was another to marry a Frenchwoman, without a single drop of Gaupali blood in her veins . . . quite another. Much as he admired and respected Rose, would he make her happy, be to her the kind of husband she wanted and deserved? They worked together in the closest harmony, it was true: Rose deferred to him and accepted his guidance and their professional relationship could scarcely have been bettered, but—Kim's mouth twisted into a wry smile. Their personal relationship was that of two polite, well-intentioned strangers, and it never seemed to alter. He knew his future bride no better now than he had known her when they met for the first time at the Embassy. She did not talk to him of the things that were close to her heart, she accepted his diffident caresses submissively but without pleasure, and never invited the slightest intimacy, even on the few occasions when they were alone together. An attitude which—correct in a woman of Gaupal perhaps, who had never left her native land—was unexpected in one of Rose's birth and upbringing, more especially now, when the secret of her birth had been revealed to him . . . revealed, in fact, to them both.

Kim Myint bit back a sigh. He bent over Father Delarge, feeling automatically for his pulse and wishing, as he did so, that he were able to ask the old priest's advice as, long ago, when he was a boy, he had been accustomed to ask it. He was a grown man now, approaching middle age and bearing on his shoulders the responsibility for this great and splendid new hospital and for the lives of the sick and injured who were in it. And yet, looking down into the lined, kindly face of his old teacher, he felt lost and alone and a child again, as much in need of reassuring counsel as he had ever been throughout their long association. But he could not expect it from a sick man who was his patient . . . Father Delarge opened his eyes. It took him a moment or two to focus them on Kim's face, but when he had done so, a smile came to hover about the corners of his mouth.

"Ah, Kim, my son," the old man said, "so you have come to me. And you have saved my life."

"No, Father," Kim denied, "not I but Rose—Rose and an Englishman called John Anson, who gave you his blood. They saved you." His trained mind noticed and registered the fact that Father Delarge was almost himself again: weak and in pain but smiling and courageous as always and in full possession of his faculties. He patted the thin, work-worn old hand that he held in his own. "What was it that you wanted to say to me? The nurse told me it was a matter of vital importance, but I don't want you to upset yourself, now that you are on the road to recovery. Would it not keep, perhaps, until tomorrow, when you will be stronger?"

Vehemently, Father Delarge shook his bandaged head.

"This will not wait, Kim," he said. "It has already waited far too long. Sit down here beside me and send the nurse away. What I have to tell you is for your ears alone, and you will have to take such action, when you have heard it, as you may deem necessary . . . violent action, if need be. But I know that I can rely on you."

"Yes, Father, of course you can rely on me," Kim assured him. He signed to the nurse to leave them alone together and took his seat on the chair at the priest's bedside, wondering what it was that the old man wanted to tell him so urgently. Some whim, perhaps, brought on by his injuries: some nightmare which had come to plague him during the long hours of bemused semi-consciousness. Or could it be to do with the matter he had mentioned to Rose when he had driven her back from the King's durbar? Kim sat up, very erect, in his chair and studied his patient's white, pain-twisted face with narrowed eyes. "What is it, Father, that may require violent action?"

Father Delarge lowered his voice. "When I met with my accident," he began, "I was on my way to give the Prime Minister the information I am about to give you and which I think you should pass on to him as soon as it is possible. I do not know, Kim"—the tired old voice rose to an unaccustomed note of anger— "whether the smash that brought me here to your hospital was accidental or deliberate, for I do not remember a great deal about it. But I do remember, just before I crashed into a line of bullock carts, that there was a large black saloon car which appeared most inopportunely from a side road and forced me to steer into the carts in order to avoid it."

"I've seen a report on the accident, Father," Kim told him, "but there was no

349

mention of a black saloon car being involved."

"Then it was deliberate," Father Delarge said emphatically. "If it had not been, the black saloon would have pulled up, the driver would have given me some assistance."

"Perhaps," Kim conceded. "But—"

The old priest waved him to silence. "You think I am raving," he suggested reproachfully, "but I am not. I have never been more in earnest in my whole life. Come closer, Kim, and listen. It is vital that you understand what is afoot . . ."

Kim pulled his chair closer and listened. He did not know what he had expected to hear, but any doubts concerning Father Delarge's state of mind swiftly vanished as gradually, word by painful word, the story unfolded. And yet it was an incredible story, a story of intrigue and evil, of treachery and horror. He might, Kim reflected, have found it harder to believe had it not had as its central figure the man he himself had so much reason to fear and mistrust . . . Thakin Maw Shwe, the King's trusted and influential Minister for War, the man who controlled the Army and the Police; the man whose over-weening ambition was a household word in Gaupal.

He let out his breath in a horrified gasp as Father Delarge talked on. He knew no details of the plot to overthrow the King, only that it existed, and that the coronation of Prince Maung Saw in his father's place was likely to be its culmination.

"I believe, Kim, my son," the old man went on, "that Maw Shwe is using the Oil Company for his own ends. The Company has not been over-scrupulous—it is interested only in obtaining the concessions it needs and does not seem to care very much by what means those concessions are obtained. Certainly a great deal of the money expended on bribes has been provided by Mr. Garrison. But Maw Shwe, from what I know of him, will not be content with any half-measures. Perhaps, who knows, he may see himself as President and dictator of a new Republic of Gaupal? Mr. Garrison will be lucky, in my opinion, if he gets his concessions from Maw Shwe, should the plot—as heaven grant it may not —ever be successful. They will move cautiously at first—Maung Saw, poor innocent boy, is a pawn in their dangerous game, to be given the crown but held prisoner until the people's reaction becomes clear."

"And after that?" Kim questioned, appalled.

Father Delarge sighed. "They would use him for as long as they needed him. Kim, go to His Excellency the Prime Minister at once, will you? Tell him everything I have told you, everything, do you understand? I do not think the coup d'état is likely to take place yet; I do not think that Maw Shwe's plans are complete, for as far as I can gather, he has not found much support for his treachery among the Army officers whom he has sought to suborn. But the abduction of the prince will be his first move. Once that has taken place, an assassin in the Palace will be given his orders and the King's life will be in hourly danger. I have not been able to discover whom they have chosen for the task, but"—he sighed again, unhappily—"it will be someone close to His Majesty, whose intentions will not be suspect until he strikes."

Kim paled. "Father, you are sure of this? You are absolutely certain?"

"As God is my witness, my son. Do not ask me how I uncovered details of this terrible thing, for I cannot tell you. But it is the truth. I am grieved that I must pass on the burden of my discovery to you—I would have borne it myself, had I been able. A hundred times, while I wandered in my mind, lying here in this hospital bed, I imagined that I had delivered my warning and that all was well. But now, since the nurse told me that I have been unconscious for almost twenty-four hours and have not stirred from my bed, I know that my warning has not been given, so I must pass it on to you and ask you to take it to the Prime Minister—or to the King himself, if need be. They must know what to expect, if bloodshed and anarchy are to be avoided. Kim, you must make them believe you. You must do this, with God's help. Now, at once, you must go to the Palace!"

"I will go," Kim promised. He rose to his feet. "I will do my best to make them believe me, Father."

The old priest fell back on to his

pillows, his strength gone and the animation fading from his eyes. The burden of his terrible knowledge had been a heavy one. He had carried it alone for as long as he could, but now he had passed it on, as he had said, to Kim. Weak and ill, he could do no more.

Calling the nurse to return to her vigil at her patient's side, Kim hurried from the ward. And then, reaching the door of his office, his footsteps slowed. An audience with the Prime Minister could not be obtained merely by presenting himself at that dignitary's official residence, however urgent he might announce his business to be. He would have first to telephone and request an appointment, containing himself as best he might until the appointed hour arrived. But . . . he wiped the perspiration from his brow with a shaking hand . . . Father Delarge had given it as his opinion that the danger was not yet imminent. The traitor's plot would take time to put into action, there would be difficulties, delays, unexpected hitches, there were bound to be.

And then he remembered having heard that Garrison had flown in that morning, in one of the Oil Company's planes, from Rangoon. What, he wondered, did Garrison's return signify? That the delays were over, the difficulties overcome, the coup d'état about to take place? Was the unknown assassin sharpening his knife somewhere, in some dark corner of the Palace, waiting only for a sign from Maw Shwe? This—in spite of the fact that only a little over twenty-four hours had elapsed since Father Delarge had been carried, maimed and broken, into the hospital, his shocked mind robbed of the secret it carried and capable only of disclosing that other secret, concerning Rose's birth . . .

Kim shivered in the warm evening air. That other secret seemed of little importance now, either to himself or to Rose: his own worries faded into insignificance. His palms clammy and his hands still not steady, he jerked open the door of his office and strode across the small room in which Ma Kyaw still bent dutifully over her typewriter. She looked up at him, her dark eyes wide with astonishment, as he bade her harshly to leave the letters and get him an outside line.

Then, as she obeyed him, he went to his

desk and picked up the telephone receiver, telling himself that there was plenty of time, forcing himself to speak calmly as he asked for the number he wanted. Why should Garrison's return mean that the danger was imminent? He, like Prince Maung Saw, was probably only a pawn in Maw Shwe's game, to be used and deceived, to be thrown aside when his usefulness came to an end. And the King was well guarded, the majority of the Army loyal—what chance had an assassin of coming within striking distance of a monarch whom his people worshipped as a god? What chance indeed! There was no reason to panic . . .

A secretary answered from the other end of the line and Kim demanded an immediate interview with the Prime Minister. The secretary demurred. His Excellency was occupied with important State papers: there was a meeting of the Council in an hour's time, after which His Excellency would wait on His Majesty the King. Perhaps if Colonel Myint were to be more explicit . . .

Perspiration again beaded Kim Myint's brow as he strove to speak quietly and without heat. He stressed the urgency of the matter, and the secretary requested him, politely, to wait. A few minutes later another, more authoritative voice came on the line and asked him to state his business. He did so, guardedly, and heard the man at the other end draw in his breath in a little hiss.

"His Excellency might be able to see you later this evening, when he returns from the Council meeting. He—"

"I must see him now," Kim declared obstinately, "*before* His Excellency goes to the Council meeting. It is most urgent that I should."

"But that is impossible," the voice returned with flat finality. "His Excellency is about to receive a very eminent caller who cannot be put off. I am sorry, Colonel Myint, but—"

"Who is the caller?" Kim demanded, so peremptorily that the other gasped. "Forgive me, Colonel Myint," he exclaimed indignantly, "but surely it is no affair of yours what callers His Excellency chooses to receive?"

"My business is a matter of life and death, as I have already told you, Duwa.

Is the caller Thakin Maw Shwe, Minister of the King?"

The gasp was repeated. Finally the voice admitted that it was. "I shall be at His Excellency's residence in ten minutes," Kim said, in a tone that brooked no argument. "Do not allow Maw Shwe to see him until I get to you, if you value your life." He slammed down the receiver and made for the door. It opened before he could reach it and Rose came in, her face white, her manner so agitated that Kim knew that something must be wrong. He held out both hands to her. "Rose—Rose, my dear, what has happened?" He led her to a chair, sending Ma Kyaw scuttling away in search of water. "Where is John? Why have you come alone?"

Rose told him, her voice taut with strain but free, he was relieved to notice, of any hint of panic. He heard, with a sinking heart, of the prince's abduction. So it had come, he thought, fighting desperately to remain calm, it had come, much sooner than Father Delarge had expected, but not too soon, surely, for them to be able to defeat the traitors? He stole an anxious glance at his watch. The minutes were ticking by, but he had to know everything that had happened, so that he might put the Prime Minister in possession of all the facts. He listened tensely as Rose told him of the finding of Narain Singh.

"He is here, Kim," Rose said. "I brought him back and he is being admitted to the hospital. John—" She broke off and now there was fear in her voice, agony in the glance she turned on him so that, seeing it, Kim forgot for an instant the urgency of his own errand and became aware, to his shocked surprise, that her fear for John Anson's safety transcended any emotion he had yet seen her display. He caught at her arm.

"Where is John?" he demanded, his voice low but miraculously controlled. "Has he gone in search of the prince? Is that why you are afraid for him?"

He felt the shudder that convulsed her. "He has gone to Mr. Garrison," she whispered. "Unarmed and alone. That is why I am afraid for him, Kim. Oh, don't you see . . ." Her voice died on a sob.

"I see," Kim answered, very gently. "I see, Rose." He gave her his hand. "You'd better come with me. I'm on my way now to an audience with the Prime Minister. Father Delarge regained consciousness and told me all that he discovered about this plot and those who are involved in it. I will tell you about it as we drive . . . come, there is no time to be lost. Maw Shwe is waiting to see His Excellency too."

"And John?" Rose cried despairingly. "Surely you are not just going to abandon him while you talk to the Prime Minister?" Again Kim heard the unendurable agony in her voice as she pleaded, "Isn't there anything you can do to help him, Kim? He is alone, he would not let me go with him, but—"

"John is a match for Garrison," Kim told her, with conviction. "He is a match for any man and he is a soldier, he knows his duty. But we can do nothing to help him until we have spoken to the Prime Minister—that is *our* duty, Rose. John may succeed in learning the prince's whereabouts from Garrison. If he does, then he will need help and I shall try to get it to him. Come."

Walking like a woman in a dream, Rose went with him, and he knew, as he walked stiffly erect beside her, that the love he had wanted from her was not to be his. She had given it to John Anson, who was an Englishman, but his friend and brother. Kim Myint recognized this and accepted it, without bitterness. But he was silent as they got into Rose's car and then, as they drove at reckless speed through the narrow, crowded streets of Tauling towards the Palace, a shadowy silhouette against the darkening sky, he forgot the pain of his disappointment and remembered only his duty to his King.

His hand went to the holster at his hip. He felt the stock of his service revolver and his mouth tightened grimly. He, too, was a soldier, and if Maw Shwe attempted to impede him, he knew his duty and he would do it. This was the first time that, as a medical officer, he had ever carried arms . . . Softly, beneath his breath, he repeated the oath of allegiance he had sworn when he had entered the King's service, twenty years before.

16

JOHN stood looking down into the white, terrified face of his enemy and said, from between clenched teeth, "I suggest you tell me the truth, Garrison. Now, at once—it's no use your looking at that door, because it's locked, and in any case my servant is standing on guard outside. He'll deal with you a lot less gently than I, if he gets the chance. *Where have they taken Prince Maung Saw?* That's all I want to know. Once you've told me, I'll be finished with you. If you value your hide, you'll get out of Gaupal . . . tonight. You'll pack your bags, order your aircraft and get out."

Charles Garrison's answer was a groan. He put a tentative hand to his bruised face and repeated obstinately, "Damn you, I don't know—how should I know, for crying out loud? You tell me Maung Saw's been kidnapped, but I know nothing about that. You come busting in here like the wrath of God and attack me without warning, but I haven't the faintest idea where they've taken the wretched boy. In fact, I've only your word for it that they've taken him anywhere. I know nothing about it, nothing, I tell you."

"You were there, Garrison, when they set on him. You and Maw Shwe."

"*Maw Shwe?* But—"

"Maw Shwe," John repeated calmly, "is probably under arrest by this time. You were both positively identified. Would you like me to hand you over to the tender mercies of the civil power or will you take the chance I'm offering you? Tell me where the prince is hidden and then get out of the country? The choice is yours, you know. I'm the prince's tutor and I'm only interested in one thing—getting him back, safe and unharmed. Tell me where Maw Shwe has taken him. If you do that, I won't put anything in the way of your escape, I promise you. You can leave tonight."

The last vestige of colour drained from Garrison's cheeks. "I *can't* leave—" he began, but John cut him short.

"You can and will, Garrison," he

returned grimly. "Or face arrest. That's your only alternative."

Garrison, as he had suspected, was a coward, and he was on the point of breaking, too frightened and too much aware of his own guilt to challenge John's bluff. When he had first entered the room, Garrison had been smiling, secure in the belief that, having left the only eye-witness of his part in the abduction for dead, he had nothing to fear from his visitor. He had, in fact, begun by apologizing blandly for Sandra's defection, John recalled, and his swollen lips twisted wryly. ". . . We're in love with each other . . . you know how it is, Anson. No reason for you to feel sore. I've known Sandra for a long time. She and I were going around together before you ever met her. Why . . ." There would have been a lot more on the same lines if John hadn't interrupted him. But, as it was, the first words he had spoken had wiped the complacent smile from Garrison's face most effectively. To begin with he had tried to lie and bluster, and then he had attempted to get his hands on a pistol which, perhaps fortunately, had been just far enough out of his reach to make the attempt unsuccessful.

John's call had taken him by surprise and he hadn't been prepared for what had followed. Even his frantic cries for help had met with no response—Bo Tin, whom John had picked up on his way to the hotel, had quickly persuaded the hotel staff that discretion was the better part of valour.

The fight, such as it was, was soon over. John flexed his fingers cautiously and winced at the pain of his lacerated knuckles. Not since his Force 136 days had he had to use his fists as he had used them tonight, and he hoped fervently that this would be the last time he would need to use them on Charles Garrison, to whom Sandra, it seemed, was now married. His mouth tightened.

"Well?" he demanded contemptuously. "Are you going to tell me? Are you going to go, while you've got the chance?"

He watched, without pity, as fear succeeded indecision in Garrison's eyes. "If I tell you," he asked, avoiding John's gaze, "will you swear that you'll stop them arresting me?"

"I'll give you the opportunity to make a run for it, for Sandra's sake. That's all I can promise you, but I think you've got time to reach the airport before the hue and cry starts. You'll be getting off damned lightly, Garrison."

"I shall be losing every penny I've got sunk in this infernal country," Garrison flung at him bitterly, "and the concessions."

"Not too high a price to pay for your skin, is it? Is it, Garrison?" John was furiously angry. "You came here and tried to cheat and corrupt a great many innocent, primitive people who trusted you. You made promises you never intended to keep and you ended up by getting involved in a conspiracy which might have led to heaven alone knows what bloodshed and horror, if it had come off. And yet all you can think about is the money you're going to lose! I ought to break your neck, instead of letting you go—" John advanced on him threateningly, and Charles Garrison cringed before the blazing fury in his eyes.

"Leave me alone, Anson," he said sullenly. "For God's sake, leave me alone."

"Only if you tell me where they've taken Maung Saw."

Garrison buried his face in his shaking hands. His voice was muffled and high-pitched as he said, "He's hidden in the Peacock Pagoda—in a cellar that runs beneath it and under the river. The guards will let you go to him if you tell them you've come from me."

John asked a few quick, brusquely-voiced questions and made for the door. Opening it, he signed to Bo Tin and the boy's anxious expression relaxed. "Where, Thakin?" he asked.

"The Peacock Pagoda," John answered, "in a cellar that runs under the river. Come on, we're going there now."

Bo Tin did not question his decision. Together they ran to where Kim's car was parked, under the tamarind trees. It was only as John hurriedly lowered himself into the driving seat that the boy asked, "We go alone, Master? Just you and me?"

"Yes," John told him, feeling for the starter switch. The powerful engine responded instantly to his touch and he swung out into the narrow street, hearing as he did so the faint sound of Garrison's voice, calling for his car. He smiled grimly in the darkness. There was nothing more to fear from Charles Garrison. He was scared out of his wits and he would run . . . back to Sandra, back to his wife. John hoped that Sandra would want him back, that she would make something of him, and ceased to regret having allowed him to escape. The mills of God, he thought, and his smile faded. Charles Garrison had a great deal on his conscience, but he, thank heaven, was not Garrison's judge. He wasn't even Sandra's.

As he reached the end of the street, he heard the roar of Garrison's car starting and, for a moment, wondered whether the man had recovered his nerve and was coming in pursuit of him. But the roar swiftly faded and he knew that his initial guess had been correct—Garrison was a coward, he had abandoned his fellow-conspirators as he would very soon abandon Gaupal.

A hand nudged his arm and he felt the cold touch of steel against his fingers. Bo Tin grinned at him.

"Better take, Master," the boy said, in English.

John took the small dagger and thrust it into his belt. "I think we may be able to bluff the guards into letting us in," he returned. "But thanks anyway, Bo Tin. My idea, in coming alone like this, is that we'll have a better chance of getting to His Highness than if we go off and collect an escort and then try to force a way in. They might harm him, if they are alarmed. But if you—" He glanced at the dark face of his servant in mute question and Bo Tin shook his head. "I come with you, Master. I know a way into cellar, too . . . one not many people know." His grin widened. "You stopping car here, Master, turn out lights. I show you."

The Peacock Pagoda, eerily beautiful in the light of the newly risen moon, loomed in front of them. It appeared to be deserted, and as he followed Bo Tin along a path which led to the river, John found himself faintly admiring whoever had chosen this as a hiding place for the kidnapped prince. It was the last place in which he would have thought of looking, for it was still largely in ruins and, since it was a sacred place, no one who had no business there would venture near it at night, few even by day. And what guards there were had obviously concealed themselves behind the lovely, crumbling walls . . .

They gained admission, contrary to all his expectations, without difficulty. A pongyi, squatting with his yellow robe gathered about him against the evening chill, waved them on indifferently as soon as he mentioned Garrison's name: two others stood aside, without speaking, when they reached the cellar entrance. Unchallenged, with Bo Tin leading the way, they traversed a long, dank, evil-smelling passageway and emerged into a large vaulted chamber, lit by two very faint oil lanterns. At the end of this stood a padlocked wooden door with a sentry, apparently sleeping, his rifle across his knees and his body, swathed in a dirty blanket, stretched prone in front of it. Bo Tin flashed him an enquiring glance and John nodded. Silently, the boy inched his way forward and a moment later the sentry rolled over on to his face, Bo Tin's brown hands at his throat. He did not stir when John fumbled amongst his robes for the key to the padlock, and Bo Tin was smiling as he whispered, his lips close to John's ear, "Go in, Master. I see he does not wake."

His hands shaking a little and his mouth dry, John thrust the key into the lock and turned it, jerking open the door. He could not afterwards have said exactly what he was expecting to see when he entered the room in which his pupil was imprisoned, but the sight that met his eyes caused him to step back with a half-stifled gasp of horror.

A strange figure, its face hideously daubed and its body draped in a cloak of shining feathers, was standing in the centre of the small, dimly lit dungeon, arms theateningly raised, as a voice he did not recognize screamed something at him in Gaupali. And then, so unexpectedly that it set his heart pounding, the figure flung itself upon him. "Colonel Anson, it is you! Colonel Anson, you have come to save me . . ." The cry ended in a sob, but not before John had recognized the voice as Maung Saw's. He held the boy to him as tears ran down the paint-daubed cheeks, and listened as Maung Saw sobbed out his story.

"Why," he asked, as the sobs at last

371

subsided, "are you dressed up like this, Your Highness? Surely—"

The boy drew himself up. "These are the robes of the sacred peacock," he answered proudly, "hidden here in a chest in this room. I had planned to escape, you see, by frightening the guards. None would touch me if he saw me thus—none would dare. I could have walked out unmolested."

"I think," John told him thoughtfully, "that's what you'd better do now, Your Highness—just that. My boy and I will walk in front of you. If anyone makes a move to stop us, show yourself and order him to let you pass. We met with no opposition when we came in, but it may be a different story when we try to leave."

Maung Saw's painted lips twitched into a rueful parody of a smile. "To think," he said softly, "that I once tried to kill you, Colonel Anson. Oh, yes, you were right— it was I, I and no other, who threw that knife at you, on the occasion of the durbar. But I lied to you about it, when you accused me." His smile flickered and died, like a small candle flame extinguished by the breeze. He held out his hand and added, his expression grave, "Colonel Anson, I ask your forgiveness in all humility. I abase myself and ask as a beggar for your friendship, if you will give it to me. I ask you to believe that I have learnt the first lesson you would teach me of the West—learnt and accepted it."

John took the outstretched hand in his own, feeling suddenly deeply moved. The prince raised his hand, first in the Gaupali gesture of submission and obedience, to his brow, then to his lips. For a moment, he clasped it tightly and then, with a return to his normal autocratic manner, he said abruptly, "We will go now, Colonel Anson, if you please." But John caught the glint of tears in the dark, intelligent eyes as he went on, "They would have given me the crown of Gaupal, they said, in place of my father. That is why the robes were here; they were planning to use them, so that the people would accept me as their King. Let us go to my father, Colonel. I want to assure him of my loyalty and to tell him that I am not yet fit or ready to be a King."

John led the way to where Bo Tin was waiting, but there, his head held high,

Prince Maung Saw insisted on taking the lead.

They walked unchallenged through the vast Pagoda and saw, in the moonlit courtyard, the King's soldiers advancing to meet them. And, in one of the parked cars, Rose was waiting . . .

John went to her, and with a little cry of thankfulness she held out her arms to him.

He hesitated, meeting Kim Myint's gaze from the shadows beside the car. Kim stepped forward, grasped his hand and linked it with Rose's small, trembling one.

"She is your betrothed, John," Kim told him gruffly. "I have relinquished my claim, even if I have not ceased to think of her with affection, but"—he sighed—"perhaps that will come, in time. It is right, you know, that it should be you and she, for Rose is of the West, just as you are. No doubt she will tell you of that, in her own good time. But you are like to her like and I am of Gaupal and the East. How does your poet, the great Kipling, put it? 'Oh, East is East and West is West and never the twain shall meet . . .'." A smile lit his brown face and touched his eyes to a soft radiance. "Like Kamal, I am proud to call you brother, John, my friend . . . 'may I eat dirt if thou hast hurt of me in deed or breath . . .'. I'll leave you together now, for there is work to be done—the prince to be restored to his father and, perhaps, the start of a rising to be quelled. Although it may not come to that, if we act quickly. Maw Shwe, who was its instigator, is dead by his own hand, and they tell me that the Oil Company's aeroplane has just taken off for Rangoon, with Mr. Garrison as passenger. He could have left before, since His Majesty the King has given the oil concessions to another British company which applied for them, through the Ambassador, a week ago. And the Ambassador"—he touched Rose lightly on the shoulder in farewell—"is on his way here now. So that all is well for us, is it not? And more especially it is well for you two."

He sketched a salute and prepared to leave them alone together, as he had promised. But, turning on his heel, he hesitated. "Earlier this evening," he said gravely, "an attempt was made by one of the officers of the guard to assassinate His

Majesty. Happily, it was unsuccessful, the King is unscathed and the traitor delivered to justice. I thought you would like to know this, John, my friend. For my part in rendering the attempt unsuccessful, I have been promoted to Brigadier and am to be decorated."

"But . . ." John stared at him in frank bewilderment. "How, Kim? What did you do?"

Kim grinned and tapped the holster at his side.

"According to the Geneva Convention, no medical officer is permitted to carry arms. Tonight I ignored the Geneva Convention and remembered that I was a soldier before I was a doctor . . . I took this with me. And my hand has not lost its cunning. I fired a fraction of a second before he did, with the result that, even if I have lost my bride to you, I now out-rank you, Colonel—and I shall expect acknowledgment of the fact, next time we meet. Good night, John—and good night to you, Rose. All my good wishes are with you both, always."

His shoulders a little bowed, but his stride brisk and purposeful, he vanished into the darkness and, after a while, the soldiers marched away with their prisoners and there was silence.

The moon rose slowly to its zenith, bathing the blue tiles of the Peacock Pagoda in a pool of silvery brilliance, and the woman he loved stirred gently in John's embrace.

"John," Rose began, her voice a soft whisper of sound, "John, I must tell you—" But, sensing what she was about to say, John shook his head.

"Not now, darling." His lips touched her cheek. "There will be time for explanations afterwards. All the time in the world, the rest of our lives, I hope. Now I want to hear only one thing from you, and that is that you love me. Do you, Rose? Do you love me enough to become my wife, to live with me, forsaking all others, till death us do part? Because I want you so, my darling, and I worship you and nothing else in the world matters to me but that. Rose . . ."

Rose lifted her face to his and her eyes were shining. "I love you, John," she told him softly, "and I shall love you always. Enough—oh, many times more than enough to be your wife, for that is the only thing that matters to me too."

He held her to his heart and his mouth found hers.

"Bless you, Rose, my darling," he whispered, lips on hers, "bless you and bless you and bless you . . ."

The Peacock Pagoda stood silent and deserted, a ghostly place of unearthly beauty that had seen a thousand years of Gaupal's turbulent history and witnessed the coronation of its first Peacock King. John Anson looked up at it and smiled. Then, retaining Rose's hand in his, he started the car. Bo Tin, who had been waiting patiently in the shadows, ran over to join his master.

They turned and drove back to Tauling, leaving the Peacock Pagoda behind them. All was quiet when they re-entered the city, and they knew then that the danger was past. There had been no rising. And now the future belonged to them both . . .

GUIDE
TO THE COLOUR CODING
OF
ULVERSCROFT BOOKS

Many of our readers have written to us expressing their appreciation for the way in which our colour coding has assisted them in selecting the Ulverscroft books of their choice. To remind everyone of our colour coding— this is as follows:

BLACK COVERS
Mysteries

★

BLUE COVERS
Romances

★

RED COVERS
Adventure Suspense and General Fiction

★

ORANGE COVERS
Westerns

★

GREEN COVERS
Non-Fiction

ROMANCE TITLES
in the
Ulverscroft Large Print Series

The Smile of the Stranger	*Joan Aiken*
Busman's Holiday	*Lucilla Andrews*
Flowers From the Doctor	*Lucilla Andrews*
Nurse Errant	*Lucilla Andrews*
Silent Song	*Lucilla Andrews*
Merlin's Keep	*Madeleine Brent*
Tregaron's Daughter	*Madeleine Brent*
The Bend in the River	*Iris Bromige*
A Haunted Landscape	*Iris Bromige*
Laurian Vale	*Iris Bromige*
A Magic Place	*Iris Bromige*
The Quiet Hills	*Iris Bromige*
Rosevean	*Iris Bromige*
The Young Romantic	*Iris Bromige*
Lament for a Lost Lover	*Philippa Carr*
The Lion Triumphant	*Philippa Carr*
The Miracle at St. Bruno's	*Philippa Carr*
The Witch From the Sea	*Philippa Carr*
Isle of Pomegranates	*Iris Danbury*
For I Have Lived Today	*Alice Dwyer-Joyce*
The Gingerbread House	*Alice Dwyer-Joyce*
The Strolling Players	*Alice Dwyer-Joyce*
Afternoon for Lizards	*Dorothy Eden*
The Marriage Chest	*Dorothy Eden*

THE SHADOWS
OF THE CROWN TITLES
in the
Ulverscroft Large Print Series

The Tudor Rose   *Margaret Campbell Barnes*
Brief Gaudy Hour *Margaret Campbell Barnes*
Mistress Jane Seymour   *Frances B. Clark*
My Lady of Cleves

Margaret Campbell Barnes
Katheryn The Wanton Queen

Maureen Peters
The Sixth Wife   *Jean Plaidy*
The Last Tudor King   *Hester Chapman*
Young Bess   *Margaret Irwin*
Lady Jane Grey   *Hester Chapman*
Elizabeth, Captive Princess   *Margaret Irwin*
Elizabeth and The Prince of Spain

Margaret Irwin
Gay Lord Robert   *Jean Plaidy*
Here Was A Man   *Norah Lofts*
Mary Queen of Scotland:
The Triumphant Year   *Jean Plaidy*
The Captive Queen of Scots *Jean Plaidy*
The Murder in the Tower   *Jean Plaidy*
The Young and Lonely King   *Jane Lane*
King's Adversary   *Monica Beardsworth*
A Call of Trumpets   *Jane Lane*

FICTION TITLES
in the
Ulverscroft Large Print Series

The Onedin Line: The High Seas
Cyril Abraham

The Onedin Line: The Iron Ships
Cyril Abraham

The Onedin Line: The Shipmaster
Cyril Abraham

The Onedin Line: The Trade Winds
Cyril Abraham

The Enemy *Desmond Bagley*

Flyaway *Desmond Bagley*

The Master Idol *Anthony Burton*

The Navigators *Anthony Burton*

A Place to Stand *Anthony Burton*

The Doomsday Carrier *Victor Canning*

The Cinder Path *Catherine Cookson*

The Girl *Catherine Cookson*

The Invisible Cord *Catherine Cookson*

Life and Mary Ann *Catherine Cookson*

Maggie Rowan *Catherine Cookson*

Marriage and Mary Ann *Catherine Cookson*

Mary Ann's Angels *Catherine Cookson*

All Over the Town *R. F. Delderfield*

Jamaica Inn *Daphne du Maurier*

My Cousin Rachel *Daphne du Maurier*

MYSTERY TITLES
in the
Ulverscroft Large Print Series